D1528503

Also by Jackie Richards

———— ◆ ————

Charlie Dog Two and Mustard
(A Children's Book)

A Most Uncommon Journey
(A Memoir—Year 1939)

THE PINNACLE SEVEN

A Political Mystery

✦

Jackie Richards

To Norm and Shirley Best wishes from your neighbor Jackie Richards

iUniverse, Inc.
New York   Bloomington

The Pinnacle Seven
A Political Mystery

This is a work of fiction. All of the characters, names, incidents, organizations, and dialogue
in this novel are either the products of the author's imagination or are used fictitiously.

iUniverse books may be ordered through booksellers or by contacting:

iUniverse
1663 Liberty Drive
Bloomington, IN 47403
www.iuniverse.com
1-800-Authors (1-800-288-4677)

Because of the dynamic nature of the Internet, any Web addresses or links contained in this book
may have changed since publication and may no longer be valid. The views expressed in this work
are solely those of the author and do not necessarily reflect the views of the publisher, and the
publisher hereby disclaims any responsibility for them.

ISBN: 978-1-4502-5638-4 (pbk)
ISBN: 978-1-4502-5639-1 (cloth)
ISBN: 978-1-4502-5643-8 (ebk)

Library of Congress Control Number: 2010912978

Printed in the United States of America

iUniverse rev. date: 9/30/10

Dedicated to the memory of my husband, Jim Richards, who always gave me the wings to go in different directions, to think new thoughts, and to become who I am.

*A politician thinks of the next election;
a statesman of the next generation. A politician looks
for the success of his party; a statesman, for that of the country. The
statesman wishes to steer, while the politician is satisfied to drift.*

—James Freeman Clark

ACKNOWLEDGMENTS

My deep appreciation to the following people:

Vera Pastore of Word Choreography, LLC, who guided me through many a comma and semicolon while badgering me to rework sentences. I am deeply grateful for her perseverance.

Editor Tom Marcuson of iUniverse for his diligence and thoughtful analysis. Susanne Lazanov for her careful proofing.

My daughter, Bonnie Schlueter, who read and reread, made suggestions, and kept me on my toes regarding the law.

Any mistakes are mine alone.

My daughter, Tere Richards, and my sons, Mike and Bob, for their steady encouragement and for never doubting that I could.

The computer gurus who kept me out of trouble—my son Mike, my son-in-law, John Schlueter, my granddaughter, Kate Richards, and my neighbors, Katie Knepley and Susie Fountain.

My entire family, not mentioned by name, who include nine grandchildren, two daughters-in-law, two great-grandchildren, and extended family, for their love that nourishes me.

Readers Julie Crews and Sharon Baldacci for their encouragement.

The very supportive Friday night ladies and the wonderful community of Falls Run in Fredericksburg, Virginia. I live among talented, caring neighbors who think age is just a number that means very little if you are busy living and learning.

The Pinnacle Seven is a work of fiction. There is no Clayton Landing or Pasqua River. There are, however, many small towns up and down the coasts of Virginia and North Carolina that once had bustling wharves in the sailing sloop era of commerce. While they cannot be called ghost towns, they are but remnants of what might have been.

CHAPTER 1

Dawn came in ominous shades of gray. Mist from the river blew softly across the courthouse green. Cassie's mood was just as gray as the skies.

As she leaned against her father's desk, Cassie stared at the front window of the *Clayton Landing Weekly*. For as long as she could remember, the name listed under "Publisher and Editor" had been first her grandfather's, Clifford Cassell Danforth Sr., and then her father's, Clifford Cassell Danforth Jr. Now the name painted on the window was hers: Cassie Danforth. She had never envisioned that her name would be painted on the window. She had never meant for this to happen; she had fought against it. Yet here she stood, staring at her name as if somehow she could change that life-altering status. The conundrum consumed her, and there was still no answer.

~ ~ ~

Two months earlier, the middle-of-the-night call had come from the hospital intensive care unit. Her father, Cliff, had just been admitted. Nurse Betsy Caldwell identified herself and then held the phone to her patient's ear.

His barely audible voice begged in a hoarse whisper, "Promise, promise. Come back to Clayton Landing for a year." They had previously had this conversation during her last trip home. Her father wanted her to take over the paper if anything happened to him. Slowly her father continued, "That's where it will begin."

There was a hoarse, prolonged cough. She heard him protest as Nurse Caldwell retrieved the phone and said the one word that sent anxiety through the wires, weakening Cassie's resistance to her father's words.

1

"Hurry."

Cassie grabbed a small bag and stuffed it with underwear and toiletries. There were plenty of jeans and blouses in her closet at her dad's home in Clayton Landing.

At two o'clock in the morning, driving was the fastest way to Clayton Landing. Traffic would be minimal on I-95 to Richmond. South of Richmond she exited onto I-64, skirted around Norfolk, where she picked up Route 17, and headed toward North Carolina's Albemarle Sound country.

Clayton Landing had become a bustling small town in the sailing sloop era. Her great-great-great grandfather on her mother's side of the family, John Charles Clayton, had owned hundreds of acres along the Sound and had established the landing as well as a dry goods store that included the local post office. Farmers from miles around brought their tobacco, corn, and other products to the landing for shipping. Long before it was really a town, folks began to refer to it as Clayton's Landing—years later, just Clayton Landing.

As she drove, her mind churned. The thought of giving up her job stabbed at her heart with much the same effect as her father's words. She and her co-host, Don Donovan, had recently been assigned as hosts on *Around and About Washington*, a half-hour local Saturday morning talk show on NBC's WRC Channel 4. Their assignment was interviewing newly arrived congressmen and senators. Eventually she hoped to go behind the scenes, zeroing in on congressional aides who wielded a great deal of Washington insiders' power. She had spent years of grunt work as a television reporter at various local stations in North Carolina and Virginia working up to a position of more exposure.

She didn't want to give up her corner apartment. It was located a few blocks from the Pentagon Mall and Crystal City in an older section of South Arlington, overlooking a park and the public library. She loved everything about her apartment—the convenience of being near downtown Washington, the coziness, her new sofa plumped with pillows, her plants. Having lived there for the past two years, she coveted her new life.

The sun had been up an hour when she pulled into the parking lot at County Regional Hospital. She dashed through the doors and impatiently waited for the elevator. The elevator reached the third floor, and the doors had barely opened when she exited and dashed toward Room 320, the number the nurse had given her.

Cassie was not prepared. Her father—normally energetic and robust—lay shriveled and drained of color; his breathing was shallow and labored. His eyes were closed.

"Thank goodness you're here, Cassie," said Nurse Caldwell.

Cassie moved to the bed and took her father's hand. His eyelids opened immediately at her touch. He tried to raise his head but could not. Cassie bent close to his lips. He feebly squeezed her hand.

"Promise ... come back ... year." He gasped the words and watched her face intently as he spoke.

She had no choice. Her tears flowed onto his cheeks as she nodded, and then she weakly said, "I will, Daddy. I promise."

He sighed and rested for several seconds before he struggled to whisper, "Good girl. It ... it ... begins ... here."

"What begins here, Daddy? What?" Cassie asked, confused and desperate for an answer.

Clifford Cassell Danforth Jr. seemed to have taken his last breath, but he suddenly rallied. His eyes opened wide, and almost frantically, he tried once again to raise his head from the pillow. He tugged at Cassie's shirt in an effort to draw her close. His words were all but inaudible as he whispered them into Cassie's ear. Then he did take his last breath.

What did he say?" asked Betsy as she bent and put her arms around Cassie.

"I'm not sure. It sounded like 'Be a brick,'" Cassie said between sobs.

Her father's doctor, Doug Chandler, entered the room. He laid his hand gently on Cassie's shoulder. "I don't know what to tell you, except that suddenly his heart just gave up."

She could not believe that her father was gone. In addition to running the small town newspaper that he loved, he had been a confidant of presidents, a political analyst, and a widely read columnist. Clifford Danforth knew Washington well. He frequently visited the city and had often visited the White House over the years. Considered a political philosopher, Cliff was often called the "Will Rogers of the South." His editorials were syndicated and widely read. Major magazines called upon him to contribute articles. He was an astute observer of human nature.

Former President John Carver, U.S. congressmen and senators, General Assembly legislators, radio and television commentators, newspaper publishers, and journalists attended the funeral, sitting alongside most of the residents of Clayton Landing.

After the funeral, Cassie returned to her job at NBC.

As she had struggled up the ladder in Washington, her father had been her prop. It was he who had suggested many topics and introduced her to celebrities. It was he who had opened doors for exclusive interviews with hard-to-get politicians. All her life she had been not only his daughter, hostess, and traveling companion, but also his student as he shared his philosophy with her.

It was not long before Cassie began to question her own stand-alone abilities. Though she cherished her independence, just how dependent on her father had she been?

Guilt gnawed at her as she wavered between the promise to her dying father and the heart-wrenching thought of leaving her career behind.

Reluctant, sometimes angry, Cassie wavered for several weeks. Guilt won. When she asked for a leave of absence, mouths dropped open. She had very little to say in the way of explanation except that she was temporarily going home to take over the small town weekly newspaper. Her boss, Ross Larson, shook his head in disbelief and tried to dissuade her. "You are a rising star, Cassie. You can hire an editor." He offered to raise her salary. The weight of the promise grew heavier and heavier, but guilt was heavier still. Finally the leave of absence was granted, but there were no guarantees that she would be able to return to her status quo.

Cassie returned to Pearl's welcoming arms and the large white house on the courthouse green surrounded by its carefully tended lawn and towering magnolias and oaks. She paced the veranda with its gingerbread trim and potted flowers or sat quietly in the porch swing with Muffin, her pure white Persian cat, waiting for the pieces to fall together. In the few weeks since her return, she had become sure of only two things. The town had not—would not—change, no matter what time frame it happened to be in. And she herself was not really who she had thought. She had been immersed in her father's life for so many years, her own had become a sideline. She had finally begun to escape when he extracted his promise.

Cassie continually asked herself the question, "When will *what* begin?" She didn't have a clue. She questioned whether she had really known her father, despite how close they had been. Why was her return to Clayton Landing so important? She could hire an editor for the paper as so many had suggested. There were so many questions. No real answers.

Thirty-two years ago, she had been born in the house on the Green—born to a frail mother, already in the first stages of cancer. She was christened Elizabeth Cassell Danforth, the name honoring both her mother and father. From the day she was born, she had been called Cassie.

Her mother died when she was two. Unlike her father's death, her mother's changed very little in Cassie's life.

Pearl had taken care of her since birth. Pearl was just twenty when she began working for the Danforth family shortly after they were married. When Elizabeth Danforth died some ten years later, Pearl held two-year-old Cassie to her large bosom and told the little girl that her white Mama had died and gone to the Lord but that her brown Mama would never leave her. She never had. At age sixty, Pearl had slowed very little. The big house on the Green stayed exactly the same—each antique in its dustless place, the spotless linens carefully accounted for.

"How can so much be exactly the same when nothing is the same without my father?" Over and over, Cassie asked herself this question.

~ ~ ~

Her thoughts drifted back to the present, and her gaze drifted away from her name on the newspaper window to the street beyond. Across Main Street at Bradley's Drugs, they were gathering.

Banker Charles Masengood rounded the corner from Center Street, immaculately dressed as always. Occasionally, at an outdoor function, he loosened his tie and removed his jacket. That was the bachelor's only bow to informality. Although now white haired, he walked as briskly as he had in his youth. His brother, John Masengood, a lawyer who handled most of the criminal cases in town, waved as he crossed the street and joined Charles on the sidewalk. While in college, John had begun wearing Western style clothes—silver belt buckles, boots, and a Stetson. He referred to his farm outside of town as "the ranch." Summers during college Cassie had often covered court cases for her father. She had observed that John's flamboyancy seemed to give him an advantage in the courtroom. Warding off the heavy mist, they waited under John's umbrella for the mayor, Gordon Everly, who parked his car directly in front of the drugstore. Gordon stood a little over five feet six inches, and like many short men, he felt he could heighten himself with superior demeanor. Cassie knew that her cousin, Mason Langdon, would be along a little later. She had never known him to arrive anywhere without being late. Mason represented the district in the House side of the General Assembly and had recently announced that he was considering a run for the Senate side in the next election. Most who bothered to observe the political scenery felt that he would eventually run for a seat in Washington.

For twenty years or more, these four men had been running Clayton Landing through the town council just as their ancestors had for generations before. Except when the legislative body was in session, the four men gathered for breakfast each morning at one of the three tables in back of the drugstore. No one in local government was elected, hired, or fired in Clayton Landing without their approval. Many in town had misgivings about their iron grip, including Cassie's father. "Thick as thieves" was a phrase he often used regarding the four.

Cassie moved to a side window and studied the courthouse green. It was similar in design to those found in New England villages; however, the Green (as the townspeople called it) sat one block over from Main Street, away from businesses and normal traffic. The Green centered the soul of Clayton Landing, making it a natural gathering place. For over two hundred years, the old county courthouse had stood at the head of the Green, facing the Sound at its foot. It was considered one of the South's finest examples of Georgian brick architecture.

Cassie smiled as she observed her aging neighbor, Maime Sanderson, busily weeding her flower garden despite the mist turning to rain. Nothing interfered with her early morning ritual. She occupied one of the six large antebellum homes that lined the Green. Maime considered herself judge and jury concerning the morals of Clayton Landing and had always felt a personal responsibility for monitoring the dress of its youth. Cassie fell under special scrutiny due to close proximity.

Restlessly, Cassie moved back to the front window, continuing her early morning observations. Linwood Johnson pulled up to the curb close to the window. When he dashed around the front of his car and under the awning to the newspaper dispenser, he noticed Cassie and gave her a thumbs-up. After he retrieved the *Raleigh News & Observer* from the bulky dispenser, he returned to his car and headed down Main Street toward Bay View Road.

Clayton Landing took a great deal of pride in Linwood Johnson, a nationally respected political analyst and political science professor at the University of Virginia. In his youth he had led Clayton High straight to the football championship for three years in a row. With a football scholarship, he went on to wear the navy blue and orange colors of the University of Virginia Cavaliers. He came back to Clayton Landing frequently to visit his mother, Lilly.

"Probably home for spring break," Cassie thought to herself.

Cassie saw her cousin Mason stop just as he was about to enter the drugstore. Cassie followed the direction of his gaze and recognized the same stranger who had bumped into her the day before as she came out of Goodman's grocery. He had apologetically gathered up the bread and box of tea that had fallen from the top of her bag. For an instant their eyes had locked, and then he had moved on down the street.

As Mason stared, she stared. There was something disturbingly familiar about the stranger. His dark rust-colored hair was clearly visible from a distance. From her brief encounter, she knew that his eyes were deep brown and penetrating. As she watched, she noticed the quality of his casual clothes, his well-proportioned body—his exceptional attractiveness. The feeling that she should be able to recall a name aggravated her reporter's instincts.

The stranger climbed into a new black Jeep Wrangler parked in front of Cyril's Antiques. Mason continued to watch as the stranger drove the Jeep down Main Street. He slowed as he turned onto Bay View Road in the same direction that Linwood Johnson had taken. Cassie observed Mason shake his head as if puzzled before entering the drugstore.

CHAPTER 2

A ringing phone jolted Cassie. She turned from the window to see sixty-four-year-old Mille Belham dashing through the back door in her usual flying fashion. She dumped her lunch bag and purse onto her desk and grabbed the phone.

The office did not open for another hour. That meant the call was likely personal or coming in from the sheriff or state police. Except for any last-minute breaking news, the paper was set for Thursday's edition of the weekly.

Cassie waited as Mille jotted notes. Her eyes lifted to Cassie's as she wrote.

Before the phone was back in its cradle, Mille said, "Cass, get down to the jail pronto. They have Peggy Slater in custody. Something about finding her trying to bury a newborn in her family's plot. They say she will only talk to you or Jilly. Better take your rain slicker. The weather report sounds very threatening, and there are black clouds gathering from the west."

Cassie obediently grabbed her slicker. Mille, an institution at the newspaper, had become another of Cassie's surrogate mothers long ago when her own mother died.

The sheriff's office and county jail backed onto the alley that ran behind the courthouse. Sheriff Jed Ryan waited for her at the alley door.

"Cassie, can't say for sure that Peggy didn't smother that baby. Claims it was premature and dead at birth. Says she can prove it but won't talk to us. Course we don't have a medical examiner's report yet. See what you can get out of her."

As Jed opened the cell, Peggy stood with her back to the cell door. It was not until she heard the metal bolt slide back into place that she slowly turned to face Cassie. Tears streamed down her swollen face. Her jaw and arms were bruised.

They both stood perfectly still for moments, each understanding Peggy's need for her friend. As Cassie reached out, Peggy collapsed on the cell cot, shaking uncontrollably. Cassie sat down beside her, holding her without speaking, waiting until Peggy got control.

Finally, between sobs she spoke. "Cassie, you and Jilly more than anybody know what a dope I am, how unattractive I've always thought myself, how much I crave fittin' in." As she spoke, she rose and stared blankly out the cell window. "I always was a pushover for any guy that crooked his finger at me."

"Peggy, Jilly and I have told you a hundred times, that's all in your head."

"And I've never believed you. But you have to help me now, Cass. The sheriff and that deputy, Tully Reese—they think I killed my baby. I didn't. I was tied up, punched up, and raped, and I think that caused the baby to be born dead."

"Did anyone know you were pregnant? Cassie asked. "I sure didn't."

"Jilly did. I'm sorry I didn't tell you, and I made her swear that she wouldn't. I was too ashamed. You know how she volunteers for everything under the sun. Well, she knows this place where I planned to go live when I got seven months along—then give the baby up for adoption. They didn't know anything about it down at the diner. That's one good thing about being too fat."

Peggy worked as a waitress at the River Bend Seafood Diner.

"Who is the father?"

"The same guy who raped me, Sadar Miles."

Cassie groaned. Sadar Miles was the town troublemaker and a bully.

Peggy started pacing. "Yeah, that no-good redneck squelcher. It happened early last August after a party at the River Shanty. I don't know what got into me. Too many drinks I suppose. Anyway, he offered me a ride home. One thing led to another. We ended up at my place in bed. I was too far gone to worry about protection."

Cassie frowned, but let Peggy continue.

"Well, you can bet I stayed clear of him after that as much as I could. He'd stop in the diner now and then and pester me some to go for a ride. I dodged him pretty well until yesterday. It was raining hard like it's been doing most every night this week. I was soaked before I walked even part way home after work. Besides that, I wasn't feeling good, kinda crampy. He stopped and yelled for me to get in his truck. Like a fool, I did."

Peggy sat down on the cot again. "As soon as I shut the door, he gunned that old truck and hightailed it out to that old huntin' and fishin' lodge near my Aunt Sara's place off Bay View where his beer-drinking buddies hang out. He dragged me out of the car. You know how big he is. He pushed me into a back room where they have cots—pretty much like the one we're sittin' on. The whole place smelled like beer and cigarettes. Then he grabbed a piece of rope off a hook on the wall and tied my hands to the cot. He was dead drunk and grinning like a hog slurping swill the whole time. That's when he had at me. Hit me in the jaw when he was finished. It knocked me out for a time I guess. When I woke up, he was asleep in one of the other cots in the room. I managed to loosen the knots enough to slip a hand through. I got out of there as quiet and as fast as I could. Lord, I was hurtin.'"

Peggy got up and started pacing again but then sat back down quickly as if exhausted. This you won't believe. I headed through the woods. It was pitch dark. There was a dim light I could see in the distance. I thought it was Aunt Sara's house. I guess I was twisted around, because I found out later that I actually headed in the opposite direction. I didn't know it at the time, but I ended up at the old Rutherford place. Anyway, by the time I got near the house, it was too late to turn back. The baby was coming. I went up on the back porch where the light was coming from and pounded on the door."

Peggy rose and went to the sink, turned on the faucet, cupped her hands, and splashed water on her face. Cassie joined her at the sink. Before they sat back down, Cassie gently dried Peggy's bruised face. Peggy took the damp towel and wound it around her bruised left wrist.

"This is the most unbelievable part. There was a man in the house that I'd never seen before. He took the situation in quick as you please. He half carried me to a sofa bed in the room next to the kitchen. He washed up in the kitchen while he talked to me—telling me everything was going to be all right. It couldn't have been more than a half hour before he delivered the baby just as easy as any doctor I ever did see."

"Peggy, are you telling me the truth?" Cassie knew there were times when Peggy stretched or twisted the truth.

"I swear on my dead mama's grave, Cassie. That's where Tully Reese found me, you know, at my dead mama's grave."

"Go on. What happened next?"

"Well, he very gently wrapped the baby in a clean white towel and placed her in my arms. He seemed real sad when he told me that the baby was dead. Then he cleaned me up some—that part was pure embarrassing. He gave me some aspirin and told me to try and get some sleep. I fell right off, I was so exhausted."

"What happened then?"

"I woke up early this morning. It was gray outside like near dawn, but I couldn't tell the time. He was all sprawled out asleep in a chair. I sat up and put my feet on the floor and sat there for a few minutes looking around. The room was shadowy and there wasn't much furniture."

Sheriff Ryan interrupted her story. He entered the cell with a tray in hand. He offered both Peggy and Cassie a cup of coffee and a sweet roll. "Don't reckon either one of you have had your breakfast. This'll do in a pinch." He closed the cell as he left.

Peggy ate hungrily before she continued. "Anyway, after I got over a little dizziness, I got up to see if I could find a bathroom. I didn't get halfway across the room before he woke up. He pointed me down a long hall. When I got back, he had coffee made and said he had better get me to the hospital. I told him I'd rather go to my Aunt Sara's nearby. I told him she was a nurse and would take care of me. I knew she wouldn't be home. Her shift at the hospital starts at six. After some fancy talking, he agreed to take me to Aunt Sara's and walked me up to the back door. I told him it was always open. I yelled in and pretended I heard Aunt Sara call back. I slipped in before he could protest and shut the door. I lied because I thought maybe there was a way to hide the baby's birth so no one would ever know."

"Peggy, do you know how this story sounds?"

"I know. I know. Sounds like one of my tall tales. But it's the truth, Cassie. I swear."

Peggy continued, "I sat down at the kitchen table and rested and thought for a few minutes. Then a plan came to me and it seemed like I could make the whole thing go away pretty as you please. I found a good-sized box on Aunt Sara's gift-wrapping shelf. I found a satin pillowcase in her linen closet and a clean sweet-smelling towel. I fixed the baby up nice inside the box. It isn't more than a half mile from Aunt Sara's to the cemetery at Calvary Methodist Church. I took the baby and headed there with a shovel from the shed. I had to sit a spell and rest when I got to Mama's grave. I opened the box and looked at my baby's tiny face.

Mama would have loved her. She was a beautiful baby. I named her Mary Margaret after Mama and me."

Cassie reached for Peggy's hand as tears flowed down both their cheeks.

"I almost had the hole dug right at the foot of Mama's grave when that brassy deputy, Tully Reese, pulled in the church parking lot."

"All right, Peggy. I believe you. I'm going to stop by Jilly's and have her come to the jail to stay with you. I'm going to Uncle Dan's and get my horse. My Mustang won't make it on that back road to the Rutherford place. It would take a Jeep."

"That's it. That's what the man who delivered the baby drove, a Jeep, a black one."

"You're sure?"

"Positive."

"Did this man have rusty brown hair and brown eyes—really good looking, somewhere in his forties or early fifties maybe?"

"Yeah, that's him! How did you know?"

"A wild guess. I'm going to try and find him. Meantime, don't say anything to anybody except Jilly and Ed Morrison about what happened. I'll call Ed before I leave town and have him come over. He's our family lawyer. He'll know what to do."

"What would I do without you and Jilly? You've always helped cover up for me. But maybe you can't do anything this time."

"I'll try to keep a lid on it until after the paper deadline at noon. That will give us another week before this breaks too wide open, if I can persuade the sheriff and Tully to keep quiet until they know the facts."

Cassie hugged Peggy and called Sheriff Ryan to the cell door.

When they reached his office, Cassie said, "See if you can round up Sadar Miles. He's involved in all this. She says she was raped and that made the baby come early. I don't doubt her story. Meantime, I'm going to get Jilly to stay with her for a while. I'll call Ed Morrison. I've got a paper to get out—then I'll be back. Jed, do me a favor, keep a lid on this for a few hours."

She knew it was wrong, but she did not mention the stranger to Jed. She dashed out of the room with no intention of returning to the *Clayton Landing Weekly* office. She dashed down the alley until she came to the back of her own house. Before she backed her Mustang out of the garage, she made a quick call on her cell phone to Ed Morrison's office.

"Good morning, Cassie—just walked into the office. I hope you are calling for an appointment."

"No Ed, not today. Peggy Slater is over at the jail. She's being accused of killing her newborn. She told me her story and I believe her, but you listen and we'll compare notes. Meantime, I'm following up a lead. I'll call you when I get back. And check out who owns the old Rutherford property, please."

She hung up before Ed could protest. Cassie knew he would not permit her to hunt down the stranger by herself. Having spent several years as an investigative reporter at WWBT's Channel 12 in Richmond, she felt in her bones that there was an even bigger story hidden in Peggy's tragedy.

Hurriedly, Cassie called Mille at the newspaper and told her to release the weekly to the printer. Mille started to protest that they should wait until noon as they always did. Cassie hung up.

She dialed Jilly's number. When she did not get an answer, she glanced at her watch. She knew Jilly's habits—she was usually back home by this time. Perhaps she had errands after she dropped the kids off at school. She decided to stop by Jilly's home on the way to get Drifter, her horse, from her uncle Dan's farm.

As she drove, Cassie thought about her two friends. Tall and large framed, Peggy struggled with her weight. She wore her skirts long, her jeans too tight. Her skin was perfection, her hair mousy brown, her spirit moody. Without Cassie and Jilly constantly monitoring her assignments, she would not have finished high school. Jilly could still pass for a high school student. She wore a petite size 4. Her dark brown eyes perpetually twinkled, her smile seldom faded, her short unruly hair matched her eyes. She had no idea how to say no to anyone, so she kept tripping over her yeses while trying to keep up with numerous community activities and her two young daughters, Mary Sue and Johna. Johna had been named for her father after Dr. Stevens told Jilly that she would have no more children due to medical complications. No boy for her childhood sweetheart, John Rogers.

The rain began in large drops. Cassie pulled into Jilly's driveway, noting that her car was in the breezeway. The space for John's big red Ford truck was empty. This meant that Cassie could freely dash into the house without knocking, a privilege that Peggy, Cassie, and Jilly had accorded each other since kindergarten days, as long as they respected the privacy of the other occupants.

"Jilly," Cassie called. "Where are you?"

A muffled reply came from the direction of the master bedroom bath. The bathroom door stood slightly ajar.

"You might not want to come in just now."

Cassie hesitated. Bathroom doors usually did not hinder the three girls, who had forfeited their own privacy with one another years ago.

"Oh well. Come on in."

Cassie stood staring in the direction of the tub. At first glance she thought some catastrophe had happened to Jilly. Then she burst out laughing.

"Jilly Rogers, what in the world are you up to this time?" Cassie asked as she tried to regain her composure.

"Dang it! This hair dye recipe has been in the kitchen drawer pestering me for months. I found it in the paper just about the same time I found a couple of gray hairs."

"Hey, we're used to you trying out crazy recipes on us, but this one beats your Catfish Jambalaya recipe. What the heck have you got on your head?"

"If you must know, it's blackstrap molasses, coffee grounds, dried rosemary, and a dash of hair conditioner."

"That's quite a combination. Do you have any idea how ridiculous you look? Never mind, get that goop off your hair and get yourself dressed. Peggy is in trouble again."

"What now?" Jilly asked as she turned on the shower.

"I don't know why I was persona non grata, you can explain that later, but I understand you knew she was pregnant."

Jilly snapped the shower curtain back and poked her head out.

"Was—what do you mean *was*?"

"Look, I don't have time to go through the whole story. Just get yourself down to the jail. Tully arrested her for trying to bury the baby. She says it was stillborn. I'm going to get Drifter and try to find a stranger who can clear her."

"Clear her of what? Tully's an idiot, always was."

"Right now Sheriff Ryan isn't sure—but he has to consider murder."

"Peggy wouldn't kill an ant if it was stinging the pee out of her," Jilly said through a cloud of shampoo suds.

"You know that and I know that, but not everyone does. You've got to get down there before she falls apart. I called Ed Morrison."

Jilly quickly rinsed her hair. She grabbed a towel as she stepped out of the shower.

"Okay. You get going. It'll just take me a minute to dry my hair. Lord knows what it's going to look like. You be careful now. The weather looks like it's going to act up."

CHAPTER 3

Cassie pulled her hood over her head as she ran toward her car. She turned on her radio just as a weather warning was issued for Clayton County. "Heavy rain for several hours, take precautions for flooding, stay tuned for updates."

No one seemed to be at home at her uncle Dan's farm. Dan Danforth, her father's only living sibling, had recently reached his ninetieth birthday. His sons now ran the farm. She parked close to the barn and dashed inside toward Drifter's stall. Drifter was skittish of storms, so Cassie felt sure one of her cousins would have put her up for the day. Drifter whinnied when she saw Cassie.

"Come on, girl. A little rain won't hurt you. We have a mystery to solve. A handsome stranger is on the loose. Can't have that. It's just a few miles down the road and if I remember correctly, there's a nice dry barn at the old Rutherford place." She spoke gently to Drifter as she harnessed and saddled her.

Just as Cassie turned into the mile long lane leading to the Rutherford place, hail began to fall. The thunder grew louder. She urged Drifter on, but the horse was getting nervous and danced to the side of the lane as much as forward. As they neared the yard, the rain became blinding. A bolt of lightning struck in the surrounding woods. The frightened horse stumbled.

"Come on, girl, we're almost there."

Cassie became frightened too. Ahead she could barely make out the outlines of the Rutherford house and the huge live oaks that commanded the front yard, the tentacles of their octopus-like roots sprawling across the surface.

Suddenly Cassie heard the tear of wood as lightning struck too close. Part of a falling tree limb struck her head and shoulder. Drifter lost her footing. They went down.

~ ~ ~

He was standing at the screen door watching the storm when he saw the horse and rider in the lightning flash. He grabbed his rain gear off the hook by the door and hastily slipped and slid across the yard.

He pushed back Cassie's hood and studied her face for a few seconds.

"Well," he said to Drifter, who had immediately gotten up and was standing nervously over her mistress. "Damsels in distress are rapidly becoming my specialty. I hoped to put off officially meeting your rider, but it looks like the timetable has been moved up."

He quickly tied the protesting Drifter to the porch railing and then effortlessly lifted Cassie. Once inside he laid her on a sofa bed, briefly examined her, and gently washed her head wound, noting her clear sun-bronzed skin. He towel dried her long blonde hair. From the back of a door, he retrieved a terry cloth robe and began undressing her. He was not above admiring her full breasts and lean athletic body as he did so.

"And so it begins—and so it begins," he whispered to the unconscious Cassie.

~ ~ ~

Sometime later, Cassie roused. A noise like a room full of little boys turned loose on drums beat in her ears. She felt the warmth before she saw the flames dancing among crackling logs in the fireplace. She realized the noise was the rain pounding on the tin roof. She was lying on a sofa bed close to the fire. She gasped as she also realized that she was wearing only her panties and bra underneath a robe.

"Hey there, you're awake."

Cassie turned her head toward the room slowly, as if she expected something might break in the process. Sitting in an old leather chair, coffee mug in hand, was the stranger. His damp hair seemed a deeper, browner red in the grayness of the room. He was good looking, no doubt about that, Cassie thought. Strangely, while puzzled, she did not feel threatened. If I am going to be rescued, it might as well be by Prince Charming, she reasoned.

"Lucky for you I made an early morning run to the bakery. Coffee and bun coming right up—be right back." His broad smile, which was almost a boyish grin, put her instantly at ease.

Cassie winced as she rose up on an elbow, looked down at her legs, and wiggled her toes. She seemed to be in one piece, nothing broken. Her head pounded. Her shoulder hurt. She noticed her torn blouse and jeans draped on a dilapidated ladder back chair at the corner of the fireplace. She sat up and pulled the robe close around her.

"Here, this will make you feel better."

Cassie took the offered mug. "Where's Drifter? Is she all right?"

"Out back in the barn." He gestured with a thumb over his shoulder. "She'll be all right, just rolled over and got right up. Lucky for you I happened to be standing at the front door watching the storm approach when you rode into the yard. I wouldn't have heard you above the noise of the storm. I got you both settled just before the storm really tore loose."

"It got worse?"

"And how. It was just getting dark and pouring when you rode in. The wind picked up, swept a couple of rockers right off the porch. I thought the roof was going to blow off any minute. It seems to be dying down some now."

"You seem to be making a habit of rescuing ladies this morning and seeing a great deal more of them than they'd like," Cassie said as she pulled the robe even tighter around her. "By the way, do you have a name?"

"Sure, everyone has a name. Just call me Coop—short for Cooper."

"Well, Mr. Cooper, it was my friend Peggy Slater that you rescued in the predawn hours, and she needs your help again. She's in jail."

"Oh boy! I knew I shouldn't have left her. I know better. What happened?"

"It's a long story, but the sheriff thinks she killed the baby because she tried to bury it."

"That's nonsense. It was a stillbirth."

"Another thing, are you a doctor?"

"No, not really. Let's just say I started out to be one a few years back."

"You will come back to town with me, won't you?"

He walked away, opened the front door, and stood looking out. "The storm's breaking up; it should be all over in another half hour."

"You didn't answer my question."

He turned around, walked back to his chair, and sat down, placing his elbows on his knees, hands cupping his face. He leaned toward Cassie.

"Cassie, I'll help your friend, but I won't come into town right away. I have an appointment this afternoon that I must keep first."

"Surely it can't be more important than getting Peggy out of jail on a possible murder charge." Cassie's tone emphasized her annoyance.

"Perhaps not to anybody but me. I came to Clayton to see three people. I have to see one of them before I become much more visible. When I have seen him, I will report in at the sheriff's office and testify on your friend's behalf. It shouldn't take more than a couple of hours or so once I get into town."

"I guess that will have to be good enough. What are you doing here at Rutherford anyway? It's private property. We do have a decent motel in town."

"I'm just camping out. I have an in with the owner."

Cassie searched her memory but could not recall who owned Rutherford. The house had just always been there—an old historical landmark—empty as long as she could remember. She decided to let it drop for the moment.

Coop walked over to the porch's screen door and looked out again. "The rain has stopped. I wouldn't be surprised to see a rainbow out over the Sound somewhere. Why don't you just lay back and rest a few more minutes? Your clothes are about dry. I'll check Drifter and get us another cup of coffee."

As soon as Cassie heard the back door open and shut, she rose and stretched and then quickly dressed. After checking out the bathroom that Peggy had mentioned, she found the kitchen and the back door. As she stepped out and headed toward the barn, the sun's brilliance poked through a cloud, and the grayness immediately gave way to a muggy haze that made it hard to breathe. She reached to pull back the barn door and winced as the sagging door stuck in uneven ground. As she entered the partially open door, she saw Coop checking Drifter's saddle, which had not been removed.

"I'll just take this off. We can leave her here for a while. I'll drive you in to the hospital. You should get a check on that shoulder."

"No need, Mr. Cooper. I'm perfectly all right. It's not as if I haven't been thrown before a few times. Drifter shies pretty easily, and now and then she takes me by surprise."

"Wait a minute now, I've already made one mistake this morning by not taking my patient to the hospital. I don't plan to make another."

Cassie reached up to adjust the saddle. Coop's hand closed over hers. It was as if an electric shock raced through her body.

"Here, let me do that," he said.

She took a deep breath and stepped aside.

After a brief discussion, Coop consented to follow her back to her uncle Dan's farm, provided he could see that she was safely in her own car before he left her.

"I'll just dash back to the house and do a quick change. Just wait here, I'll be right back," Coop said.

When they reached the farm, Coop took Drifter's saddle to the tack room in the barn while Cassie released her to the corral out back.

As Coop headed toward his car, Cassie asked, "What shall I tell the sheriff?"

Coop looked at his watch. It was a little past eleven. "Cassie, tell the sheriff I should be able to drop by his office around five this afternoon. I'll be in touch."

Cassie occasionally glanced back at his Jeep as he followed her into town. The vague feeling that she should know Mr. Cooper gnawed at her. Then the realization came to her that he did not ask her name; he already knew it. She would get to the bottom of this mystery, she promised herself.

He followed her into town and then continued down Bay View Drive toward River Road when she turned into the alley behind her home. She was tempted to back out of the alley and follow him, but she thought better of it. Mille would be nearing a stroke if she did not get back to the newspaper office soon.

CHAPTER 4

Linwood would be around for breakfast with his mama any minute now. Lilly had the coffee made, and the biscuits were on the counter ready for the oven the minute she heard his car turn into the lane.

"It's some kind of special having Linwood home during the week." She moved to the old pie safe in the corner and took out a new jar of damson preserves. She glanced down at the hound dog lying close to her rocking chair. She continued talking to him.

"It's high time for that boy to settle down." It was Lilly's favorite lament. "Linwood has some kind of fester that just keeps festering." She used to say that regularly to her husband, Ben.

Lilly moved to her ancient stove and turned the sausage simmering in the pan. "Poor old Ben," she said. "Too bad he didn't live long enough to see his son get his professorship. I guess he was pleased rightly enough to see him a football hero though. What do you think?"

The old dog raised his head in response. Nocount hadn't been much more than a puppy when Ben died. His long sad hound face somehow reminded Lilly of Ben. She thought it was quite fitting that she talk to Nocount much as she would have to Ben. It was Ben who gave Nocount his name. He said he'd never seen such a lazy puppy before.

Lilly and Ben Johnson both worked the Anderson land all their lives, as had their parents before them. When he had died ten years previously, Maxwell Anderson had willed them a fifty-acre piece that included the five-room house they had lived in for most of their married life.

Linwood was Lilly's only child, her pride and joy. He was born late in her life, just after her thirty-third birthday. He was also the pride and joy of Clayton County, his black skin forgiven by the white community and celebrated by the black community. Football had made him a hero to both. He'd earned a football scholarship to the University of Virginia. Unlike most of his teammates, he wanted the scholarship for the education, not for the glory it might bring. Nonetheless he distinguished himself on the field while at the university. Seduced by scouts from the NFL, he agreed to play pro football for the Washington Redskins, accepting a four-year contract, playing as a running back. At the end of his contract, he walked away. Sports commentators had a field day for a few weeks, begging for interviews, guessing at reasons. Then the football world moved on and forgot about Linwood Johnson.

He returned to the University of Virginia, completed his masters and doctorate, and stayed on, accepting a position as a professor in the political science department.

Shortly after settling down at the University, Linwood built a small cottage on his mother's property on a rise of land down by Leaking Creek. There he spent many weekends and vacations fishing, reading, and studying while also caring for Lilly.

Lilly moved to a corner of the kitchen where two rocking chairs sat near a wood-burning stove. A small television sat on top of a bookcase facing the two chairs. She turned it to the news channel. Linwood liked to watch the news while he ate his breakfast.

The TV screen threw its images into a kitchen cluttered with accumulations from the past. Among them, an old churn stood in one corner as if ready and waiting for the cow to be milked. A tin dipper hung by the back door even though modern plumbing had long ago replaced its use. Lilly resisted letting go of the past as if she did not quite trust the future.

"Think about it, Nocount, we've gone from picking cotton to cable TV. Come on now, get yourself out of here. You know Linwood doesn't appreciate dogs in the house." She threw a couple of day-old biscuits out the back door and shooed Nocount after them.

The dog gulped down the two biscuits and flopped his body into a dirt hollow under an abandoned chicken coop that tilted haphazardly on a cracked leg.

Lilly stood on the doorstep stretching, her eyes roving her land. The garden space got smaller every year.

"Seems like I don't hoe so fast anymore, Nocount. A body could get plain useless like you."

Lilly looked up at the sky. "No telling which-a-way it's going to be today, maybe the sun will shine and maybe it won't, but my bones are telling me it won't. Seems like it's getting darker instead of lighter." A glance at the old dog confirmed her suspicion that he was already fast asleep. It began to rain.

Turning back inside, she glanced at the peeling green metal alarm clock on top of the refrigerator. It was almost seven. She had been up since five-thirty, old habits being hard to break. The day stretched long ahead. She ladled the sausage into a dish and set it on the back of the stove to keep warm. Minutes later she heard the familiar sound of Linwood's car coming up the lane signaling that it was time to put the biscuits in the oven.

CHAPTER 5

Linwood always seemed to blow into the back door rather than just enter. He quickly hung his dripping raincoat on a hook beside the kitchen door. Turning to Lilly, he said, "How's my little old mama?" His hug lifted her off her feet. Being the only child of this frail precious woman was a responsibility Linwood met head on.

"I'm glad to see you, that's how I am. How's my son this morning?"

"Hungry, Mama. I thought about your biscuits while I was driving here from Virginia last night. Nobody makes biscuits like my mama." Linwood fed her ego as often as he could. It was small payment for the years she had fattened his.

While Lilly busied herself at the stove, Linwood dropped to the kitchen floor in front of the sink to check the repair of a leaky pipe he had made on his last visit.

Breakfast was served and eaten quickly.

As Lilly began clearing the breakfast dishes, Linwood leaned back in the chair to concentrate on the morning news. Suddenly his mood changed. His fist came down hard on the table, the remaining dishes rattled, and a spoon fell to the floor.

"Linwood Johnson, what ails you? If you break your grandmamma's blue sugar bowl, I'll have your head, son."

"Did you hear that, Mama? Did you hear what he said?"

"Who said?"

"That boy Gene Riley was interviewing. He said, 'I axed the gentlemens if he war hurt but like I done tole you, he jus lied dere.'"

"That does not give you call to be slamming down your fist on my table and nearly breaking your grandmamma's dishes."

"It does, Mama. It surely does. Gene was interviewing that young man after an accident. He appears to be around fourteen or fifteen at most. Surely he's still in school."

"I have heard your speech before, Linwood, and I know what's bothering you. Son, like I have said before, some black folks have been talking like that for a long, long time. It comes natural, part of their heritage."

"Mama, you know better than that. It's not part of any heritage. We've got boat refugees in our country, Mama, who did not know a word of English a few years ago and who are not only speaking English perfectly but going to the head of the class as well. They have a heritage too. No, these kids believe it sets them apart. That thinking is wrong—dead wrong."

"I suppose you think you are going to be able to change it all somehow. One man can't do that. You are frustrating yourself needlessly, Linwood."

"Needlessly, Mama? We've got a few—precious few—black leaders around who are waking up, aware of the situation. Way too many black children have been slipping and sliding through school imitating a hip-hop language along the way."

"I know that shouldn't be, but the black child seems to need some separate identity to hang onto, son. He does not want to mimic the white man's society."

"What does that mean, Mama? So he rejects an educated society? Most of the white people in this country are but a product of melding ancestors. Most of them will tell you they are an ethnic mix. The young whites rarely know where their ancestors originated from nor do they care. Most second- and third-generation immigrants strive not to sound like their forebearers. So, what is there to mimic except a mixing bowl of people who have left the old behind in a common effort to meld with one another?"

Linwood stood and began pacing.

"Our ancestors suffered mightily; we owe it to them to be the best that we can be."

Lilly unconsciously glanced out the window, checking to see if anyone was about, an automatic response to Linwood's impassioned speech.

"It used to be that you worried that some white person would hear what I was saying. Now you worry some black person is listening."

"Linwood, it just isn't right that you should be talking against your own people like that."

Agitated, Linwood shifted in his chair and crossed his legs.

"Hell's afire, Mama. I'm not talking against anyone. I want all people to move on, move out, move up—grab every opportunity, every inch and make the most of it. All my life you have taught me to do right—to strive toward making something of myself."

"You sure are getting high and mighty, Professor Linwood Johnson."

"Now don't go getting your backbone up. Just take me, for instance. Old Mr. Anderson took a shine to me, everybody in town knows that. If it weren't for him, I might be right here in this town scratching here and there for work. Think about it, Mama. You and Papa started working on this farm as youngsters and stayed all your lives. You both worked hard from the beginning, and from the beginning Mr. Anderson took an interest in you."

"You aren't telling me something I don't know, son."

"Maybe you've forgotten something, Mama," Linwood continued as he walked over to the stove to refill his coffee cup. "Papa told me many times that when he was working out in the fields with Mr. Anderson, he would have to stop and think about what he had to say because that man just would not talk to him unless he spoke properly. Papa began to listen to good speech and imitate it, he told me so. By the time I came along, the two of you began a pattern of correcting each other's speech. So, proper language came naturally to me."

"I suppose that's so, son."

"What you may not know is the grief it caused me. Back then it did not seem natural for a black boy to speak correctly here in the South. At school I was accused of trying to act like a whitey by blacks and of being uppity by whites. So I became a loner until I took to the football field. It's ironic; sports become the grand mixer of all races."

"You were good, Linwood, a hero in this town."

"Sure, Clayton Landing High won championships those years. Chasing a ball—football, baseball, or golf ball—makes heroes out of people with any skin color. It's a crazy world, Mama."

Linwood took his cup and stood by the back door. Through the trees to the north, he could see the rooftop of the old Anderson place. His child's eyes had seen it as a mansion. In reality, it was to this day an attractive large brick farmhouse with white trim. It was now renovated and modernized, owned by a weekender who farmed out the land.

"I won't forget that day old man Anderson called me up to the house; it was close to high school graduation. He set me to thinking about my future that day. He said I had too much going for me to get the football fever lodged in my gullet. 'Use it, son. Use it to get something better out of life,' he said."

"And you've done just that, son. Your Pa and Mr. Anderson would burst their suspenders if they could see you now."

"It's not enough, Mama. Papa always said to do the best I knew how every day so nothing would be left gnawing at me when I put my head to the pillow at night. Well, something gnaws, Mama, every blasted day, something gnaws."

"You beat all, Linwood, not enough indeed! Hush up now and let me listen to this weather report. It's beginning to look mighty threatening," Lilly said as she peered out the back door.

Linwood poured his third cup of coffee and sat down at the kitchen table, obediently quiet. He leaned back in his chair and thought about his mentor, Maxwell Anderson.

Over the years, Anderson acted as a third parent might. He gave advice in a steady stream. "Linwood, use this sports thing to get yourself a good education. You've got personality, people have confidence in you. Always remember, life doesn't owe you a thing. When your mama puts seeds in the ground, she tends them, and in return she gets an abundance of vegetables and flowers. Life's like that. You have to sow some seeds and do the tending, and then you have to share the crop."

Lily returned to the table. "You're mighty quiet all of a sudden."

"I was just thinking about Mr. Anderson."

Lily said, "He surely was a surprising man. I didn't know until after the funeral, but he paid the hospital bills when cousin Silas had his leg cut off in that tractor accident. Silas said Mr. Anderson told him he would just as soon leave it be between the two of them. And I never will forget the time a new preacher came to town and tried to talk him into going to church. I overheard him tell the preacher, 'It's not the hearers of the law that are just before God, but the doers of the law.' Then he said, 'you'll find that in Romans, you know.' That man had an answer for everything."

"That's what I've got to get on with, Mama, the doing. All I've been accomplishing is getting the field ready to sow the seeds."

"It seems to me you're doing all the time—traveling all over these United States."

"I've been learning, Mama—learning too much about things gone wrong. Everywhere people keep talking about a need for change, but no matter who we elect to run the country, change isn't happening."

Linwood rose from the table, walked over to the sink, and rinsed his cup. He opened the back door and checked the weather. "It's raining harder."

The alarm clock's shrill bell clanged suddenly and insistently. Linwood jumped, recovered himself, and moved to shut it off. As he did so, he picked up Lilly's medicine bottle from the back of the counter and handed it to her.

"That old clock is enough to stop your heart, Mama. You ought to let me buy you a new one."

"I don't want any of those fancy digital things. My clock does just fine, and it doesn't flash on and off and have to be set every time it storms and there's an electric blip, which we are likely to get any minute now."

"Speaking of the weather, it's thundering again. I had better get on down to my place. I have a paper to work on."

Nocount scratched at the back door.

Lilly glanced up at Linwood but did not make a move to let the dog in.

"Mama, what would you say if I decided to go into politics?"

"What do you mean? You are already in politics, Linwood. You have a steady job teaching politics. I can't see why you would want to change that. That's high-toned thinking."

Linwood didn't answer. He moved to the wall peg by the back door where his raincoat hung. Lightning flashed off in the distance. Nocount's scratching became more desperate. Linwood eased the door open, and the dog pushed its nose in and squeezed through.

"Mama, you have spoiled this dog rotten."

"He's company, Linwood, he's company."

Nocount settled in the corner on a rag rug, his eyes glued to Linwood.

"High toned or not, I've been thinking a lot lately. The political arena is the best way to accomplish change. There's a crisis, Mama, no doubt about it—a worldwide crisis. It's like we're sitting on top of a fiery bubbling caldron likely to boil over. It's time to defuse the pot. We have to dissect the cause of all this turmoil and somehow change the effect. There is distrust between neighbors next door, next state, and next country."

"Linwood Johnson, you are getting worse all the time. It seems like you want to carry the troubles of the world on your shoulders. Best you be getting yourself back to the church and start praying, son. That's what you need to do."

"We who are on this blessed earth today aren't owed, Mama, we owe. We owe all those who have gone before us a huge debt—to become the best that we can be. Booker T. Washington said, 'There's no escape—man drags man down or man lifts man up.'"

As if to accent those words, a bolt of lightning streaked across the sky, its flash momentarily lighting the whole kitchen. Nocount buried his head with his paws.

"I've delayed long enough. I'd better get on down to my place." Linwood threw his raincoat over his shoulder and walked through to the front room.

Lilly stood on the front porch and watched her son's car until it disappeared at the edge of the woods that separated her house from his. The wind grew stronger; the daffodils blooming by the front steps were bending to the ground. Lilly grabbed two of her potted ferns and returned to the kitchen.

"I reckon this is about the noisiest storm I ever heard, Nocount."

She settled into her favorite rocker near the corner window to watch the storm. Nocount inched over and laid his head on her feet. She reached down to rub his head.

"All the same, I had better get myself to church and do some tall praying for that boy. No telling what he will get himself into spouting off like that. Are you listening, Nocount?"

The dog's heavy lids were tightly closed. Despite the rumbling thunder and the roar of the wind, he felt safe at Lilly's feet.

Lilly reached for her Bible, read a few pages, and then laid it open on her lap. One hand rested on it as she closed her eyes. Her head began to nod, and she drifted off to sleep.

Sometime later, while Lilly dozed, a menacing black funnel cloud ripped across the treetops in the nearby woods and then dipped to carve a splintered path through Lilly's yard. It screamed past the old chicken coop, flicking away the broken leg, before slamming into the back corner of Lilly's house—the kitchen corner.

CHAPTER 6

Cassie parked her car in the garage off the alley in back of her house. Guessing that Pearl would be less likely to see her if she came in through the seldom-used front door, she skirted around the house through the flower garden, ducking down below the massive lilac bushes. She made a quick dash up the walk and across the veranda, hoping no one saw her tattered condition. She winced as she closed the front door a bit too hard in her haste.

"Cassie, is that you?"

Cassie quickly headed for the stairs and her room to avoid Pearl's inquisition.

"Cassie Danforth, you know better than to slam your mama's door," Pearl called up from the foot of the stairs.

When the original had become badly cracked, Elizabeth Danforth had designed the door's fragile stained-glass insert, which Pearl lovingly guarded.

Cassie took a quick shower, partially dried her long blonde tresses, and dressed in a fresh blouse and jeans. She would have to appease Pearl before she left again.

"What's cooking? Smells divine." Cassie gave Pearl's arm a fond squeeze as she stepped beside her. Pearl stood at the kitchen table rolling out butter cookies.

"Jilly asked me to make a bunch of cookies for parents' day at school. Lordy! It doesn't seem like it's that time of year again. What are you doing home in the middle of the day?"

Cassie ignored Pearl's question. "I agree, time is flying by. Did we have any major damage from the storm?"

"I've been so busy I haven't done much more than look out the window. I didn't see anything busted. The yard is full of leaves and twigs, though. I'll have to get Joe over here to rake up."

"I've got to run, Pearl. Oh, by the way, Peggy is going to stay with us for a few days." Cassie picked up her tote bag and grabbed a cookie from a cooling pan before Pearl could ask any questions.

Cassie walked briskly up the alley behind her home and went through the back door of the jail to the sheriff's office. She found Tully sitting behind Jed's desk.

"Where you been? Arrested Sadar—he musta' been smokin' something besides drinking." Tully always talked out of the side of his mouth, head thrown back in a manner that suggested swaggering even while sitting still. "He was drunk as a skunk."

Since childhood, Cassie had wondered where that expression had come from, having never heard of a skunk really being drunk. It was one of Tully's favorite expressions, since arresting drunks was the biggest part of his job.

"How's Peggy?"

"Jilly was just stormin' after she saw Peggy—shamed the sheriff into releasing her to the hospital. Jilly took her. He didn't cotton to her doing that, but you know Jilly. She's some kinda force when she sets her mind."

Cassie laughed; she could picture Jilly's onslaught.

"The sheriff has been looking for you; he just went over to see Larry."

Without comment, Cassie turned back down the hall, went out the door, and crossed the alley, entering the backdoor of the old courthouse. She was taking a shortcut through the courthouse to the office of Larry Stillman, the district attorney.

The dark wide floorboards of the historic courthouse were kept oiled and shiny. The walls of the large center hall were lined with portraits of Clayton Landing's distinguished residents. Suddenly one of the portraits caught Cassie's eye.

"My God," she said out loud. Suddenly Cassie felt she knew why the stranger had looked so familiar. Coop appeared to be a clone of the man in the portrait, Dr. Martin Lansfield. The portrait, commissioned years ago by the Lansfield family, had been hung just weeks earlier when the town honored its long-time faithful physician at the Founder's Day ceremonies. Generations of Lansfields had lived in Clayton Landing. Cassie knew all the living ones. Mr. Cooper was not one of them; of that she was positive.

Disturbingly, an elusive thought kept flicking into her mind; she could not quite grasp it as yet.

Mulling over this latest development, Cassie went out the front door of the courthouse and turned left through the alleyway leading to Larry Stillman's office on Court Street.

Cassie saw Jed Ryan standing beside Linda Hale's desk. Larry's white-haired secretary held longevity in the court system. Cassie knew that every detail of Peggy's plight would soon spread throughout the courthouse system via Linda's computer, and from there e-mails would fly throughout the town within minutes. Despite the fact that her job called for discretion, Linda seemed unable to help herself when it came to keeping Clayton Landing informed.

"Hi, Cassie. Linda here says Larry will be back from late lunch any minute. The storm held him up. I've got to get with him about Peggy's case. I can't hold off any longer."

"I know, Jed. Could I talk with you a minute out in the hall, please?" She did not want Linda overhearing anything she had to say to Jed.

She motioned him away from the door and down the hall by a window. "Peggy told me that a man she had never seen before was camping out in the old Rutherford place. He helped her after she got away from Sadar. I went out there to confirm her story. The fact is, he helped to deliver her baby and can testify that Peggy's little girl was stillborn. He can also testify to Peggy's physical condition. I don't think there's any doubt that she is telling the truth."

"Where is this man?"

"He said he had an appointment to keep before he came into town. He assured me that he will be in to give a deposition to you by five this afternoon. He said to call him Coop; his last name is Cooper, I think. I didn't get his first name."

"Hell, Cassie. What's wrong with you? You know better than to go after a witness like that—a transient camping out like that in abandoned property—no telling why he's hiding out or what he's done. You didn't get a full name? Did you get a license or anything? He's likely halfway to Virginia or South Carolina by now. You call yourself a reporter?"

For a moment Cassie felt herself panicking. Yes, inexplicably she had gone about it all wrong, yet she was sure, dead sure, that Coop would be at the sheriff's office at five.

"Jed, he's been in town a couple of times the last day or so. He's well dressed and drives a new black Jeep. Believe me, he's no transient," she said defensively.

Jed shook his head. "Makes no never mind, you've done wrong and you may have to pay for this."

"I just know he'll show up to verify Peggy's story."

"He'd better, Cassie, or your head's in the noose."

Jed looked over her shoulder. "Here comes Larry now. You want to go in with me and try to explain yourself?"

"No, I'm heading back to the newspaper. As far as I know, I'll be there until five. Then I'll come over to the jail. He'll be there. You'll see."

"It's high time you got back to your own job. Mille's in a tizzy. She even called me. My deputies and I have been out all morning covering the storm. Tornado dropped down up near Leaking Creek—bad scene."

CHAPTER 7

Cassie left Larry's office on the run, picking her way through the debris scattered along Court Way. As Cassie opened the back door of the newspaper office, Mille blasted off.

"Damn! It's about time you showed up. Do you know what it's like sitting around here chewing my pencil while everything in town busts loose? I mean, I sit here day in and day out taking in gossip items and sorting advertising, and then a day like this comes along and I'm just sitting and waiting. Where in tarnation is your cell phone?"

Cassie reached for her jeans belt and then realized she had accidentally left her phone in her car before she saddled Drifter at the farm and had failed to retrieve it in all her dashing about. Another screwup, she thought.

"Jed said you were in a tizzy; looks like he was right. What's going on that I don't know about?"

"Your father always said, 'When bad news is rolling, it comes in like a tidal wave.' Besides Peggy and town storm damage, a tornado dropped down out Leaking Creek way. Folks dead and hurt we hear, not sure of all the details yet. Ace is on it."

Just then Ace Coleman slammed the back door on his way into the office. Ace was the only official photographer for the paper as well as the sports editor. Ace had begun working part-time for the *Clayton Landing Weekly* while he was still taking photography classes in high school. He had a natural ability with the camera, a sunny disposition that seemed reflected in his tousled blonde hair, and a knack for melting Mille's wrath.

"This may be my chance to hit the AP, Cass. I got some great pictures—human interest stuff. I'm going to shoot the best off to CNN and MSNBC," he said excitedly as he entered his cubicle.

34

"What happened? Who got hurt?" Cassie asked.

Ace began entering pictures into the computer and scrutinizing them as he talked. "A tornado touched down between the Anderson place and Leaking Creek. It tore through the woods behind Lilly Johnson's—took down her house and went on across the road and took out most of Brown's Country Store and completely destroyed two other homes. One side of the Mt. Zion Baptist Church had roofing blown off, windows broken, and shutters scattered."

Cassie stood behind Ace and watched as picture after picture appeared on the computer screen.

"Course the worst part, there are three dead and two injured. It hasn't been confirmed yet, but near as I could get the facts, it was Lilly Johnson, Grandma Tillie Carter, and a man name of Millard Jones who apparently had a heart attack in the store from fright. Grandma Tillie's two grandchildren were injured, but not badly. Hey, that one's a humdinger," Ace said, pointing to the computer.

It was a picture of a small child sitting in the wreck of a house with the roof blown off. The child and his dog were peeking out from under a blanket that was over their heads.

Cassie turned to Mille. "I'll get over to the hospital and check on the dead and injured. Then I'll go out to Leaking Creek and do a follow-up, particularly on the child's picture. I know Linwood Johnson is in town. I saw him just this morning. He'll be devastated. I'll see if I can find him."

"Not before you tell me about Peggy. What went on there? This is supposed to be a newspaper office where we know all the breaking news, you know," Mille said.

"Look, I'll explain later. There is an investigation going on, and we can't be sure of the facts right now. Peggy did have a baby, and it was stillborn, but Jed isn't too sure of her story yet. He's working on it, and as soon as he gets things straight, I can start working on an article."

Mille frowned. "And just when do you expect that will be?"

"I believe I'll have enough facts by morning. There's just a lot of speculation right now. I'll be over at Jed's office at five o'clock this afternoon. The facts should be clearer by then. I'll grab my cell phone and keep in touch." There were times when Cassie felt like reminding Mille just who was editor of the paper.

"We could have delayed the paper a few hours if you hadn't insisted on sending it to the printers early. It's not every day we have this much excitement in town," Mille grumbled.

"Strike three," Cassie mumbled to herself as she picked up her tote bag and left.

CHAPTER 8

As Cassie pulled into the hospital parking lot, she suddenly had a flashback, remembering the morning that her father died. She sat in the car taking in deep breaths before reluctantly going through the entrance doors.

Cassie went to the administrative office, where she verified Ace's report of the dead. She witnessed a few more injured straggling into the emergency room. Before leaving, Cassie stopped by Peggy's room.

"I hear you're doing all right. I talked to Jilly a few minutes ago to tell her that I will be taking you home tomorrow. Pearl will be delighted to have someone to fuss over for a few days."

"Thanks, Cassie. I feel good, considering. They aren't telling me much. Do you know where my baby girl is? Did they get Sadar?"

"The baby is downstairs in the hospital morgue. The coroner has to check her and write a report. Yes, they got Sadar. He's over at the jail where he will be staying for some time. Is there anything you need?"

"No, I know you have a lot to do with the storm and all. Jilly said she would come by this evening. She went over to the school to help with the kids."

"Yes, I know. Jilly said all's well; the elementary school missed the brunt of the storm."

Cassie left the parking lot and headed for Leaking Creek.

Most of the damage she saw along the way was due to downed electric wires felled by tree limbs. As she neared Leaking Creek, signs of damage increased: felled trees, furniture strewn about, parts of blown-off roofs lying in the ditch. She stopped at Brown's store where a group of people were gathered. There she filled her pad with notes and learned the name of the child in Ace's picture—Jimmy, Tillie Carter's grandson.

It wasn't difficult to find Linwood. He was sitting on the brick steps at Lilly's house. Behind him, the entire house had collapsed. Friends and neighbors were roaming among the debris, collecting a few items that were salvageable. As she approached him, Cassie noticed that tears were streaming down his face. In his hands he held Lilly's Bible.

"I'm so sorry, Linwood. I know that your mom meant everything to you."

Linwood nodded but said nothing.

Cassie gazed at the destruction around her as tears welled in her eyes. She sat down beside Linwood without speaking. She wanted to take his hand but wasn't sure if that would be the right thing to do. Linwood was a good deal older than Cassie. Her father had followed his career and befriended him as a youth. After Linwood became a professor, they sometimes sat and talked for hours.

Feeling helpless, Cassie rose, and Linwood spoke.

"If only I had taken her to my place. Maybe if I had stayed with her I would have recognized the sound when the tornado approached—got her under the kitchen table. I just left her there all alone."

Cassie knew that nothing she could say would console Linwood. She laid her hand on his shoulder. After a few moments, he reached up and laid his hand over hers.

"I had better get back to town. Pearl and I will be there for the funeral. I'm sure Pearl will come laden down with food for the after-service gathering. If we can help in any other way, please let me know."

Her voice choked as she spoke. Her words felt trite and completely inadequate.

At that moment, a woman Cassie did not know approached Linwood. She was holding a fully intact blue flowered sugar bowl. She deposited the bowl in a small pile accumulating beside the steps.

Linwood bent forward, rested his elbows on his knees and covered his face in his hands as he tried to maintain control.

Cassie barely reached her car before she began to shake with uncontrollable tears. She drove a little way down the lane and then stopped. Cassie sat weeping for Lilly, for Peggy, and for the baby. But mostly, memories of her father had suddenly overwhelmed her. Right now she felt inundated. She needed him.

After some time, Cassie got control of herself. She reached for a tissue and then fumbled for her compact and comb. She glanced at the dashboard clock. She had just time enough to check in with Mille and drop off her notes before going back to the sheriff's office.

"Some hard-nosed reporter you are," she said aloud as she started her motor once more.

CHAPTER 9

Cooper drove slowly as he approached his turn off River Road. As he turned into the lane that led to Wahala Hall, he slowed the Jeep to a crawl and then came to a stop where the edge of the woods met lawn. Thoughts rushed through his mind like a wind storm. No amount of anticipation of the meeting ahead of him had truly prepared him. Déjà vu rippled through his veins, pumping his heart. Despite all reason, his senses were conjuring up feelings out of nowhere that he belonged in these surroundings. His soul was coming home, and it seemed to soar toward something familiar even as his body warily approached the unknown.

Still in the shadows at the edge of the woods, Cooper got out of the car and leaned against the fender, surveying the scene before him.

Wahala Hall was typical of many antebellum Southern mansions, with its white columns and wide veranda. Also typically, at some point in its history, wings had been added on either side of the brick main house. Twin chimneys rose between the wings and the original building. Set back and off to the side of the west wing, a tennis court had been added. The lawn was presently strewn with storm debris from fallen limbs of old magnolias and towering oaks. The wide lane turned in a circle just beyond the point where Cooper was parked. It led up to brick steps in front of Wahala, and then doubled back on itself as if inviting you to come and expecting you to leave.

Fresh thoughts leaped about in Cooper's head. In his mind, he had practiced many scenarios leading to this day. Now his emotions seemed to be writing a new script.

He knew some of the history of Wahala Hall. It had been built in the late seventeen hundreds and had always belonged to the Lansfields—

sometimes shared by two families. Through the years, the inhabitants of Wahala had distinguished themselves mostly as lawyers, politicians, and doctors. Not unlike many distinguished families, there had been an occasional black sheep.

The rear of Wahala Hall overlooked terraced gardens that ran down to the Pasqua River. About halfway down and off to the side, close to the woods, stood a preserved smokehouse, testimony to another time.

From Cooper's vantage point, the scene was exactly as his mother had described. The rest he had gleaned from the *Clayton Landing Weekly* and research. For several years, Cooper had been a regular reader of the *Weekly*. During garden week, the paper featured locally famous homes, and Wahala Hall had been among them. Pictures of the main house, the front hall with its winding stairway lined with family portraits, the dining room, and the terraced gardens had burned into his brain—a healing source he needed and yet had inexplicably fought against with all his conflicted being.

Cooper's thoughts turned to the present inhabitants. Until his recent retirement, Dr. Martin Lansfield had been a physician and medical director at Clayton County Regional Hospital, which the Lansfield family had originally built and endowed. It had been expanded and sold to a major health organization several years ago. According to the *Clayton Landing Weekly* article, Martin was the last remaining Lansfield.

The other inhabitant was Mavis Ludlow-Lansfield. Her mother, Adelaide, had married Martin some fifteen years ago. Cooper had seen Mavis's name many times listed among attendees at charity balls, tennis meets, and other social activities. A picture frequently accompanied articles. Cooper had studied the pictures. Mavis appeared to be in her mid-twenties, with dark hair that was just short of coal black. Her wardrobe apparently leaned toward the low-cut, showing ample bosom. Each picture captured the same frozen sorceress smile.

Cooper came out of his reverie. He brushed a bit of dried mud off his otherwise crisp tan chinos.

"Must have come from Drifter," Cooper said aloud. "Well, I guess I had better get on with it before I back out."

He turned toward the back door of the Jeep and retrieved a tie and then proceeded to contort himself so he could use the side mirror. He grabbed a jacket that lay on the front seat. Satisfied that he looked presentable, he climbed back into the Jeep.

The motor turned over smoothly and idled for several minutes until finally Cooper's foot slowly touched the gas pedal.

CHAPTER 10

Mavis was in a fret. A clap of thunder had awakened her long before her accustomed hour. She was a night person who rarely awakened before noon. She lay listening to the storm until it abated. When she did venture to turn her head toward the bedside table, she found that the clock was blinking a meaningless time of day. Her arm slid across the pink satin sheet and brushed the clock to the floor. She rose up on an elbow and looked around. The pink flowered drapes were tightly closed. The shadowy light in the room gave little clue as to the status of the weather outside. The bedroom was warm and stuffy.

"Drat."

She threw the sheet off with the force of her displeasure, and it landed in a heap by the foot of the bed. Long, perfectly tanned legs swung to the floor. Carefully manicured toes rummaged in the thick carpet until they found her waiting slippers.

As she crossed the room, she paused before the full-length mirror that drew her like a magnet. She gazed at her reflection. The room's dimness emphasized the short white satin nightgown that covered her full bosom, her small waist, her flat stomach. The tiny pearl earrings in her lobes shone against a tennis-tanned oblong face framed by jet-black hair. Without turning away from the mirror, she fumbled for the drapery cord on the adjoining wall and gave it a yank. Light streaming across the mirror unveiled a hard-set-jaw and cold, dark green eyes.

Mavis turned to the window. The lawn was littered with broken tree limbs and scattered leaves. Soaked pillows blown from the veranda furniture were scattered about. A broken pot lay surrounded by its former geranium tenants.

Mavis crossed the room and threw open the door, stepped into the hall, and leaned over the banister rail.

"Cor-ley."

She did not expect an answer. She expected Corley to appear with coffee and a toasted muffin while she showered.

There was no Corley, no coffee, and no muffin when she finished her shower.

"What the hell?"

Mavis quickly dressed in her favorite tennis outfit, leaving a trail of nightgown, slippers, and wet towels behind her.

As she entered the kitchen, she glanced at the battery-operated clock above the sink—it was nearly noon. Corley was not in the kitchen.

Her annoyance grew. The back door slammed as she left the kitchen to inspect the tennis courts. The courts were a mess. Leaves and twigs covered the concrete and were imbedded in the net. In the far corner, Wardin, the grounds man (as Mavis referred to him) was beginning to clean up.

"I knowed you would want this court cleaned up first thing, Miss Mavis. That sho' was some storm."

"You're right for a change. Where the hell is Corley?"

"She done gone down by Leaking Creek, Miss Mavis. The storm done tore up the hollow. She was worried about her kinfolk. She said to tell you the coffee is made and the muffin be in the toaster oven buttered and all—jes' push that button what starts it. The electricity came back on jus' a while ago."

"See you have this court cleaned off by four. I may bring friends back from the club this afternoon." She delivered these instructions over her shoulder as she stalked off the court.

Wardin stared after her.

"Things just ain't been the same since that girl and her mama put foot on this here place," he mumbled to himself.

Mavis yanked the screened back door open to its full breadth as she reentered the kitchen. It slammed resoundingly behind her. As she poured her coffee, she gave a minute's thought to where the old man might be. He was probably in his office staring at the portrait that he'd recently brought down from the attic. He had been acting strangely since that letter came. It was locked in his desk drawer. He kept the key on a ring secured to his belt. She often thought there must be a way to get her hands on that key.

"Drat it." She rushed to the sink to dab water on a spot of coffee staining her impeccable white shorts.

Mavis retrieved a muffin from the toaster oven and sat down at the kitchen table. She was not used to sitting in the kitchen and felt out of place. A frown creased her brow; she tapped a brightly polished fingernail on the table while her thoughts turned to her mother. It had been quite a triumph for both of them when the widow Adelaide landed Martin Lansfield. Her strong-willed mother had quickly gotten Martin in line. Everything had been going so well until Adelaide became ill. It had been a terrible shock to Mavis when her mother died a year ago. Adelaide was so much younger than Martin. He should have died first, the way it was supposed to happen, and then her mother would have inherited everything since there was no heir to Wahala Hall. Now Mavis wasn't too sure what the old fool would do.

The doorbell rang. Mavis listened. Corely was gone, Wardin was in the yard. Martin had not appeared.

"Drat."

The doorbell rang again. She flounced to the front hall, her agitation mounting.

She had opened the door barely a crack when her whole demeanor changed. Her stomach muscles drew in and hardened, thrusting her bosom upward. Habitually, one leg moved slightly forward, throwing her pelvis into an inviting angle. The man at the door missed none of this.

"Afternoon, although not such a good one," he said, while gesturing toward the lawn behind him. Turning back toward Mavis, he smiled and added, "The description of your beauty has been understated."

Mavis was rarely caught off guard when it came to men, but for a moment she found herself actually flustered. The man was exceptionally handsome. His body was perfect. The crooked smile topped off by a teasing twinkle in his eye instantly ignited her steamy blood. A familiar tingle simmered.

"I'm Cooper Canaday. Dr. Lansfield is expecting me."

"He didn't say anything about expecting someone. I really don't know where he is at the moment, but do come in. Have we met before?" Mavis's exaggerated southern drawl was counterpoint to Cooper's slight New England accent.

Cooper ignored Mavis's question. He stepped into the grand hall. His eyes immediately swept every corner, checking details that were etched into his mind as if he had seen them many times before. Fresh flowers arranged in a low Chinese bowl highlighted the round center table. An oriental carpet ran the length of the hall. Wide plank flooring bordered the carpet. Family portraits lined the long hall as well as the walls leading to the second floor. At the foot of the stairs, in the allotted space for the mistress of the house, the portrait of Adelaide was in place. The portrait of a young woman in a white dress carrying a bouquet of daisies was nowhere to be seen.

CHAPTER 11

Martin Lansfield sat in his office in the east wing. He silently thanked his ancestor, Senator Robert Lansfield, for incorporating this book-lined study into the addition to Wahala. It was strategically located adjacent to the dining room, affording a great deal of privacy. The formal dining room was seldom used. A small family dining room off the kitchen overlooking the terraces was used daily. During the past few years, the office had become a haven, a refuge from entanglements with Adelaide and Mavis—now just Mavis. He was at peace here among his books and memorabilia.

Until just months ago, the hospital had been his life. The young whippersnappers had begun to run circles around him. When the town held a testimonial to his long service, he figured there was also the hint that he was too old, past his time. Of late he contented himself with showing up at board meetings and reviewing a case now and then.

Martin spent most of the morning watching the storm through his binoculars. When the worst was over, he settled into his desk chair, lit his pipe, and took the well-worn letter from the desk drawer. He still found the contents unbelievable, but he clung to the hope that it was true. He looked at the portrait that he had recently brought down from the attic. It now hung on the wall opposite his desk. He studied it. The pretty young woman in the portrait wore a flowing white dress and carried a bouquet of field daisies. She barely resembled the renowned actress Madalaine. It was small wonder that he had never connected the two. Again he glanced at the letter. "God willing, let it be true," he thought to himself.

He rose once more to look out the window. He had a clear view of the driveway where he was easily able to see anyone approaching the house.

He had wanted his visitor to see Wahala at its best, but now debris was everywhere.

"I'll call what's-his-name to come and help Wardin," he mumbled aloud to himself. For a moment he concentrated on trying to remember what's-his-name's proper name, but he gave up before it came to him.

Martin stepped into the small office bathroom and studied his face in the mirror, inspecting his earlier shave. His hair was pure white. His skin retained its pale hospital pallor. Strange, he thought, that the Lansfield men had clear fair skin despite the dark auburn hair of their youth. No freckles. His eyes were dark brown, his forehead permanently creased.

The sound of a car caught his attention. Quickly stepping to the front window, he saw a Jeep enter the long circular driveway. It stopped just short of the veranda. Cooper hopped out, went to the front of the Jeep, picked up a magnolia limb blocking the driveway and tossed it aside on the lawn. He then stood for a few minutes surveying Wahala Hall.

As Martin raised his binoculars for a better look, the sun broke through the fast-moving clouds. Cooper lifted his head to meet the streaming light. His dark auburn hair soaked up the sun and reflected it back here and there in glints of gold.

She had said in the letter, "There will be no doubt when you see him." Martin's heart skipped a beat.

Martin had planned every detail of this moment. He carefully adjusted his tie and reached for the coat hanging on the wall rack. He went through the kitchen, made his way to the back stairs, ascended to the second floor, and then stood at the top of the grand hall stairway. Standing there, he mustered all the dignity the moment required. Below he could hear Mavis administering her particular brand of charm, sprinkled heavily with the sexual intonations she typically employed with all the subtlety of a cat rubbing against its master's leg when desperate for dinner.

Martin drew in his breath, stretched himself to his full height, and began his descent down the wide staircase. Despite himself, tears began to well. He made a conscious effort to hold them back. The two men locked eyes. Mavis became aware of a peculiar electricity in the air and suddenly felt as shut out as if she were not in the hall at all.

When Martin reached the last step, Cooper stepped closer with his hand stretched forward, but his intent changed and in the next instant he folded the teary-eyed man in his arms. When they separated, Martin motioned for Cooper to join him in the sitting room. Without a word, the two men left the hall, and Martin closed the heavy wood sliding doors of the sitting room behind them.

Mavis, open mouthed, was left standing alone.

CHAPTER 12

Martin took his time with the doors, making sure they were tightly closed to ward off any eavesdropping possibilities. Mavis would surely try.

Cooper's gaze quickly roamed the room. An oriental rug in hues of blue dominated the room. On either side of the fireplace were two comfortable sofas upholstered in pale blue with a large coffee table between them. A magnificent grandfather clock caught his eye. Bookcases along one wall held the collection of books and memorabilia coveted by several generations. Side chairs in gold and a baby grand piano of indeterminate age filled the remainder of the room. Despite himself, Cooper felt a sudden warmth come over him—again a strange sense of belonging.

The men turned to face each other. Martin motioned Cooper to one of the sofas. He sat opposite and was the first to speak.

"My life has been right here and at the hospital among my patients. Until recently, each day has been much like any other, except for the days of varying predictable catastrophes and panic that every hospital expects. Overseeing Wahala Hall now takes up my time. I thought it would be ever thus. But life can change in a moment, and that moment came with your mother's letter."

"I'm sure it was quite a shock to you, as it was to me some thirty-four years ago when I turned eighteen."

"Yes, I'm sure it was. Believing you know who you are and then learning that you have the genes of another family would be most traumatic. I can also understand your rebellion," Martin said.

Both men were quiet for a moment, both reflective.

"Well now, I understand you know a great deal about Clayton Landing, Wahala Hall, and the Lansfields. But there is much I need to learn about you, someone I never knew existed until your mother's letter came in the mail a short time ago."

And so Cooper began.

He began back as far as he could remember. There were recollections of life in a New York apartment; of playing in Central Park with other children marshaled by nannies; of trips to the theater where ropes, lights, and backstage excitement impressed more than the stage performances. Theater in one form or another was the family business. Sam Canaday was a well-known wheeler and dealer, Broadway director, producer, and writer. In Cooper's eyes, his mother, Madalaine, was two people—the beautiful fairytale actress and the adored mother who changed from one role to the other like a chameleon. The summer following his graduation from elementary school, the family moved to a mansion in Westport, Connecticut. Life changed. His high school contemporaries moved in circles that included tennis courts and horseback riding, and he moved with them. Despite all the social distractions, he managed to be a good student.

"It was shortly after my high school graduation, the day after my eighteenth birthday, my mother and dad—Sam ..." Cooper stumbled in the telling at this point and glanced at Martin, who just nodded and signaled him to continue.

"As I was saying, I remember waking up that morning thinking life was mine to explore, to taste, and to revel in. The world was wide open to me. Those were the thoughts of a carefree young man who had known nothing of life but luxury, protected in a shell of material bliss. Mother and Sam expected me for lunch on the terrace; they needed to talk with me, they had said the night before. While I was glad I was not expected until noon as I had celebrated my birthday late into the night, I was also hoping they would make it brief. I had a tennis match planned in early afternoon. I dressed in preparation and took my tennis racket with me. I was not feeling apprehensive, more euphoric than anything else. I expected to talk about college plans or summer plans. When we finished lunch, Mother leaned closer to me and rested her hand on mine. She took a deep breath and her hand began to tremble."

Martin noticed that Cooper seemed distressed at this point, as if reliving the scene. He rose and went to the dry sink disguised among the bookcases. He poured two glasses of wine. Carrying a small tray, he returned to the sofa and set the tray on the coffee table. Cooper took a sip from his glass and then continued

"I remember being stone silent once mother began speaking. She began by telling me of her life here in Clayton Landing. I had no idea what she was leading up to, but I had never heard her talk about that part of her life, and I found it interesting as well as startling. Then the bombshell came. Mother tried to explain how she and Sam had agonized over this moment, but by that time I had stopped listening."

Cooper stood and walked over to the window. For a minute he was quiet, reflective.

"I remember suddenly standing, my chair falling over. I hurled my tennis racket as far as I could. I ran to my room, tossed a few clothes into a duffel, and left. It was some sort of grand defiance, I suppose. By the time I returned home, I had joined the army. There was nothing Sam and Madalaine could do. They were devastated."

Cooper returned to the sofa, took another sip of wine, and continued.

"After a smattering of training, I was shipped off to Vietnam. It was near the end of the conflict."

"Thank God you returned," Martin interjected.

"I was there less than a year. I got careless and lagged behind in a village fight trying to save a buddy. I caught a bullet in the leg and another one in my upper chest, which fortunately hit nothing vital. I was shipped home a changed person from the playboy I had been."

Cooper leaned forward and rested his elbows on his knees.

"I apologized to my parents, who I knew truly loved me and had given me a fairy-tale life to the point of Vietnam. I told them that I would forget that previous conversation. I shut my mind on the subject and vowed never to open it again"

Restless, Cooper leaned back and stretched his legs. He paused for a few moments, thinking of the best way to explain his present life.

"I greatly admired the skill of the medics in Vietnam; they saved many lives. I suppose that's why I enrolled in college and went on to medical school. But the year before my residency was to occur, I felt compelled to take a different tack. I could not forget about Vietnam. I didn't want it to ever happen again. So I returned to the university and took another approach to seeking a meaningful career—one far more difficult to achieve. I have announced my candidacy for the United States Senate."

"I think you have done enough research on the Lansfields to know that a number of the men in the family have been politicians, and quite distinguished ones at that," Martin said.

"Yes, sir. That is what finally persuaded me to ask my mother to write you a letter. My life must be an open book. There can be no secrets. That is a requirement."

Cooper glanced at his watch. "I didn't realize how late it had gotten to be. I promised I would be at the sheriff's office by five. I'd better get along. I got myself involved in a case."

Martin said, "Oh, so soon on arriving in Clayton Landing?"

"Unfortunately. I am camping out at Rutherford. A young lady appeared in the middle of the night in the state of rapidly approaching childbirth. I'd had enough training to be of assistance. The baby was stillborn, but the sheriff needs an affidavit from me."

"Who was that?"

"Her name was Peggy—that's all I got out of her. I took her to a house that she said was her Aunt Sara's, if that gives you a clue. She pleaded with me to leave her there. Stupidly I did. My only excuse is that I did not want to answer a lot of questions at the hospital."

"Peggy Slater—had to be. Her aunt is a nurse at the hospital. Peggy is good-hearted but a little on the irresponsible side. Keeps her Aunt Sara worried now that Peggy's mother is gone."

Cooper rose.

"May I have your bags brought in?" Martin asked. "We have plenty of room. It can't be too comfortable out at the old Rutherford place. I didn't know your mother still owned it. She fell in love with it shortly after we were married. I bought it for her. Will you be back tonight in time for dinner? I expect Corley will be back to cook for us."

"No sir, not tonight. But I may take you up on that invitation later. For now, I need to meet with two more people in Clayton Landing before I become too public. I'd appreciate it if you kept our meeting in confidence for a few days at least."

Martin raised an eyebrow. He was puzzled as to who those two people might be, since as far as he knew, Cooper had never been to Clayton Landing before. Not wanting to press too much, he let it go. He watched Cooper drive away until he was out of sight. Martin removed Madalaine's letter from the desk drawer and began to read it once more.

CHAPTER 13

Dear Martin,

This letter will come as a shock. I apologize for that. In the beginning, it was my wish to hide the truth from you, and then later it became the wish of someone else. But let me begin when our lives first became entwined. Some of it you will know of course, but not from my perspective.

I remember our first meeting. I was feeling particularly euphoric—pleased with my performance that night. Having a small speaking part as well as being a dancer in a Broadway musical was indeed a dream come true for a twenty-three-year-old from Brooklyn.

You came backstage with some friends that you met at a medical convention and mingled with the cast. I remember that you looked so out of place, and I made an effort to make you feel comfortable. You were so handsome. I think I was instantly smitten. Apparently you were too. I was delighted when you asked me to join you for a nightcap at a club close to the theater. I'm sure you remember that for the rest of the week that you were in New York, we saw each other every chance we got. I loved those late night walks on city streets, afternoon rides on the Staten Island Ferry, and the mornings in Central Park. We were in my world, but our conversations were about your world.

You returned to Clayton Landing and left me with an invitation to join you there for a visit after the closing of the show. It was a month of waiting that seemed like an eternity. I began to romanticize. Of course I had seen pictures of southern mansions. My vision of life in such mansions was colored by movies where ladies wore hoop skirts and strolled on beautiful lawns—silly, of course.

Pictures in magazines did not capture the essence, the smell, the feel that hovers over and seeps into Wahala Hall. I was immediately enchanted. I began playing a role as soon as I stepped into the grand center hall with its polished plank floors and its ornate curved stairway. I pictured myself sweeping down that stairway in a flowing white dress carrying an armful of daisies. Weeks later, I did just that as I became Mrs. Martin Lansfield, mistress of Wahala Hall. I was thrilled with the portrait of me that you had painted. For months I was delirious with happiness. Then suffocation crept into my euphoria. Inside and out, Wahala Hall was run by servants much like a well-trained stage crew. I felt useless; I had no real role. Invitations came to church socials, picnics, and endless teas. I felt out of place, off kilter. Your life was medicine, day and night. Overseeing the building of the new hospital took even your spare time.

Too, I began to see another side of you—a different person than the one I thought I had married. Alone, you were still my romantic lover. But when we were together at functions, you watched me closely and began questioning my every move. You accused me of being a flirt. I had to account for every hour of the day. Your anger flared at my slightest transgression. After a time, I began to picture myself coming down the grand stairway, suitcase in hand.

Then, an announcement in the Clayton Landing Weekly caught my eye. There were to be tryouts for a play sponsored by the local drama society. The play would open the fall season. Without telling you, I jumped at the chance to act once more. I planned to surprise you in hopes that if the play was successful, you would be proud of me. Of course that was a mistake.

I had previously met Cliff Danforth but was surprised to see him at the tryouts. I knew he was the son of the editor of the Clayton Landing Weekly and Clayton Landing's most eligible bachelor, according to the endless gossip at the endless teas. He had recently returned to town after several years away at college and graduate school. Like me, he was restless. It seems he had dabbled in drama in college, among many other interests, and he came to the tryouts out of curiosity and boredom.

I feel that I must again explain what happened. I tried to tell you all this at the time, but you would not listen.

Cliff and I were selected for the lead roles. Cliff was one of those people who never knew a stranger—the party began, the atmosphere changed the minute he entered a room. It worked on stage as well as off. Our chemistry was good. We quietly developed a strong friendship. I had found someone to talk to, someone familiar with a world outside Clayton Landing.

It wasn't long before we were meeting for private rehearsals, since so many of our scenes involved just the two of us. I suggested the grand hall at Wahala because it was a perfect setting. I reasoned that there were ample chaperones around, and I had explained what was taking place to the servants.

As you know, it was during one of these rehearsals that it happened. The scene required a kiss, more of a peck on the cheek. When we broke away, you were at the door. I had never seen such rage. No explanation would placate you. I dropped out of the play. Your coldness and silence went on for over a week. Cliff phoned every day. He felt totally responsible and helpless. I knew our marriage was over.

Finally I called Sam Canaday in New York. Dear, dear Sam. He was Broadway's jack-of-all-trades—producer, director, sometimes actor, and always benefactor to stage fledglings. Our whole cast had considered him a friend as well as our director. Shortly before the show had closed, he stopped me backstage. He said he'd seen a spark in me, encouraged me to work hard and not give up.

You did not just discuss with Sam. He went into action.

"Come home by the way of Reno, darling, it's very simple—Reno, the place to lick wounds and shed mates," he said.

In a few days, he had made all the arrangements for a quick divorce. When I told you, you turned your back and walked away. For the next few days, you acted as if I did not exist.

I withdrew all my savings from the bank, the remainder of a small inheritance from my parents plus what I had saved of your generous allowance. It would see me through a fast Reno divorce, I reasoned.

Cliff saw me off. We promised to keep in touch.

Eight weeks later, my divorce decree in hand, I arrived back in New York with little money left. I was very pregnant. There was never a doubt in my mind that you would never know about my child.

Once more Sam came to my rescue. I remember his words so well. "My dear, everyone suspects that I am not of the persuasion that leads to marriage. They are right. However, my adorable mother would go to her grave much happier to see me married and settled. She would treasure a grandchild. So, see, both our problems will be solved. In addition, I will make you a star. It can be quite a partnership."

And quite a partnership it was. We slipped out of town and were married by a justice of the peace. Sam announced that we had been married months before in Reno. Broadway questioned very little when Sam spoke.

My mousey brown hair was changed to champagne blonde, highlighting my natural deep blue eyes. Makeup was applied until just the right combination brought out my best features. Sam hired a voice coach and scheduled drama lessons with the best professionals. Even in pregnancy, I was not allowed to waddle. I learned to walk with a majestic flair. The pretty girl from Brooklyn magically became a beauty. When I looked into the mirror, I saw a stranger and I liked her. Susan Marie Fletcher from Brooklyn was no more.

"Madalaine, I like that—emphasis on 'laine'—pronounced like lane. No last name, just Madalaine." With those words, Sam christened me anew. Shortly after the baby was born, I was ready to step into the limelight, and Sam opened all the doors.

We christened the baby Cooper Canaday, but his birth certificate read Cooper Lansfield Canaday. Some small voice inside me would not let me strip Cooper's heritage entirely.

Sam adored Cooper with a special kind of sensitivity. Cooper bonded our peculiar relationship. To the outside world, we were the perfect family, a rarity in show business. Oddly enough, our unconsummated life together worked privately as well. Freed of the sexual battleground and its parameters of jealousy and frustrated desires, we were able to concentrate on our careers. Our friendship and respect for each other created a winning combination.

As I rose to stardom, the life I had lived in Clayton Landing was soon forgotten, except for Cliff. He came to Washington and New York often. He said his father sent him off to poke around in the halls of the Capitol to see a different side of politicians than was known at home and to write about what he saw. He came to New York to watch the world walk by, a background for many of his articles.

Sam liked Cliff, and the three of us were seen about New York on rare occasions. Sam always introduced him as a cousin. He never expanded. Cliff frequently visited our New York apartment. We rarely mentioned Clayton Landing. Cliff and I touched with our eyes, sometimes with our fingers, a greeting kiss on the cheek—never with our bodies. It would have spoiled something so rare as to be undefined.

Cliff was the only person other than Sam and me who knew about Cooper's birthright. We could not hide it from him. My little tyke was a carbon copy of his father, and Cliff was a link to both. Sam and I knew that someday we would have to tell Cooper the truth. The three of us often discussed this. Someday kept stretching on and on.

We finally told Cooper about his birthright following his graduation from high school. It traumatized him for months and threatened our relationship. He joined the army, went to Vietnam, and came home wounded. Slowly his wounds healed, inward and outward. Cooper was born with a deep-thinking maturity that was always beyond his years. I believe it was that maturity that brought him finally to my room one night, where he told me that he thought it mattered very little how his life began; it mattered only how it was lived and how it would end—what purpose it would serve. I think perhaps I have never loved my son so much as at that moment. He also said it was his wish never to discuss his lineage again. As far as he was concerned, Sam was his father and always would be.

Something happened to change his mind. I will leave that for him to explain. A few months ago, shortly after Sam died, he came to me and asked me to write this letter to you.

As I said at the beginning of the letter, all that I have written will be a shock to you. You will probably feel very angry at first, and of course cheated. Bear this in mind. Cooper would not be the man he is today had he been torn between us and our incongruent lives. As a grown man, his own man, he will now come to you by choice. You will be very proud as you come to know him. When you see him, there will be no denying that Cooper Lansfield Canaday is your son.

Once yours,

Madalaine

CHAPTER 14

Cooper arrived at the sheriff's office a little before five o'clock. A clerk was busy at the copier. A uniformed man sat behind a low counter. He wore a badge that identified him as Deputy Tully Reese.

"Well, I expect you are that stranger Sheriff Ryan is expecting. Didn't I pass you on the road up near Calvary Methodist Church a couple of days ago driving a black Jeep? I keep my eyes open around here. Not much gets by that I don't spot."

"There is a church near where I'm staying; not sure it's Calvary though. Is the sheriff here?"

"He'll be coming in. You're early. Come on in to his office, he'll be here directly. Heard you claim to know something about Peggy Slater's baby."

Tully led the way as he talked.

Before Cooper could reply, Sheriff Jed Ryan entered the office and introduced himself. He motioned for Cooper to sit in the chair opposite his desk.

"Tully, go on out front and mind the store. Close the door behind you—all the way."

The sheriff waited until Tully had reluctantly complied and then asked, "What is your name? Just what is it that brings you to Clayton Landing? What can you tell me about the birth of Peggy Slater's baby?"

Although he pulled no punches, Jed Ryan's tone was not harsh.

"My name is Cooper Canaday. As to why I'm here, I've come to see a couple of people about a business proposition and to get acquainted with Clayton Landing. As for Peggy, she was obviously in distress, and by happenstance, I was available. I don't know what she told you, but she stumbled in at the Rutherford place in hard labor in the middle of the night.

With no minutes to spare, I set about delivering the baby. Unfortunately, the baby was apparently early. The little girl was stillborn."

"You got any credentials for delivering a baby? Peggy says you seemed to know just what to do."

"I have no more official credentials than you would have if you stopped a car barreling down the road and found a woman in the middle of childbirth inside. But I've had several years of medical college that did include delivery. I can verify that." Cooper knew what the next question would be.

"And why in tarnation did you not take her to the hospital?"

"For one, she protested vigorously. She assured me that her Aunt Sara who lived just down the road was a nurse and would take care of her. For another, I was trying to avoid showing my face around town too much until I had settled my business. She seemed strong and she was very determined. You know, modern medicine now measures the time new mothers stay in hospitals in hours instead of days—up-and-at-it mentality prevails."

Jed tapped his pencil on his desk for a few seconds.

"What are you doing at the Rutherford place? It seems like you are trespassing to me. I know Ben Jones is looking after the place. I called him. He said he knew you were there—had permission from some corporation that owns it, the one that sends him a check now and then. I checked over at the county records; seems a corporation by the name of Canaday Enterprises has owned it for many years. I never thought to look it up before. I suppose you somehow relate to this Canaday Enterprises."

"In a manner of speaking. A relative of mine owns the company."

Jed resumed tapping his pencil.

"Well, for your information, a friend of Peggy's, Jilly Rogers, insisted that Peggy belonged in the hospital. I let her take her over to the hospital to have her checked. I called the hospital to make sure they kept her until I got things settled in my mind. My deputies and I were too busy to do much else except monitor storm damage for a while there. I just got a preliminary report from the county coroner. He's right busy. We had some folks killed in the storm. Anyway, he said it appears that Peggy is telling the truth about the baby being stillborn; he'll do a full autopsy later. That opinion along with your testimony makes me comfortable enough to drop any charges as far as Peggy is concerned. I've got Sadar Miles, the bastard that raped her, locked up out back. He's going to be here for a while."

"That's good. Sorry I didn't use better judgment. I guess we all have a lapse now and then."

"Well, just don't make it too often, not while you're in my territory. I hear you met Cassie Danforth. She wasn't using good judgment this morning either. Seems the whole town is turned upside down. You can go along now, but I hope you plan to stay in town a few days in case something comes up."

"You can find me at the Rutherford place. I'm sure your deputy will keep an eye on me."

When Cooper returned to the front office, he saw Cassie leaning on the counter talking to the deputy.

"Oh, there he is now," she said to Tully. Turning to Cooper, she said, "I was waiting around to catch up with you."

Cooper smiled, took Cassie's arm, and led her outside without speaking.

CHAPTER 15

"Hey, don't I even get a hello?" Cassie said as they stood on the sidewalk in front of the sheriff's office.

"Sorry, I just wanted to avoid that deputy making too much out of anything we said."

"That's understandable. You judged him correctly. He seems to think everyone's business is his business too."

"How's Peggy?"

"My friend, Jilly, took over and demanded that the sheriff release her to the hospital. Peggy checked out just fine. I stopped by the hospital to see her just about an hour ago. She'll be released in the morning, and she's coming to my house for a few days. My housekeeper, Pearl, will love mothering her."

"Good. I'm feeling very guilty about not taking her to the hospital myself."

"Now let's get to you. My investigative instincts finally kicked in, and I went online to confirm my suspicions. So if you aren't Mr. Cooper L. Canaday, Lt. Governor of the State of Connecticut and recently announced candidate for the U.S. Senate, then you are his twin brother who doesn't exist."

"Guilty," Cooper said sheepishly but with a big grin. "Look, is there some place we can go for dinner and talk?"

"I would very much like that. I have a lot of questions—like why are you also the spitting image of a younger Dr. Martin Lansfield?"

"Not here on the sidewalk. I promise I'll explain everything, but not here. I'm still trying to lay low for a few days. Besides you, I have one other person I should meet with before all this becomes fodder for the press."

"Besides me? I am one of the three people you mentioned that you had to see in Clayton Landing?"

"Yes."

"More mystery. Well, I've already told Pearl that I might bring someone home for supper. She's thrilled. We haven't had guests since my father died. I told her to set up supper on the back veranda."

"Sounds great."

Pearl would join Cassie for meals on the veranda or at the kitchen table but never in the dining room, so they rarely used the dining room.

As Cassie and Cooper walked from the sheriff's office down the back alley to Cassie's house, she explained her closeness with Pearl.

"She is more like a mother to me than a housekeeper, but she prefers that title. It gives her some sense of authority, she says."

On entering the kitchen, Cooper smiled broadly as he took Pearl's hand in his. "What is that wonderful aroma? I've heard that you are the best cook around these parts. I'm honored."

Pearl was immediately disarmed.

To include Pearl in the conversation, talk at supper ranged from the storm damage to some of the history of Clayton Landing.

"I've read quite a bit about Clayton Landing's history, but that's not quite like really getting acquainted with its character or its peculiar layout."

"I'll tackle its character," Cassie said. "I know you've driven around town. I'm sure you've noticed all of our large historic homes. Most were built in the mid-seventeen hundreds to mid-eighteen hundreds by the more prosperous of the times. Many are still owned by ancestors of the original builders. Since I've been out in the world more, sometimes when I come home, I've wondered if these dwellings have some kind of undue influence on their inhabitants, leaving them in some kind of time warp."

Pearl interjected. "Land sakes, Cassie, I've never heard you talk like that. I always thought you were proud to live in this house. Now you own it. Anyway, Mr. Cooper, the town has made some progress over time. The warehouses that used to be behind the old courthouse were torn down about ten years ago, and now we have a modern jail behind the old one, a new courthouse facing Church Street, and a new school up off Main Street, not to speak of our hospital with its new modern wing."

"I think Coop knows what I mean, Pearl. Sometimes people are just better able to cope with life if they wrap a shell around themselves. Now I'm sounding philosophical. I didn't mean to get off on that tack."

"I wondered why so many alleyways connected the Green and the new courthouse complex," said Cooper. "I can see that they do accommodate the new buildings without opening up the Green area to too much traffic."

Pearl rose and began to clear the table. "Now you two young ones just run along while I take care of these dishes. I plan on retiring to my room and catching *Jeopardy* as usual."

As they made their way through the kitchen, Cassie said, "There's a secluded corner on the front veranda where we can be away from eyes and ears."

The night rhythms had settled in by the time they reached the porch. The waves in the Sound slapped at the rocks and the stone retaining wall. Crickets and tree frogs lent their brand of music to the night. Flitting fireflies scurried about as if conducting it all. Cassie took the wicker rocker while Cooper settled in the padded porch swing, the squeak of metal chains adding to nature's cacophony.

"The trelliswork and ivy at this end of the porch gives us some privacy. Weekends, I often curl up with a good book undetected."

Neither spoke for a few minutes, soaking in moments of respite from an exhausting day. Muffin pushed open the screen door and made her way to Cassie's lap.

"I suppose I should apologize for not recognizing you, especially since I am supposed to be a political reporter. But then, it's not everyday I find the Lt. Governor of Connecticut in an old relic of a mansion having just delivered a baby. Now will you explain why you're here?"

"Only if you agree that what I am about to tell you is strictly off the record for now."

"Do I have a choice?"

"No. I will promise you that when the time comes, you will get an exclusive. When a politician decides to dump his skeletons on the public, he might as well choose his own media."

"That's fair enough."

"As you now probably know, I am the son of Madalaine, the famous actress. And, as far as anyone knows, I am the son of Sam Canaday, her equally famous husband. Although my birth certificate indicates that as a fact, it is not the truth. Actually I am Martin Lansfield's natural son, though he never knew I existed. Until I was eighteen, I didn't know either. Until recently, I have not acknowledged him as my father in any way. He learned of my existence just weeks ago. Until this afternoon, we had never met."

"Lordy, Lordy, as Pearl would say." Automatically, she mentally began framing questions for her exclusive.

"Don't think I haven't heavily weighed my decision to make this public. But politics is a dirty business. Some super sleuth commissioned to dig just might connect my looks and middle name to the Lansfield family. It would be used to my opponent's benefit. If I come forth, I can present the true facts. Conceivably, opening the family closet could work to my advantage."

"You bet it could. The South loves its dramas, especially among its favorite sons. Soap operas merely imitate life. My father often repeated that old cliché."

"The time has come for me to rewrite the script. Secrets are not compatible with public life if one wants to survive. I have to get this out in the open before I start campaigning in earnest."

"I'll be only too happy to oblige when you give me the word. What a boost this exclusive would give me if I were still in Washington. Right now I'm on leave. Maybe my boss will let me conduct an exclusive interview."

"I suppose such an interview is inevitable. But there's more you need to hear."

"You've also robbed a bank or have six kids hidden away."

Cooper laughed. "No, nothing like that. The rest of my life is already an open book. My wife died of breast cancer several years ago. No kids. I've never felt the need to rob a bank."

"Good. One major disclosure is enough."

"You see, I'm here to see you as well as Martin Lansfield. I need to explain what part your father has played in my life."

Cassie cocked her head and looked puzzled.

"I don't understand."

"Your father and my mother had a platonic friendship here in Clayton Landing many years ago. In fact, that relationship contributed to the breakup of my mother's marriage to Martin, although according to my mother, the divorce would have eventually happened anyway."

"That may explain why my father and Dr. Lansfield were so distant with one another. So your mother was actually married to Martin? I don't see how Martin could have been married to the famous Madalaine without that fact being known in Clayton Landing."

"She was not Madalaine then. She was Susan Marie Fletcher, a fledgling actress and dancer who Martin met while attending a medical conference in New York. He was smitten, as was she. At his invitation, she joined him in Clayton Landing. They were married for a little over three years. She was pregnant when she left, but she never told Martin—that is, until a few weeks ago. I suppose it was easy for people to forget a mousy northern misfit, as Madalaine described her former self."

"When Martin married Adelaide, I vaguely remember Mille mentioning that he had been married before. Dad never brought up the subject. I can't imagine how this secret was kept for so long. It doesn't make any sense. Wouldn't Martin have recognized Madalaine?"

"No, her appearance was entirely changed. Sam Canaday let it be known around Broadway that she was his long-time protégé. They were secretly married shortly after my mother's Reno divorce. I was always accepted as their son; no one was ever the wiser—except your father."

Cooper moved to the end of the swing close to Cassie's chair. He took her hands in his.

"Do you remember visiting New York with your father when you were about five?"

"Vaguely. I remember being fascinated by all the Broadway lights. We went to several plays and fancy restaurants. I had some new dresses and felt like a princess."

Cooper laughed and then turned serious again.

"Do you remember going backstage at one of the theaters and meeting the cast? Madalaine and Sam were there, and so was I. It was an opening night, and I came down from Connecticut for the weekend."

"Again, vaguely. But, sorry, I don't remember you. There were so many people."

"Well, it wasn't your father's first visit and certainly not his last. He and Sam and Madalaine remained good friends and confidants all these years until Sam died a few months ago. Your father went to the funeral and then visited my mother once after that before he died."

Cassie was silent for several minutes. Cooper rose and walked to the steps and scanned the sky while she digested the events he had just recounted.

"As close as I was to my father, what you have just told me is difficult to believe. I've been in the media business long enough to know that people do lead double lives—but not my father. What purpose would he have?"

Cooper turned back to the swing and sat close to Cassie. Again, he took her hands in his.

"Cassie, you meant everything to your father. I'm sure he did not remotely think of himself as leading a double life. He just needed to separate this one aspect of his life for my protection, Madalaine's protection, and your protection. What you did not know, you could not disclose."

"So you're saying my father kept your family informed about Clayton Landing and Martin Lansfield?"

"No, I am not saying that. Actually, I think it was taboo to talk about the past except for their dilemma where I was concerned. At least, that is what my mother tells me. However, he always had new pictures of you to show us. We knew how you were doing in high school, your college choice, career choice. He was so proud of you. I just thought it natural that a friend would share his daughter with us. I know mother kept him informed about my doings. Our relationship changed after I was told the truth. Although I professed no interest in ever contacting Martin Lansfield, I frequently questioned Cliff about Clayton Landing and my natural family. As I leaned more and more toward politics, he also became a mentor on the subject."

"I have to have time to think about all this. This day has been too much. I can't think right now. I have to give it some time," Cassie said.

"I understand. But I hope in a day or two we can meet again and include the third person I came to see."

"Who might that be?"

"Remember this is off the record and in confidence still. Linwood Johnson is the other person I am to meet."

"I suppose you will eventually tell me how you are connected to Linwood, but you will have to wait a few days to see him. His mother, Lilly, was killed by a freak tornado earlier today."

"I'm so sorry to hear that. I know he was devoted to Lilly."

Cassie raised an eyebrow, started to ask another question, and then thought better of it.

"I just can't take any more in tonight. This has been a mind-boggling day. My head is spinning. Just let me know when you want to meet again. I think I'd like to call it a night for now."

"I understand. I've thrown quite a bit at you." As he spoke, he handed her his business card. "Call me when you feel like talking."

Cooper reached down and touched Cassie's shoulder as he rose. He left the front porch and walked back toward Main Street, where his car was parked.

Cassie sat thinking and stroking Muffin's head for a few minutes before she went inside.

CHAPTER 16

It was an unusually hot spring day. Humid air hung heavy and still over the congregation as its members gathered in the churchyard to bid farewell to two of its cherished members, Grandma Tillie Carter and Lilly Johnson. Linwood thought it fitting that these two lifelong friends share their funeral. He arranged to pay for both.

A large blue tarp covered a section of the roof that had been torn away by the tornado. Volunteers completed the installation of window glass shortly after dawn. Shutters were replaced and the churchyard cleared of debris.

Most of the congregation waiting for the funeral to begin had attended the morning services. Many brought picnic baskets. They made use of the long tables and folding chairs set up under the shade trees for the reception following the funeral. Those with abundant baskets invited friends to join them.

Cars lined the roadside where later arrivals had parked. The churchyard was filled with milling friends and neighbors when someone signaled that the funeral procession was nearing. A hush fell over those gathered.

Two identical black hearses pulled slowly into the gravel driveway and stopped at the front steps of the church. Following the tradition of Mount Zion's funerals, the congregation slowly followed as pallbearers silently carried the twin caskets into the sanctuary. They paused in the narthex until the caskets were placed at the altar among numerous flower arrangements. Funeral directors then seated members of the church. Ladies wearing the traditional white attire, the gentlemen in appropriate black, were seated close to the front. Those who were not members of the church filled the back pews. Linwood and the Carter family entered from the door to the left of the altar and took their places in the front two rows. Linwood was visibly shaken.

Cassie, Pearl, and Mille sat in a back pew. Cassie was surprised to see Cooper enter and remain standing near the church door. He gave no indication that he saw her.

The service followed the established rituals of the ceremony. The minister invited family and friends to pay tribute to the deceased. Linwood rose and spoke eloquently of a woman who had given much and asked little, who out of love had demanded that he steadfastly pursue his education for the betterment of himself and out of respect for his heritage.

Others rose to speak highly of both women, who together during their lifetimes had ministered to their own and the community as well. It was when the gathering tried to sing the final song that voices choked and tears freely flowed. "In the Garden" had been Lilly's favorite hymn. She had often sung it as she labored in her own garden.

Pallbearers slowly retraced their steps with the caskets for the short walk to the cemetery in back of the church. As they reached the narthex, Cassie noticed Cooper step to Linwood's side, touching his arm as he did so. He then fell into step behind Linwood. To Cassie this seemed the act of a close friend rather than a casual acquaintance. Her curiosity grew. As the caskets were lowered, each in a different part of the cemetery, Cassie glanced around in hopes of speaking with Cooper, but he had already gone.

Mille and Cassie returned to town while Pearl stayed to help with the reception.

CHAPTER 17

When Martin called to invite him for dinner, he suggested that Cooper spend the night at Wahala Hall. "There is a great deal of family history to catch up on," he said. Martin sounded overjoyed at the thought of sharing family stories with Cooper.

Cooper packed a small overnight bag before attending Lilly's funeral. He parked some distance down the road from the church so he could leave the funeral quickly without being boxed in.

It was still exceedingly difficult for Cooper to think of Martin as family. He thought about his belated role in the Lansfield family as he drove toward Wahala Hall. The whole situation was awkward and would create a hailstorm of gossip among the political world, the entertainment world, and Martin's world when the news broke. That day was getting close.

There were a number of cars parked at the west end of the driveway near the tennis courts when Cooper arrived at Wahala Hall. Several people were milling around. He parked at the corner of the east wing as Martin had instructed and made his way to the outside entrance to Martin's office. A small canopied porch identified the doorway.

Martin opened the screen door and ushered Cooper in. Martin motioned Cooper toward the comfortable chair beside the front window as he sat behind his desk. Cooper immediately noticed the large portrait of a young woman standing on the great-hall stairs holding a bouquet of daisies. He knew of course that this was his mother as he had never seen her before. He rose to examine the painting.

"She was lovely in those days," Martin said. "But not the renowned beauty that she became. I have done a bit of research about Madalaine and her career. She has been astoundingly successful."

"Yes, she has. Fortunately for me though, she has managed to keep a very private life off stage and screen. Escaping from New York to Westport made that possible. People there are used to celebrities and afford them both friendship and respect."

Cooper returned to the easy chair. He took a cursory glance around the office. The wall adjacent to the dining room was lined with bookshelves. There were more bookshelves between the windows. A rich oriental rug covered most of the room, edged by dark-stained wood floors. Martin's massive desk took up most of the remaining space, barely leaving room for the leather chair in which Cooper was sitting. A floor lamp and a small table stood beside the chair.

"Well now. Where shall I begin? Perhaps back to the early seventeen hundreds when Sir Richard Lansfield died. He owned a vast estate in Yorkshire, England. He had four sons. The elder son, as is the custom, inherited the estate. However, each of the three remaining sons was given a large endowment with which to seek his own fortune. One chose to stay in England. Henry and Malcolm Lansfield chose to strike out for the new world. Through a grant, they obtained this land along the river close to the Sound and decided to build twin homes. Henry's home became North Hall. Malcolm, intrigued by Indian lore, chose to call his home Wahala Hall, meaning 'South Hall.' In the early nineteen hundreds, North Hall burned to the ground. Henry's two remaining great-great grandchildren had by this time scattered west with their progeny and chose not to rebuild. I bought the land. The hospital now stands where North Hall used to be."

"Wahala is quite impressive. When were the wings added?" Cooper asked.

"The west wing was completed in 1859. The east wing, where we're sitting now, was added in 1890."

Martin swept his hand around the room. "In many of these books and diaries you will find the family history, including the English ancestry. The family seat is in Yorkshire."

Cooper raised an eyebrow. "Strange. Years ago I visited the Yorkshire area and toured the York Cathedral. While I was there, I experienced strange instances of déjà vu. I've always wanted to go back, but never have."

"Perhaps you should. Your distant cousins will welcome you as they did me on the two visits that I have made. Anyway, back to Wahala. You will find the family history in this room among these books. There are also wills, drawings, and even account books."

"As you might guess, this is all a bit overwhelming for me," Cooper said as he turned in his chair, attempting to take it all in.

"And for me as well. I suppose every man harbors a wish for a son to carry on the family name. Of course I felt that time had passed me by. I find myself saying the words 'my son' over and over to myself." Tears welled in Martin's eyes as he spoke.

Both men were silent for a few moments.

Martin rose. "I thought we would make the rounds of Wahala before dinner. Mavis will be entertaining her crowd for a while yet, but she will join us for dinner. With your permission, I plan to break the news this evening."

"If you don't mind, sir, I would prefer you wait a few days. I have promised Cassie Danforth an exclusive. The announcement of our relationship will cause quite a stir in some circles."

Hesitating for a moment, Martin said, "Perhaps it would be less cumbersome for both of us if you just call me Martin." He continued, "I guess you are right about announcing our astonishing news. It won't hurt Mavis to be mystified for a few more days. Would you mind driving your Jeep? We have a few trails to back fields and pastures that are little more than logging roads."

"Of course," Cooper said.

"My farm manager, Otis Kingsley, usually takes me around for inspection now and then. He drives our four-wheel-drive farm truck."

Cooper and Martin spent a pleasant two hours inspecting timber stands and newly plowed fields, as well as pastures where prize Hereford cattle grazed. Martin explained that in Colonial days the main cash crop had been tobacco, the majority of which was shipped to England from Clayton's Landing.

"The two Lansfield brothers used indentured servants as field hands. Some stayed after their seven years were up. They had a decent place to live, all the food they needed, and sufficient pay for incidentals. They also had the run of the land for fishing and hunting. Later, freed black families crossed the river fleeing plantations inland. They worked for five cents an hour. My gardener, Wardin, is a descendent of those former slaves. A wooded area was set aside where they built small log homes. Quite a few are buried near those homesites. Some managed to buy small pieces of land nearby and took up fishing and crabbing for a meager living."

The two men got out of the car and meandered along the banks of the Pasqua River for a short distance. Over the years, fishermen had developed well-worn paths. Not far from where they parked, a small clearing under some shade trees obviously served as a picnic site, complete with a fire pit.

"I spent a lot of time down here fishing and camping out—sometimes for days in summer. This is the widest part of the Pasqua before it melts into the Sound."

Cooper said very little. He was content to let Martin talk. He felt Wahala seeping into his bones like much-needed marrow.

Dinner that evening was strained by Mavis's continual questions. She vacillated between flirtatious crescendos directed toward Cooper and annoyance at Martin's avoidance of her questions about the purpose of Cooper's presence at Wahala.

"If I had known Cooper was expected this afternoon, I would have arranged for him to join us at the tennis courts," she said to Martin while turning to Cooper. "I am sure you would have enjoyed my friends much more than Martin's tour of *our* back forty."

The emphasis Mavis placed on the word *our* escaped neither man.

"Perhaps you will join me for lunch at the club tomorrow?" Mavis asked.

Cooper made his excuses, claiming a busy schedule during his few remaining days in Clayton Landing.

"I don't recall just how you and Martin are connected," Mavis continued. "Are you here on hospital business?"

"No," Cooper replied without elaboration.

Seeing that she was getting nowhere with Cooper, Mavis excused herself before dessert. A few minutes later, the two men heard gravel scatter as her car left the driveway.

Martin chuckled. "Mavis is in a stew. Like her mother, when she is not in control, she is out of control."

Later, when they returned to Martin's office, Cooper hastened to assure Martin that his coming to Wahala was not to claim any rights or inheritance.

"I hope you know that my purpose in being here is to become acquainted with you, Martin, and to explore my bloodline. I do not wish to place any claim on Wahala. I hope you will assure Mavis of that when the time comes."

"Those matters will be taken care of in time, Cooper. Right now it suffices to say that Mavis was never to inherit Wahala Hall. I would not have broken the promise made many years ago between the two brothers who settled this land that it would stay within the family. I do keep up with the descendants of Henry Lansfield, original owner of North Hall. Now I will leave you to explore my bookshelves. I trust you can find your way back to your room. I will see you at breakfast."

~ ~ ~

Cooper's head nodded as the old grandfather clock in the dining room struck two. Reluctantly he laid aside the diary he was reading and made his way up the grand staircase to the room that had been assigned to him earlier. Two lights illuminated the curving stairway. They created shadows on the portraits of his many ancestors. He studied each one as he made his way slowly to his room.

The next morning, the house seemed strangely silent. Cooper wandered downstairs and found coffee and buns in the sunroom off the kitchen. He poured a cup of coffee and then stepped through the door that led to the veranda, where Martin was having coffee and reading the paper.

"Well, good morning. I'll signal Corley that we are ready for some bacon, eggs, and her hot biscuits."

"Sounds great. Sorry, I seem to have slept in. I read until rather late last night."

"No matter. I don't get up as early as I used to myself now that I have officially retired. I may have told you before that I've been assigned a small office at the hospital. Occasionally I wander over, review a case or two, and show up for board meetings. Otherwise, my time is fairly free these days. I trust you found the diaries of interest."

"Very much so. The Lansfields have much to be proud of."

Martin chuckled. "Mostly, but there were a few in the family whose history got swept under the rug. Nothing to be ashamed of, mind you, they just wouldn't comply with Lansfield standards."

"I will be leaving on Saturday and returning to Connecticut. But I would like to see you sometime on Friday. By then I will be free to reveal my plans to you, and within days those plans will also be released to the press."

"Fair enough. May I plan lunch on the back veranda around noon on Friday?"

"That will be fine."

After a leisurely breakfast, Cooper left with a couple of borrowed volumes of family history under his arm.

CHAPTER 18

Cassie always arrived early at the paper on Mondays. As she entered the back door, Mille yelled from inside the massive safe where the newspaper archives and supplies were kept.

"Cassie, come here! Someone's been at it again."

Mille stood in a pile of fragile old folders containing back issues of the *Clayton Landing Weekly* that had obviously been slung off the shelves. A container of more recent archival disks was upturned on the floor, and others had been pushed aside haphazardly. Supply boxes were empty, the contents strewn about.

Mille had reported a similar incident to Cassie shortly after Clifford Danforth's death. Cassie was in Washington at the time and had asked Mille to handle it. Cliff's desk had been rifled, his briefcase disappeared, and his computer stolen.

"Don't touch anything. I'll call Jed Ryan. Maybe he can get some fingerprints this time," Cassie said.

Sheriff Ryan arrived quickly. "I doubt we'll find any fingerprints. The only ones we found last time were a jumble of employees and people who had come in to review old articles for one reason or another. There was nothing that we could trace to any criminal type—probably wore gloves even though I don't think this is the work of a professional. It has to be someone looking for something. Nothing of any value has been taken."

"I can't figure why anyone would want anything from this safe," Cassie said.

"Hard to say what's going on with Cliff gone. He might have had a clue," the sheriff surmised.

Mille said, "For a while, we kept the safe locked after the last break-in. I remembered that Cliff found the combination under the slide extension above his top desk drawer. Sure enough, it's still there. He found it several years after the bank closed when the newspaper expanded into this building. The bank president's desk was left behind, along with a few other items. Cliff loved that old desk. Same one Cassie is using now."

"Why'd you stop locking the safe?" Jed asked.

Mille answered. "It was a dang nuisance. We thought it was a one-time event. We constantly need supplies, and folks stop by fairly frequently researching one thing or another. Guess we should close it at night, though. Besides, I can't figure how anyone gets in here at night without a sign of a break-in anywhere."

"That is puzzling," Jed said. "Well, there is little else I can do here. I'll send Tully over with the fingerprint kit."

While Tully worked in the safe, the frantic race to beat the Wednesday afternoon deadline began. For the next two days, Mille fielded phone calls, mostly reports of additional damages around town. Cynthia Millhouse happily found herself swamped with advertising related to Easter clothes as well as additional ads for tree and damage removal services. Ace sat at his computer studying every detail of the storm pictures as he sorted for a pictorial page.

Cassie stewed over the Sadar Miles arrest article. She knew that the rumor mills had churned facts into a salacious mush of half-truths. When Cassie finally pressed the print button on her computer for proofing, she was satisfied that she had cast Peggy in the best light that she could. She did not mention Cooper in her article, merely stating that there was an ongoing investigation. Cassie briefly let her mind wander to Cooper, wondering what he was doing. She had not seen him since the brief glimpse at the funeral.

She moved on to the article that covered the storm damage around town, which was to be augmented with Ace's prize photographs. She was concentrating on a human-interest story about the deaths of Lilly Johnson, Grandma Tillie Carter, and Millard Jones when her cell phone rang.

"You look busy." Cassie recognized Cooper's voice.

"Did you say I *look* busy?"

"Yes, turn around—I'm sitting in my Jeep across the street in front of the drugstore. I'm hoping you can spare a few minutes for some lunch."

As Cassie turned her chair to face the window, Cooper waved.

"Not sure I can do that. The first three days of the week are hectic around here."

"I've been apprised of that, but I had the drugstore fix their special club sandwiches. I'll swing by and pick you up. I promise, I'll return you in thirty minutes flat."

Cassie glanced over at Mille, who was in total concentration poring over phone notes.

"Okay. Stay where you are, I'll dash across the street."

Cassie picked up her tote bag and said casually to Mille, "Back in a few."

When Cassie reached the Jeep, Cooper said, "I spotted a turn-off overlooking the Sound just up the road. You probably know it." He pulled away from the curb. In minutes they were parked just off the road at a local fishing spot where trails led off along the shore. Fortunately, no one was around.

Cooper dug into a bag of sandwiches and handed Cassie her share of chips and a pickle, as well as a large paper cup of iced tea.

"I hope you like your tea sweet. The lady behind the counter said everyone drinks sweet tea around here."

"Mostly they do, and yes, I do like sweet tea."

"How is Peggy?"

"She's doing just fine. Sunday evening she went to her Aunt Sara's to stay for a while. My friend Jilly, Pearl, and I have been hovering around her all weekend."

"That's good news. I've been in contact with Linwood. He and I feel we can wait no longer, we need to meet—the three of us, that is."

"I don't suppose you care to elaborate and at least give me a subject matter."

"Not yet. I understand you pretty much wrap up the paper by Wednesday evening. I have to get back to Connecticut by Saturday, and Linwood will be returning to Charlottesville then as well. So, will you meet with us Thursday around six-thirty for dinner?"

"Yes. It's time I knew what all this mystery is about. Do you want to meet at the Country Club?"

"No, it's too public. Linwood says he'll barbecue and toss a salad. His place is fairly secluded. I'll bring wine."

"I've never been there, but I know about where it is. I'll get Pearl to bake a pecan pie for dessert. It's one of her many specialties. Will you answer one question? I get the feeling that you and Linwood have known each other for a while. How did that come about?"

"We met through mutual interests, you might say. It was at development seminars that we both attended. Over dinner one night, I discovered his relationship to Clayton Landing. Naturally I drew him into many discussions about its history until the time finally came when I shared my own relationship to Clayton Landing. I know this is a bit unfair, but we'll tie it together for you over dinner."

"I guess I have to be satisfied with that for now. Cassie glanced at her watch. "You have precisely five minutes to return me to work."

Cooper grinned. "Will do," he said.

Mille came over to Cassie's desk shortly after she arrived back from lunch.

"Your cousin Mason dropped this article off while you were out. No surprise, just more of his propaganda about his state senate run. You'd think he was God the way this reads. I expect you'll do some chopping. That picture looks like he had it taken by one of those glamour photographers."

Cassie dropped the article on her work pile without glancing at it. Before she turned to her computer and the story she had promised Ace, her mind began to churn with adjectives that she would like to add to Cousin Mason's article. Words like obnoxious, arrogant, egotistic, dogmatic, overbearing. She had to will her mind to stop and return to the task at hand.

CHAPTER 19

Cassie rose early on Thursday. She found Pearl having a cup of coffee on the back veranda. As usual, Pearl's hair was smoothed neatly back into a bun. It shone from the dab of Vaseline that she spread through it each morning. She wore one of her many starched white aprons over a blue housedress, her daily uniform.

"I thought you might sleep a little later this morning. You did finish getting the paper out yesterday, didn't you say?" Pearl asked.

"Yes, just have a lot on my mind. So much has been happening in the past week."

"Seems like that's the way life is. It goes along smooth for weeks on end and then all of a sudden—boom. I guess it's the Lord's way of testing us. I'll get you a cup of coffee and we can sit a spell. It seems to me we don't get the chance to do that much anymore."

Pearl brought juice, coffee, and freshly made cinnamon rolls to the veranda and settled into her rocking chair. Muffin sat nearby, patiently waiting for crumbs.

"I've been so busy. Did I mention to you that Monday someone broke into the office safe again?" Cassie asked. "This time they weren't so subtle about it—stuff strewn everywhere."

"Somebody is sure looking for something. That reminds me. I can't rightly account for things being shifted around in your dad's office here at home since you told me that you haven't touched anything in there as yet. It's downright puzzling. And the other day when I went to get a tablecloth from the dining-room buffet—when that Cooper fellow came, you know—I would swear there had been some rummaging in that drawer. Some napkins were ruffled, and the top tablecloth had a corner folded over.

I had to press it again. I put it down to me getting old and less tidy when I put things away. But somehow I don't quite see it that way."

"Somehow I can't see it that way either, Pearl. You've been an everything-in-its-place woman ever since I can remember. On the other hand, it's scary to think that someone might be rifling among our cabinets and drawers. Do you think we need to lock the house? We've never locked up in daytime in the past."

"We might have to consider doing just that. It would be a shame though. Jilly, Peggy, my cousin Corley, your Aunt Martha, and any number of your dad's friends have always felt like they could just poke their head in the door, give a yell, and come right on in. That's just the way it's always been. My goodness! You don't think it might be one of those folks?"

"Why would any of the regulars start nosing about? No, either our imagination is getting the best of us or someone is looking for something. What, though?"

"I can't even begin to imagine. Nothing is much of a secret around here except my Sunday Go-to-Meeting Coconut Cake. I'm not about to give that recipe to anybody."

Cassie laughed. She knew that her cake was not the only one of Pearl's closely held recipe secrets.

"I guess I had better get my shower and get going. We always have some loose ends to wrap up on Thursday mornings, and there's planning to do. Anyway, I need you to make one of those secret recipes for me. How about a pecan pie for me to take to a dinner at Linwood Johnson's house tonight? Cooper is going to be there too."

"Well now, that's a strange combination if I do say so. What's that all about?"

"I haven't a clue. Just add it to the mystery list for now. Anyway, I've got to get my shower and get scooting."

CHAPTER 20

Considering the events of the past few days, Cassie was pleased that Thursday remained fairly calm. The newspaper came back from the printers on schedule and in good shape despite the burden of extra pictures and stories.

The sheriff called to report that they got a fingerprint off the desk slide that could belong to the thief. "I think he or she might have looked for the combination and then put on gloves for the actual search. That leads me to believe whoever it was is an amateur who might not have a record. We'll run the prints, of course."

As the sheriff talked, Cassie wondered whether she should mention her concerns about the happenings at home. No, she thought. There was no real evidence, more like an uneasy feeling.

While she returned phone calls and began a priority list for the next week's assignments, she kept glancing at the office clock. She planned to leave early to keep a rare appointment at Sue's Salon for the works—hair, nails, pedicure.

"My, don't you look beautified," Pearl said when she came through the back door. "You haven't taken the time to take care of yourself since you came home. Any special reason now?"

"Hush. Can't a girl get her hair done once in a while without having some ulterior motive?"

"Hmm. I'm thinking an ulterior motive might just have a name—like that Mr. Cooper who you just happen to be seeing tonight."

"I'll have more to tell you about him after tonight. I'd forgotten what it's like to get my hair done, much less my nails and toes. I had a standing appointment in Northern Virginia. Taking my father's place has not been easy, Pearl. I feel like a tadpole in a fish bowl."

Pearl laughed, remembering the time when eight-year-old Cassie had tried raising tadpoles in a fishbowl. All went well until they started jumping out all over her bedroom.

"I know. I'm just joshing you a bit. The pie hamper is loaded and ready. I'm glad to see you getting out a little. Spending all your spare time with Jilly and Peggy is not very invigorating."

"Invigorating? I'm not sure what you mean by that. But yes, there should be at least a welcome change of conversation tonight. Much as I love them, Jilly's reports on all her committees and board meetings and Peggy's gossip from the River Bend Diner are hardly stimulating."

"You miss Washington, don't you?"

"I have to admit that I do. I just can't see myself in this role for very long, Pearl. I love the excitement of politics and political creatures."

"We've got plenty of those creatures around here, just not as grandiose— though some of them think they are. Take your cousin Mason, for instance. My! What a peacock, that one."

Cassie laughed. "I got his announcement about switching over to the Senate side of the legislature yesterday. For all his huffing and puffing, his name around the state is highly recognizable. He sees to that." Cassie glanced at the kitchen clock. "I'd better go change. What do you think— my new sundress or white slacks and a blouse?"

"Sundress I think. Men like a feminine look now and then."

"In that case, sundress it is."

CHAPTER 21

Linwood called earlier to give Cassie directions. She slowed her Mustang as she passed Mt. Zion Baptist Church, watching for an opening among the trees. She turned onto the narrow gravel lane that ran between the wooded creek bank and the denser woods to her left. The sides of the lane were lined with oyster shells. It gradually swung left and up a knoll. Linwood's log home sat nestled among tall pines and oaks. She saw that Cooper's Jeep was already parked in the horseshoe-shaped driveway.

As Cassie opened her car door, Linwood appeared from around the corner of the house, drink in hand.

As she approached Linwood, Cassie said, "I know this must be hard for you, Linwood. I'm sure you're still deeply mourning. It's so soon after your mother's funeral."

"You are so right, Cassie. We've both had a lot to bear recently. Although the timing is not good, I feel I must carry on. Much is at stake. Come, join us around back. Cooper just got here."

Cassie followed Linwood along a slate path. As they rounded the back corner of the house, she saw Cooper hovering over a large grill set off to the side of the yard on a concrete patio.

"Hi there. I'm just trying to fan up a blaze here. I think I have it going now," he said as she approached.

"Let's sit inside on the screened porch while we wait for the coals to catch. Mosquitoes are a problem near the woods even this early in the spring," Linwood said.

Cassie opted for the porch swing while Cooper settled into a comfortable wicker rocker.

Linwood offered drinks. "I'm drinking iced tea, but I have wine, vodka, and fruit juice. Sorry, not much else in the way of hard stuff."

"I think iced tea for now, thanks, but I'll put in a request for wine with dinner," Cassie said.

"Ditto that order," Cooper said.

"I love your home, Linwood, the setting is so calm and peaceful," Cassie commented.

"That's the idea. It's my refuge from professorial bickering, student skepticism, and reporters' questions about anything political that they do not wish to research themselves."

Cassie laughed. "Can you entirely cut yourself off?" she asked.

"Pretty much. I have two cell phones. One I habitually tell people I forgot to turn on so I didn't get their call. The other—well, there are a very few people who have the number, and they are trained to call only when absolutely necessary—like a student uprising or something of that nature. Janice, the secretary I share with another professor, funnels office call messages through my laptop, and I check them periodically."

"Now that sounds like a plan," Cooper interjected.

"I gather you two have been friends for some time. So when are you going to let me in on whatever it is we're gathered for tonight?"

"Seems to me we could enjoy a nice steak before we get down to business," Linwood said. "Meantime, maybe Cooper will tell us what he thinks of Clayton Landing now that he's had a few hectic days in residence as a son of Wahala."

Cooper leaned forward, hands clasped between his legs. "To say that it's been strange is an understatement. At the risk of seeming overly emotional, as I study the portraits at Wahala and read diaries of my ancestors, I see similarities in expressions and traces in personalities that I relate to. Or, I ask myself, am I just imagining it? But I must say my soul seems drawn in while my brain tells me it would never work."

"I guess Cassie and I know what it's like to be torn between two environments."

"I don't know about you, Linwood, but it seems like Clayton Landing is where I anchor, but out there in the cities beyond is where I've been able to improve and even excel at my craft. I'm not sure I can do that here. Life here seems so—repetitious, for lack of a better word. Right now I'm also conflicted in my feelings," Cassie said, surprising herself by her openness.

Cooper glanced at Linwood, who nodded, acknowledging the silent message.

"Well, those coals should be about ready. What do you say we put the steaks on the grill and toss the salad? The table is set inside," Linwood said.

Cassie and Cooper went into the kitchen, which (except for a dividing counter) was part of the large open living space. The furnishings leaned toward the comfortable and masculine and were suited to Linwood's large frame. A massive stone fireplace dominated the room.

Cassie tossed the salad while Cooper opened the wine. A minute later, Linwood brought in a platter of steaks. Dinner conversation included Linwood's reminiscing about life with his mama. At times his eyes glistened with held-back tears.

After dinner, Cassie rose to help Linwood clear the table. "You are in for a treat, gentlemen; next up, Pearl's pecan pie," Cassie said as she scraped steak bones from the plates.

Linwood poured coffee. As they ate dessert, tenseness seemed to permeate the room.

Cooper broke an awkward silence. "It doesn't take much imagination to know what life was like with one of our country's most beautiful and talented actresses. Our family vacillated between the whirlwind and glamour of Broadway and Hollywood and the serenity of Westport, Connecticut."

"And now we three are here, raised differently and arriving at the same point," Linwood said.

Cassie raised an eyebrow. "And it's about time you two let me in on what that point is," she said.

"You're right. Shall we move to the porch again? It's not too cool," Linwood said.

They cleared their dessert dishes from the table and deposited them in the sink as they made their way to the porch.

CHAPTER 22

Cooper began. "Cassie, your beat has been mostly in the political arena during your career. Do you think that was your own preference, or do you think you were steered in that direction?"

"That's an odd question," Cassie replied.

"Think about it for a minute. What were your dinner conversations like—as far back as you can remember?"

"Well, sometimes they were about my day at school or college. As I got older, they were about my work. Sometimes about happenings around town that were newsworthy. Elections were a big deal. Often our conversations were on political developments—what was really taking place behind the headlines. Those sessions occurred mostly when we had visitors. That was fairly often throughout my life, come to think about it."

"Exactly," Cooper said.

"What do you mean? I just considered those discussions pretty normal in our house. After all, my dad was sort of the sage of the South. His opinions were sought by many high-ranking politicians, including a few presidents."

"How many political statistics could you rattle off, if asked?" asked Cooper.

"Now that is an impossible question to answer."

Linwood chuckled and nodded his head. "Even I wouldn't know where to begin to answer that question, and I teach political science."

"Well, I'll back up and take a different tack. You would agree that political discussions during your formative years were way up on the scale compared to most households."

"Well, sure, when you put it that way—probably in the upper one percent if we're talking about the whole United States. So where is this inquisition leading?"

"Cooper, you're beating around the bush. I've known Cassie most of her life. She is intelligent, well educated, and nobody's fool. Just get down to it," Linwood said.

Cooper rose from his chair and stood leaning against a porch post while he collected his thoughts. Cassie noticed the strong set of his jaw and the way the setting sun highlighted his rusty-colored hair, turning it more toward gold.

"Cassie, have you heard of the Soronto Institute, the Rothmeer Foundation, and the Americas World Academy?"

"Yes, of course. I've also heard rumors that those groups are affiliated with some sort of new movement, possibly a third political party. I don't know how the Americas World Academy fits in with those rumors. I do know that the brightest of high school students have been given scholarships. The campus is outside Washington in the Winchester area, and I've heard there is a good deal of building going on."

"Right on all counts," Cooper said.

For the next few minutes, Cooper explained the work of the two institutes. The Soronto Institute is in downtown Washington with small working groups located in offices all around Washington in the suburbs. Each of the offices is a branch of the whole. Their focus is on world economics, and each office is devoted to a different country or region. The major powers have a separate office. Some offices concentrate on the whole of a continent or region. There is a South American office with its sub-groups, another for the African countries and its sub-groups. The Rothmeer Foundation concentrates on the governments of the same sets of countries and shares the same satellite offices.

"I see," Cassie said when he finished his explanation. But what is the purpose of all these studies, and how does the Americas World Academy fit in?"

"I was just about to get to that. The academy students study the politics of these same sets of countries. After their first year, they are separated according to their choice of countries or regions. From there they are immersed in the languages, religions, politics, and customs of their chosen areas."

Linwood added, "That first year Cooper mentioned—the students get a basic advanced education. Two hours of each day for the next three years are spent on normal college courses. Right now, the campus is still under construction. The completed core building houses the academic studies. When completed, the campus will resemble a wheel with the spokes leading to residence slash study buildings. Each of these buildings is where students will live and study as if they were in the foreign country of their choice. They will speak the language, adopt the customs, study the history, politics, and become knowledgeable in their religions. They will in effect be in a foreign country for approximately twenty-two hours a day, five days a week."

Cooper went on to explain that in the fifth year each student spends an entire year in the study country. They will be housed with local families. They will visit museums, shrines, historical sites, and where available, governmental sessions. They will speak the language at all times.

"Wow. Students can actually be found who are willing to undergo that grueling routine?" Cassie asked when Cooper paused.

Cooper laughed. "Believe me, on graduation, these young people will be offered an avalanche of career choices. However, because all are on scholarship, their contract calls for them to work for the Rothmeer Foundation for a minimum of ten years. There they will learn about the economic and hard-core business relationships between their choice country and the United States."

"What then? Where is all this leading, and what does it have to do with me?"

Linwood laughed. "Cooper will get around to that. He just likes to beat around the bush. What say we have another glass of tea—or if you wish, another glass of wine?"

CHAPTER 23

After pouring Cassie and himself a glass of wine, Cooper settled into his chair. Linwood passed around an assortment of mints and nuts and then returned to his seat.

"Cassie, you mentioned rumors about a possible third party. Yes, I can confirm that all of what we've been talking about is in preparation for a third party launch. Heretofore, as I'm sure you know, most third parties have been created due to breakaways on issues within the major parties or have been launched due to a cause. Few have had any real impact. Linwood, help me out here."

"I doubt Cassie needs a refresher course, but to emphasize the difficulty of such an undertaking, I will shorten a semester into a few sentences. Third party attempts go back as far as 1844, when James Birney ran as a Liberty Party candidate against James K. Polk, a Democrat, and Henry Clay, a Whig. Birney received 2 percent of the vote. Since then, there have been attempts by other parties, such as the Free Soil Party, the American/ Know Nothing Party, the People's or Populist Party, and the Progressive Party, to name a few."

He went on to explain that most third parties have garnered somewhere between 2 percent and 27 percent of the popular vote. Theodore Roosevelt, running as the Progressive or Bull Moose Party candidate, had thus far made the most inroads with 27 percent of the popular vote and a very respectable 88 electoral votes. But, Linwood was quick to point out, Roosevelt was a highly popular past president, which heavily weighted the outcome. In his case, experience counted, as many of the Progressive Party platforms were later incorporated into the mainstream and passed into law—women's suffrage and the Social Security system among them.

"As an issue candidate, George Wallace ran as a segregationist on the American Independent Party ticket in 1968 and made a decent showing with 13.5 percent of the popular vote and 46 electoral votes," Linwood said, tapping his fingers together. He was at ease in this role, a college professor expounding on his favorite topic just as he might have done during his office hours with highly attuned students. "Then there have been the perpetual gadflies like Eugene V. Debs, a Socialist, who ran in five elections from 1892 to 1920, receiving a fairly steady 3 percent of the vote. Most recently, Ralph Nader has assumed the gadfly role. Ross Perot received a decent 18.9 percent of the popular vote in 1992 but no electoral votes. His 1996 campaign was much less successful."

"Thanks for the refresher course, Linwood," said Cassie. "I don't know how you can possibly remember all those numbers. But again I ask, what does all this have to do with me?"

"Patience, Cassie," Cooper said. "We're heading in that direction—there's just a lot of background information you need to know first. There is yet another group known as the Pinnacle Seven. This group has been meeting quietly for some years, mostly at the estates of some of the members in and around Washington. They've been researching in detail the fallen major powers of the past, Greece and the Roman Empire first and foremost. They've also been researching what went wrong with past third parties in the United States. The idea is to apply their psephological studies to a possible future third party. The press has gotten wind of some of their research work—for instance, the personality profile studies of the most successful political figures, particularly our past presidents. The original Pinnacle Seven group has grown, of course, and it now includes many powerful politicians, businessmen, and journalists, among others. They're all extremely concerned about the future of our country. Your father was one of them."

"Well," said Cassie, "that certainly doesn't pack the wallop of learning of his relationship with your mother. Anyway, he did mention something about a Pinnacle group—one of the many meetings he had when he was in Washington. And we often had what-if conversations about parties and unsuccessful candidates. Political history was often the topic of the evening around our house."

"Exactly my point," Cooper said. "Politics might as well have been stirred into your Pablum. One way or another, politics was always in your future. I seem to have come by my obsession through genes I only recently knew existed. I wasn't consciously programmed, though politics was often a topic of conversation, especially during your father's visits."

"Wait a minute, are you intimating that I was somehow programmed toward politics?"

"Members of The Pinnacle Seven who had young people in their lives were encouraged to indoctrinate those they selected with an in-depth knowledge of political history so that one day those children would become natural, knowledgeable politicians. This group was to be the core group of a third party. Of course, in your case, political discussions would have been your father's natural inclination in any event."

"Unbelievable," Cassie said.

"Believe it, Cassie," Linwood interjected. "I'm another one."

Cassie turned toward Linwood. For a moment she studied his face, noticing for the first time the traces of white in his sideburns. His brow was permanently creased. His brown body remained muscular and lean, no doubt due to a discipline of exercise, she thought.

"Meaning no disrespect, Linwood, you know I thought highly of Ben and Lilly, but they just weren't known for being interested in politics."

"You would be right, although they always went to the polls. They considered voting their duty. However, it was Maxwell Anderson who led me down the path. Having no children of his own, he latched onto me, since I was so often at his farm with my parents. They kept me morally straight, and Maxwell guided my education. Neither much approved of my sideline into sports, but I remained grounded and they were satisfied that their influence would eventually lead me to another occupation. Maxwell harped on political history and history in general—sometimes to the point that my brain reeled. I must say, though, that I am proud that football allowed me the independence of earning my own education. Maxwell had offered to foot that bill."

"And Maxwell Anderson and my father were very good friends. Now I see the connection."

"Precisely. And now here we are, the three of us woven together in a cloth not entirely of our own making."

"What do you mean by that?"

Cooper spoke. "He means that the three of us are being asked to consider careers in politics, leading to a third party entry on the scene in possibly 2012. Some major players are already onboard. As you know, there have recently been a smattering of Senate and House members who have announced that they have become Independents. Having been discouraged with the future of their own parties, they are actually sidestepping—getting prepared to declare as third-party candidates."

Cooper and Linwood both fell silent, and Cassie took a long, slow slip from her wineglass before she responded. "Out of the blue you expect me to swallow all of this? Let's review where each of us stands in our careers. You are already in the running, Cooper. Linwood is a respected political science professor and political consultant, as well as a well-known former NFL football player. I can see where he would be a very viable candidate for a political office."

"We hope you are looking at the next governor of Virginia," Cooper interjected. "All right, another surprise. Okay, so where does that leave me? Even if I were the least bit interested in some political position—and I certainly am not committing myself just how would a rising television correspondent launch a sudden career in politics?"

"It's easier than you might think, Cassie," Cooper said. "Easier than you might think."

CHAPTER 24

Linwood checked his watch and rose to his feet. "I have coffee ready in the thermos decanter. Shall we take a break? It's close to ten o'clock."

"Thanks. I could use a break. Cream and sugar, please." Cassie excused herself and made her way down the hall to the bathroom.

Both men went into the kitchen.

"What do you think? Did we pour too much on her all at once?" Cooper asked Linwood.

"We'll soon see, after the next round."

Linwood placed cups on the counter along with a tray of coffee, cream, and sugar. When Cassie returned, he said, "Let's stay inside; it's getting cool on the porch. Besides, the bugs are bombarding the screens with the lights on."

After they were seated at the dining table, Cooper reopened the conversation. "Cassie, just how much do you know about the activities of Mason Langdon, Gordon Everly, and the Masengood brothers, John and Charles?"

"Now that's a trick question if I ever heard one. You probably know perfectly well that Mason is my cousin. But I gather you think you know more about him and the others than I do."

"I know that Mason is not a blood relative. Your Aunt Martha raised him as her son when she married his widowed father, George Langdon. I have access to a long dossier that includes microscopic details of his political career. Some of it seems pretty shady. So far he seems to have covered his dealings well, even though his wealth has grown way beyond the income he should have from dabbling in real estate."

"For that very reason, there has never been any kissing-cousin fondness between Mason and me. My father despised him, and I always found that a little strange since he always gave a person the benefit of the doubt."

"We've been dissecting him for some time, trying to find some way to end his career. He seems to have an iron grip on state politics," Cooper said.

"It's that ever present smile and his ability to remember the names and family histories of just about everyone he meets. It makes the less astute feel like he's a big brother who knows what's best for them. As far as Mason is concerned, what's best for him is always best for them. I just got his formal announcement today that he will be switching to the Senate side of the state legislature. I'm sure he plans to spend a term and then head for the House of Representatives or even the Senate. He is that calculating."

Linwood said, "He's always been a painful entity in North Carolina's politics, wielding far too much power as Speaker of the House. There have been rumors for years about personal gains from some state contracts."

"My father used to say some of the bills Mason pushed were like well-bagged garbage. They didn't stink unless you slit the bag open. I understand John Masengood is angling to take Mason's place in the House. I would say they're political blood brothers. It is rumored that John actually writes many of the bills Mason introduces. So far he seems to have played second fiddle to Mason, but some people think Mason is a puppet with John finagling the strings. I'm not sure if Mayor Everly has any loftier ambitions, but it wouldn't surprise me. The three of them and John's brother, Charles, have a stranglehold on local politics, and they influence state politics as well."

"I understand there's a dossier on John in the works," Linwood said. "John and his brother Charles are like two peas in a pod, always together."

Cooper's cup sat untouched at his elbow—he had been following the conversation too intently to bother with coffee. "Now for the bombshell!" he said. "Cassie, your father had something on one of them that will throw a dead bolt on their political careers. About a week before he died, he phoned Jordan Mitchell, administrator of the Pinnacle Seven group, and told him he had concrete criminal evidence against one of them that would immediately sink any political ambitions. He said he had information that would put one of the two guys in jail for a very long time. Jordan said Cliff seemed very agitated. But he didn't say who it was, what the crime was, or what proof he had, only that he would be back in touch after checking on a few facts that might implicate someone else."

Cassie gasped and returned her coffee cup to its saucer with a clatter. "So my father was in the middle of an investigation when he died? Could that have brought on his heart attack? It does account for the rifling of the office safe and the mysterious happenings at home."

"What do you mean?" asked Linwood.

"Twice now the office safe has had a going-over, stuff strewn all about. My dad's briefcase and computer were stolen in the first break-in, along with some other office equipment. Pearl has been reporting things mysteriously out of place at home. You wouldn't understand the importance of that unless you knew Pearl like I know her. Come to think about it, Ed Morrison reported that some of his office files had been searched last month. He's our lawyer. Fortunately, most of his really sensitive files are kept in his secret office safe. You may have seen the police report in the paper, Linwood."

"Then whatever evidence Cliff discovered must be carefully hidden somewhere, or whoever is looking would have stopped looking by now," Cooper said.

"But why would an office search be so evident and the searches at my home so subtle?" Cassie asked.

Linwood stroked his chin as he spoke. "Seems to me it indicates that whoever this person is wants the newspaper office search to look like it might be a petty thief looking for penny-ante stuff. Did you say that a computer was taken in the first break-in?"

"Yes, and there was some small stuff missing from desks—calculators mostly, and one of our laser printers. But why so careful at the house, if it really has been searched?"

"The thief didn't want the two searches to be connected. Besides, you never reported your suspicions. Except for Pearl's eagle eye, what proof do you have that there was a break-in at all?" Cooper asked.

"You're right. There is none," Cassie replied.

"Who all has access to your home, Cassie?" asked Cooper.

"That would be a long list—it's always been pretty much open house. A good many of our friends and relatives just stick their heads in the back door and yoo-hoo as they come in."

"And if they know anything about Pearl's or your habits, they would know when no one would be home, correct?" Linwood asked.

"I guess so. Pearl has a regular meeting at church on Thursday afternoons, and she always shops on Wednesdays for specials when the store prices change. Of course everyone knows when I'm at work—especially tied there Monday through Wednesday."

"So Wednesdays and on Sunday when you are both at church would be pretty safe, and the back door would be open," Linwood suggested.

"Sure. The back door is always open except at night—last one in locks the doors."

"Mason, being family, would also know about Pearl's affinity for having everything in its place where a common thief would not. Would the Masengoods or Mayor Everly?"

"Yes, I guess so, but then so would a lot of people. It's not uncommon for the more historical homes in Clayton Landing to be maintained impeccably. The one exception at home is my room. Pearl and Dad have always given me special dispensation. Our home was left to my mother by her parents and then to my dad. She grew up in that spotless atmosphere. Dad adopted the lifestyle. I'm not a slob, but I seem to always be in a hurry and careless about putting stuff away right away. My drawers aren't all that neat, either. Friday is Pearl's cleaning day so I pick up sometime during the day or evening on Thursdays—lifelong habit."

"Do you have any idea if your room was searched?" Linwood asked.

"I haven't thought about it. I don't know if I would have noticed, but I can't imagine why anyone would search my room."

"Perhaps because yours is the only room that is not pristine," Cooper said.

"What do you mean?"

"Think about it. If Cliff wanted to hide something at home, it just might be in a room where Pearl is least likely to notice something out of place," Linwood surmised.

Cooper reflected for a few moments and then said, "I don't think so. I don't believe he would have put Cassie in danger, no matter how remote."

"Can we get back to how all this connects me with possibly getting into politics?"

"All right, that's our next topic, Cassie," Cooper replied as he glanced at his watch. It was getting late.

CHAPTER 25

Cooper continued the conversation. "What we've been leading up to, Cassie, is that there will be a dedicated effort by a large number of participants in the next few years toward creating a viable third party. Powerful and rich men are waiting in the background. They are ready and willing to devote themselves as well as a good deal of their personal wealth to restoring our country to its greatness."

"I still don't see where all this concerns me unless there is another big story in it for me. I already have a promise from you, Cooper, for one exclusive."

Linwood spoke up. "Cassie, it boils down to the fact that we, and others like us, very much want you to be a participant in the third-party movement. You and I aren't the only ones who have been spoon-fed U.S. history and politics. If you think about it, you could name a number of these households yourself—congressmen's children and presidents' children among them. There's a growing field of the disenchanted. Some highly regarded journalists are ready to embark on a political challenge as well."

Cooper added, "And we believe Cliff hoped that you would eventually become involved."

"And I guess you two have been delegated to rope me in. Gentlemen, my mind is reeling with all that has happened in the last two months. I've lost my father; given up my career—temporarily, I hope; the town's just taken a huge whack from Mother Nature; Linwood has lost his mother; Peggy was attacked and had a stillborn baby that Cooper delivered, not to mention revelations about his family ties with my father; and now I have to worry that some lunatic is searching my home and office for I know not what."

"Hey, take a deep breath, Cassie." Cooper was grinning despite the inappropriateness. Cassie is damned cute when she's stirred up, he was thinking.

"All right. Here's the plan we envision—*we* meaning the head honchos at Pinnacle. Somehow, we find this evidence Cliff had or uncover it ourselves. We're pretty sure the culprit is politically involved. He drops out of the race, and at the last minute you step in as a candidate in his place." Cassie started to protest, but Cooper didn't stop. "You will have a staff of professional political managers," he went on, "and hopefully some local help. You are well-known statewide, fairly famous by local standards, you have the educational background, and you've been covering the political beat for most of your career. Ergo, you are well-qualified and electable." He broke out in another grin. "And voters seem to appreciate it when candidates are good looking."

Cassie's mouth dropped open. When she regained her composure, she turned from Cooper to Linwood and back again. "You two are serious, aren't you?"

"Yes, ma'am," Linwood said.

"Absolutely," Cooper added.

"First, this is all out of the blue. Second, I grant you I might be recognizable to those who remember me while I was on the air in Virginia and D.C., but that hardly makes me a household name. And third, although I have never had to worry about money, I certainly would not be one of those filthy rich participants you mentioned. And fourth, at this point it would take a lot of convincing."

Cassie rose, walked over to the foyer table and picked up her purse. "I'm going home now. I've absorbed about all I can take for one evening. I know you must have a good deal more to dish out, but it will have to wait. Good night, and thanks for the hospitality, Linwood."

"Whoa, wait one minute more please, I have one more request to make," Cooper said.

Cassie glanced at her watch. "Sixty, fifty-nine, fifty-eight."

"Call Ed Morrison's office tomorrow, you have an appointment," Cooper said hurriedly. "He is expecting your call to confirm."

The door banged as Cassie left.

CHAPTER 26

Tully sat partially hidden in the shade along the side of Mount Zion Baptist Church. He hoped to snag a speeder before returning to town after his regular afternoon patrol. He'd be off duty in twenty minutes and was looking forward to a cold beer. Tully was just about to start his motor when he spied a black Jeep driving too slowly to warrant a ticket. He was a little puzzled when the Jeep turned into the hidden lane where Linwood Johnson lived. He sat and contemplated the significance. Good thing he didn't rush off, he thought to himself when he saw Cassie's red Mustang coming down the road a few minutes later. She too turned into Linwood's lane along the creek.

"Jackpot," he said aloud as he pulled out his cell phone.

"I've got Cassie and that Canaday fella in my sights," he said. "Dumb luck to sight them both while I was just sitting here. I was just about to go back into town to check on their whereabouts when they both showed up here."

The voice on the line asked, "Where's here?"

"Oh. I was sitting in the Mount Zion Baptist Church lot just observing traffic when I saw them two come along. Guess where they were going?"

"Just get to it, Tully," the voice responded.

"I was getting to it. They turned into Linwood Johnson's lane. Can you imagine that? Now just what do you suppose those two have to do with Linwood?"

"Well, why don't you just get your ass on up to the house and see if you can figure that out, Tully? It will be dusk soon, but be careful that you aren't detected."

"Will do. I'll get back to you."

"Hot damn," Tully said aloud when he turned off his cell phone. "James Bond step aside, here I come."

Tully decided he would have to walk up the long lane. When he got close to the house, he skirted into the thick trees and proceeded tree by tree until he reached the back of the house, where he observed the three on the porch. When they moved inside, he calculated that if he crouched low he would be unobserved for the few feet between the woods and the house while they were distracted eating their supper. He couldn't hear a word they were saying; the air conditioning was on and the windows were shut. Luckily they moved back to the porch after eating.

When he saw them leaving the great room after dinner, he quietly hunched down and made his way along the walk to the edge of the porch. He crouched at the edge of the house close enough to listen. What he heard didn't make a lot of sense. Sometime later, he cursed to himself when the three moved back into the house, leaving him unable to hear anything.

He dashed across to the woods once more and made his way down the lane farther away from the house. He was close to the road when he felt safe enough to make another call.

When his call went through, Tully whispered into the phone, "They was talking politics. I couldn't make much sense of most of it. Something about schools teaching a bunch of foreign stuff, and then that Canaday fellow said something about a group—Pinnacle something. After dinner it was more political stuff. I remember Theodore Roosevelt's name came up."

"Hold it, Tully. In the first place, why are you whispering? You aren't where someone can overhear, are you?"

"No, but you can't be too careful in this detective business."

"In the first place, you are not in the detective business. I just pay you to keep your eyes and ears open around town. Was my name mentioned at all?"

"No, why would it be? Seemed like they was just having a highfalutin' get-together."

"You're sure."

"Course I'm sure. I couldn't hear what they were saying inside the house, but judging from the talk on the porch, it probably wasn't all that interesting. It was mostly about politics."

"Nonetheless, it seems like a strange trio. I'm more than curious about this Canaday fellow. Get back to your squad car and let me know tomorrow what time they break up. Don't call me again tonight."

"Okay. Will do."

Tully stealthily made his way back to the road. Standing behind a tree, he peered up and down the road for headlights before dashing to his squad car. He wrote down the time when Cassie's Mustang turned out of the lane. A short time later, he jotted down twelve-fifteen on his pad as Cooper's Jeep turned onto the highway. He waited a few minutes before returning to town. His thoughts turned to how he would go about explaining why he hadn't checked in at the sheriff's office that evening.

CHAPTER 27

Cassie made sure all the doors were locked and then quietly made her way through the house and upstairs to her bedroom. Her head was pounding. After dropping her clothes onto her bedroom chair, she went down the hall to the bathroom. She took two Tylenol out of the bottle, filled a glass with water, and sat on the toilet. For a few moments she just stared at the old-fashioned tub with its claw feet as if in a trance. Then tears began to roll down her cheeks. She grabbed a tissue and let the tears come. She was tired of keeping up a brave front. She was confused about the direction of her future. She wanted so badly to be able to talk to her dad. Minutes passed before she opened her left hand and swallowed the Tylenol one by one, washing them down with water.

When she returned to her bedroom, she looked around. How would she know if anything was out of place? She frequently moved things around on her bureau and dressing table. Her desk and the bulletin board above it looked much the same as they had during her high school and college years. She glanced at the old pictures pinned to the board. They never failed to bring back fond memories. She hadn't added new ones in years.

She slept fitfully, finally dozing off toward dawn. It was nearly eight when she entered the kitchen the next morning.

"I was just about to go checking on you," Pearl said. "You came in mighty late last night. Linwood and Cooper must have been good company. Go on out on the veranda, the fresh air will wake you up. I'll bring a tray."

Cassie chose a lounge chair rather than sit at the table. She leaned her head back and closed her eyes. Muffin jumped into her lap and started purring. Cassie obliged with a hug.

Pearl appeared minutes later with a tray of fruit, muffins, and coffee. She set it on the small table beside Cassie's chair. Cassie opened her eyes and smiled in appreciation.

"What's troubling you, child?"

"I guess all the changes have caught up with me, Pearl. And last night, Linwood and Cooper just added to it."

"How? What do you mean?"

"They think someone has been breaking into the newspaper office and into our house looking for some evidence that Dad might have had."

"I just knew it. I mean the part about breaking in. But why?"

"It seems Dad may have known something that would put a stop to one of our local politician's careers."

"Must be someone in that drugstore gang, bunch of roosters they are, except they don't even know when to stop crowing. I never could understand why your dad mingled with them."

"Of course you do, Pearl. Remember he used to say that in the newspaper business you often had to 'fraternize in order to circumvent fabrication.' He was often able to thwart some piece of legislation he was against by keeping his eyes and ears open. His editorials carried a lot of weight."

"I can't stand the thought that maybe one of those weasels has been roaming around this house while we weren't here. I reckon we have to keep locked up all the time now. Do you think we need to get one of those alarm systems?"

"I don't think so just yet. Do you know where the keys are?"

"Yes, of course I do. There's two in the pantry on a hook and one in the garage on a hook on the left side of the door."

"I think you should have a couple more made. I'll take one from the pantry and put it on my key ring. You do the same. Let's hide the one in the garage in a can or something. Keep the air conditioning on and close all the windows and lock them."

"Lord have mercy, I wouldn't have thought of that. Guess I'll have to spend a lot of time on the back veranda. I don't cotton to being without fresh air."

"Hopefully it will be for just a little while. I lay in bed last night trying to think where Dad might have hidden evidence in a place no one would think to look. Well, I've got to make a couple of phone calls to Mille and Ed. I'm not going in to work today."

"First you sit right there and eat some breakfast."

Cassie picked at her food for a few minutes and then put Muffin on the floor and went upstairs. She made her phone calls, showered, and dressed.

As she passed back through the kitchen, Pearl said, "Here's your key. I'll be off to my meeting after lunch, and I'll lock up. I'll put the garage key in a coffee can and put a few nails on top. It will be on the shelf on the right."

Cassie gave Pearl a hug. She left by the back door and bypassed the garage. She decided to walk to Ed's office.

CHAPTER 28

Ed Morrison's office was located in one of the historical homes at Main Street and Church Street, just a block from the new Clayton County Courthouse. The massive double doors contained panels of ornate beveled glass. A small bell attached to the right door made a melodious sound as Cassie entered the wide hallway. She turned toward the left, where Ed's secretary's office was located. The gold-plated sign on the partially open door read "Reception," indicating that this was a first stop before clients entered Ed's office. He was quite a talker, and it wasn't unusual to see someone sitting in the hallway in one of the comfortable Queen Anne chairs waiting a turn. There was no one there today.

Cassie poked her head in. His secretary, Jane Hanson, was on the phone. Without interrupting her call, Jane pointed across the hall to Ed's door and then motioned with a wave that Cassie should go right in.

Before entering, she tapped lightly on the door. Ed immediately responded.

"Well, it's about time. How many times have you put me off, Cassie?"

"I know. I'm sorry. I just didn't want to deal with legal stuff. It seems so final. You've always handled the family finances. I don't see any reason why you can't just keep on doing that. I get my check right on time each month. I don't need anything more."

"Let me go get your files, Cassie. Jane is busy dealing with a mighty upset wife in the middle of a divorce action who seems to think all my time is hers."

Cassie proceeded to the leather wingback chair sitting to one side of Ed's massive desk. She never failed to notice and admire the deeply piled Oriental rug woven in red and beige hues. The room was lined with bookcases. Off-white drapes hung from the two windows that opened onto busy Main Street. She studied the picture of Ed and Laura that sat on the corner of his desk. The picture had been printed in the *Clayton Landing Weekly* on the occasion of their fiftieth wedding anniversary five years ago. They looked very much alike, as if the years had melded them into one. Both had short white hair, round faces, twinkling eyes, and wide smiles.

When Ed returned to the office, he said, "Jane has been after me to put the few accounts I manage on the computer. Somehow I just can't bring myself to trust that dang machine yet. Besides, most of the accounts I handled in the past are in the hands of a financial manager or an accountant now. Cliff and I had an agreement that I would continue to handle his affairs and yours. He wanted some privacy that he couldn't get from just anybody. I think you know, though, that by agreement I have the books audited each year by a small trustworthy accounting firm over on the other side of the state, and they make out the income tax statements."

"I'm aware of that, and I also know you have powers of attorney for both of us. I don't see any reason to change that arrangement for me."

"I do, Cassie. I'm watching the calendar these days, and the years are mounting up. I turn seventy-nine next month. It's time for your affairs to be handled by professionals. By the way, I don't know who this Canaday fellow is, but I'm sure glad he nudged you in here."

"I'll fill you in on that later. I was unaware of a longtime connection he had with Dad."

"That's understandable. Cliff had a lot of friends outside Clayton Landing."

"Before we discuss my business, Ed, and before I forget to ask, was there anything of value missing when your office was broken into?"

"No, not really. The backdoor lock was ruined. Some files were rifled, books pulled from shelves—that sort of thing. But then all the confidential files are kept in my safe, and only a handful of people know where that is located. These old houses in town have many secret nooks."

"Well, it's strange. The newspaper office has been searched twice now, and Pearl is sure someone has been methodically searching the house. Did Dad mention anything about some evidence he had?"

A thoughtful look came over Ed's face, and he folded his delicate fingers together on the desk in front of him. "No, but then I hadn't sat down and talked with him for a while before he died." He shook his head as if to clear his mind. "Now before you get me distracted and put this off again, let's get down to your affairs. Young lady, you are a mighty rich woman, and it's getting way beyond my capability to manage it all."

"What do you mean? I know I have more than the average person my age; I get a very handsome allowance each month. Dad said it was from interest on money my mother left me. I've been very grateful for that. It allows me to dress for TV and mingle in the best restaurants. You'd be surprised how many news tidbits I pick up in Washington's most fashionable eating establishments."

"Well, now you can buy one if you wish. I've condensed your holdings to a one-page synopsis. There is a figure under each heading—stocks, bonds, CDs, real estate." As Ed spoke, he shoved a piece of paper across the desk toward Cassie. "Take a look at the bottom line."

Cassie's jaw dropped. "My God, Ed! This is unbelievable. How could I be worth millions and not know about it?"

"Your father was up to a little skullduggery. When you reached college age, he led you to believe that your mother had left a small trust fund for you, hence the allowance. You were happy with that arrangement. Actually, your mother was quite wealthy and left a very large trust fund. Cliff was trustee, and I handled the nitty-gritty with a good deal of advice from outside sources who assumed I was asking about my own finances. Then too, over the years, taking a lesson from the Clayton holdings, Cliff invested funds from his book deals, consulting fees, et cetera and built up a sizeable estate of his own in trust. Now it all belongs to you, and danged if I haven't had a time getting you the least bit interested."

"I realize now what all those talks were about. Every time Dad read about some young person losing their sense of values by becoming too rich too quick, I got a lecture."

"Yes, he intended to keep you levelheaded as long as he could. And you always came on pretty strong about wanting to make it on your own. You might not have done that if life had been too soft—if you didn't think you'd have to make a living."

"I'd like to think I'm a better person than that, but I guess one never knows. Anyway, what do I do now?"

"We need to get you a top-notch financial manager, and I guess you have some thinking to do regarding how this amount of money will influence your life."

Cassie slid the synopsis back across the desk. "Come to think about it, Ed, I believe I know a couple of fellows who might be very interested in how this money will influence the rest of my life. They've got some more explaining to do."

CHAPTER 29

Cassie stopped by the newspaper office Friday morning to check in and tell Mille that she would be gone most of the day. Then she called Cooper on his cell phone.

"I need to see you and Linwood this afternoon. Can you reach him?"

"We thought you might want to get back with us soon. Do you want us to come to you?"

"Yes. How about around two o'clock? Pearl will be at a meeting until around five." Cassie's tone was all business.

"I'm sure that will be all right with Linwood. We're in sort of a standby mode, hoping that you would get back to us today."

"Come in the back way down the alley from Church Street. As you know, there are two parking places beside the garage."

Cooper and Linwood arrived within five minutes of each other.

Cassie led them to the dining room. When they were all seated at the table, Cassie turned to Cooper. She offered no drinks and made no social pretense.

"Just how is it that you seem to know more about my affairs than I do? What prompted you to make an appointment for me with Ed Morrison and how did you know that he was my lawyer anyway?"

"You're irritated, and I don't blame you. I know nothing about your personal or financial affairs. The last time I saw Cliff, we talked about how much money it would take to launch a third party. At the end of our conversation he said that if anything happened to him before he introduced you to the Pinnacle Seven group, he would like Linwood and me to brief you. As sort of an afterthought, he said that I might also have to push you into settling his estate, because you always brushed off his attempts to talk about the possibility of his death. It seems like my just knowing who Ed was did the trick."

"I have to admit it got my dander up. I thought you perhaps knew a little too much about me. I also remembered that you stressed in our previous conversation that it would take a great deal of money to launch a third party and that a number of individuals were willing to dedicate a sizeable chunk of their own wealth to do so. For the past hour I have been fuming over the thought that perhaps your interest in me was really all about money."

Cooper said, "Not true, Cassie. The Pinnacle group is looking for the best candidates to lead this country, and perhaps the world, into a new tomorrow. This is not a fly-by-night movement. This is a visionary movement. Sure, there are idealistic and even unrealistic ideas in the hopper right now, but we are gathering the talent to move forward, and we are counting on the momentum and enthusiasm of individuals and eventual public support. Our forefathers had a dream and risked their lives and personal wealth to see that this country came about. At a time when the United States is in danger in a way it has never experienced before, there are those of us who feel we can do no less."

Linwood said, "It so happens, Cassie, that a few years ago when Maxwell Anderson died, I got a call from Ed. With the exception of the house and land that he left my parents, his entire estate was left to me. He had a great many real estate holdings, dabbled in the stock market, and had a hefty bank account. I haven't touched any of it. I like my way of life and am comfortable with my own income. I plan to dedicate his funds to this movement, and I feel in my heart that is exactly what he had in mind."

"My recent wealth came from Sam Canaday," Cooper said. "With the exception of their joint real estate holdings, my mother requested that he leave his estate to me. You see, they have always kept separate accounts. Their talents created both fame and fortune for each of them. I too will dedicate a high percentage to my campaign."

"Linwood, you seem to be hinting that the way you and I were brought up has been leading us to a path of public service all along. Do you believe that?"

"I think so, Cassie. Not in a mandatory way but in our shaping. We are finding that there are many others like you and me. Many who seem to have a strong sense of destiny."

Cooper reached across the table and took Cassie's hand. She made a slight movement as if to take her hand away; his grip tightened. His eyes were penetrating as he looked into hers.

"My mission here is to fulfill a promise to your father that I would introduce you to the Pinnacle Seven group. No one expects to railroad you into a decision to join a third-party movement. They would, however, appreciate a chance to elucidate—to broaden your knowledge of the progress thus far. The mission is not so much to proselytize as to inform."

Cassie did not remove her hand but rather relaxed under his touch. She was quiet for a moment, looking from one man to the other.

"Just suppose I become interested in switching careers. It would take a great deal of political maneuvering. It would take a well-seasoned and organized staff to get my hat in the ring on short notice. Would all that be available for a state delegate? Wouldn't most of the new party funding be on the federal level in the House and Senate?"

"You have been thinking, haven't you? Yes, on the surface it would seem that would be the logical approach," Cooper said as he turned to Linwood. "Would you care to elaborate on this question?"

"You see, Cassie, in the past, third party emphasis was mostly placed on a few individuals with a platform that did not have sustainable long-range vision. As we mentioned last night, Theodore Roosevelt's Progressive Party came the closest. These parties by and large also did not involve the grass roots to the extent of making lasting headway in state politics as a viable party."

Cooper added, "Don't forget, there are several members of the U.S. House of Representatives and a couple in the Senate who will do that side-step I mentioned. Those that haven't already declared as independents are prepared to jump ship directly to a new third party. In addition to our stable of professionals, we will need a good many volunteers for each new candidate. These should be trusted and influential locals who can rally the independent voters and persuade some diehards to new thinking."

"Jilly," Cassie said.

Cooper said, "Who's Jilly?" Speaking at the same time, Linwood asked, "Jilly Rogers?"

"Mind you, I am in no way committing myself. But if I were, Jilly would fill that bill perfectly. She knows half the state. She volunteers all over the place with a number of organizations. If anyone can persuade independent-thinking voters, Jilly can."

Linwood laughed. "You've got that right. My arm still twinges from the last time she twisted it."

"What about our mysterious break-ins? Do I talk to the sheriff about Pearl's suspicions that may tie the paper incidents to my home?"

"Yes, I think so. However, speak to him in confidence. We can't risk our culprit being warned," Cooper said. "If, as we strongly suspect, it is either Mason Langdon or John Masengood, they will be vicious in protecting their political futures."

"All right, I'll speak to him. Now, may I call my Washington Bureau and tell them I would like a shot at going on the air with an exclusive regarding candidate Cooper Canaday?"

"Yes, I will be going to Washington myself next week and can meet you there—Wednesday or Thursday is best for me. If you want an on-air interview either of those days, let me know by Monday latest."

"Good enough," Cassie replied, taking her hand away.

"And may I make an appointment for you with Jordan Mitchell at the Pinnacle office?"

"Yes, make it Friday morning, if possible. Meantime I have some thinking to do, a sheriff to see, and schedules to rearrange."

Cassie walked the two men to their cars. She stood and watched as they proceeded down the alley.

Tully, who had been taking a smoke break while sitting in his squad car in the alley, suddenly started his engine and followed Cooper and Linwood out of the alley and onto Bay View Road.

Curious, Cassie thought.

CHAPTER 30

Cooper met with Martin at his hospital office just before he left to return to Connecticut. They agreed that no one would be told of their connection until it was officially made known through Cassie's interview. Cassie would then have an article ready for the next issue of the *Clayton Landing Weekly*. Martin walked with Cooper to the hospital front entrance. The two men embraced as they parted. Martin stood watching as Cooper started his Jeep and left the hospital parking lot. He wanted to hold on to his son, keep him close by. He knew he could not. His shoulders sagged as he reluctantly returned to his office.

Linwood took one more turn around Lilly's yard before leaving. The grounds had been scoured thoroughly by friends and neighbors, but Linwood searched each day, hoping to find just one more of Lilly's meager possessions. He wandered toward the woods at the edge of the front yard and poked with a stick among the leaves that Lilly accumulated each year as mulch. When his stick met with an object, Linwood reached down and brushed the leaves from his mama's old green alarm clock. Tears streamed down his face, and he returned to his car with the clock. He sat for a few moments, reached for his coffee in the cup holder, and thought of the many mornings his mother had made his coffee. After one last look around, he started his motor and turned toward the highway, Virginia bound.

Cassie and Pearl spent the weekend house cleaning. At least that's what they told Jilly and Peggy when they stopped by to see if Cassie wanted to take in a movie with them. Actually, they were making a careful search of the house, beginning with Cliff's office. Ed's remark about the old houses in Clayton Landing having secret crannies had reminded Cassie that there was such a place in the office bookshelves behind Cliff's desk.

"Let's take down all the books and dust them while we're looking," Pearl said. "There might be something in a book."

"I suspect someone may have been searching the books, but I know you like help dusting them, so sure, let's dust as we go."

They started with the two middle shelves in the built-in bookcase behind the desk. Those removed, they pulled a shelf from its side grooves and found a small indentation that fit Cassie's index finger. She slid the panel to one side. Inside were several pieces of antique jewelry that Cassie knew had belonged to her mother, along with her mother's journal. Cassie had read it a few times when she was a teenager. She hadn't thought about it for years. Cassie carefully laid these items on the desk and reached for what looked like a scrapbook. Inside were newspaper clippings apparently gathered over several years. Cassie gave them a cursory glance, noting that they all seemed to be related to the four drugstore politicians. Most dealt with news releases from town or state business in which they were involved, but many dealt with their travels. Cassie found that puzzling.

"I'll read these in depth later," she said to Pearl. "Right now, let's dust these books and put everything back. I don't want to leave them out in case they're important, and I don't think anyone has found this nook."

The two women continued working methodically in the office. Later in the day, they moved into the dining room, dusting and polishing as they searched every possible hiding place. By Saturday evening they had found nothing to add to the scrapbook.

Exhausted, they took a break and had a sandwich on the back veranda.

"It would help if we knew what we were searching for and why it's important," Pearl said.

Cassie thought for a minute and then decided she should share the events of the last few days with Pearl, including her visit to Ed's office.

"I haven't been as forthcoming as I should have been," she began. "It seems that Linwood and Cooper have known each other for some time. They met at a conference sometime back, and while they were talking they realized they both had a connection to Clayton Landing."

"And pray tell just what connection does Cooper have to Clayton Landing?"

Cassie explained the need for strict confidence for at least the next week and went over the entire scenario with Pearl.

"Lord have mercy! So that's why we're searching and searching and why somebody else is searching and searching! And we don't know what we or they are searching for?"

"That's right. But whatever it is, we think it will end the career of at least one for the Clayton Landing town council. That scrapbook might give us a clue. I'll read it tonight."

"Now for that part about them maybe wanting you to run for a state office. Are you considering doing that?"

"I don't know, Pearl. I'm going up to Washington next week and meet some people who are involved in this third-party movement. My head tells me that I have a good start on a great career. Having covered politics and the national news for some time, my heart tells me this country needs people in public office who will put the interests of the United States ahead of partisan politics and private gain. We ask our young men and women to sacrifice and put their lives and their income potential on the front line for freedom. It is time for those of us safely at home to do the same. That thought keeps nagging at me."

"Didn't you say something about Cooper and Linwood being willing to use their wealth to support this idea? I didn't know Linwood was wealthy. Lilly sure didn't ever mention it. And she surely didn't show it. You would think Linwood would have done better by his ma."

"Lilly didn't know the extent of his wealth, but any time he tried to make her life a little easier, she resisted. She could be very feisty about not wanting her life to change."

"I guess so." Pearl chuckled as she spoke. "She could be downright fussy about the linens and altar at church being just so."

Both women were lost in thought for a few minutes. Pearl then said, "I knew you are mighty comfortable money-wise, but you said you just found out that you are wealthy?"

"I finally went to see Ed on Friday. I have been putting that off. It seems so final. There are two trusts, one from my mother and the other from my dad. Together they amount to millions. Dad advised me to give Ed my power of attorney years ago. I've never bothered with finances at all, with the exception of balancing my own personal bank book."

"I know that's the truth. I can't even get you to go over my house accounts."

"With the exception of a few people, I don't want anyone to know until I decide what path to take. Ed will be going ahead with all the paperwork now. I understand Dad left a chunk of change for you too. It should keep you in those fancy Sunday go-to-meeting hats for many years to come. Now that he has my attention, he'll be settling the estate properly very soon."

"My, oh, my! Life can sure be discombobulating at times."

"You can say that again. But for now, keep all of this under one of those hats until I can get it sorted out myself. Meantime, we'll keep looking for some kind of evidence and just hope that we find it before someone else does. It sure would help if we knew what we were looking for."

CHAPTER 31

Cassie did not want to raise any hackles at the newspaper by rushing off to Washington before the *Clayton Landing Weekly* was put to bed. Sunday evening, after she and Pearl finished their dinner, she sat down at her bedroom desk and made a list of items to take care of in preparation for the following week. First on the list was a call she would make early Monday morning to her boss, Ross Larson, at NBC. She felt certain that he would allow her to break Cooper's story. Without raising too many questions, she needed to have Ace Coleman pull file pictures of Wahala Hall and Martin Lansfield. She would call a couple of local writers to see if she could hire them part-time to fill in for her. She made a note to look into her father's files and find the name of the editor of a small-town newspaper in West Virginia whom he had admired. She could not recall his name but did remember that he had led the way for some legislative changes that benefited low-income cancer patients, among other good deeds. She needed to get back with Ed to sign some papers. She added a note to call Linda, her neighbor at her Arlington apartment, who had a spare key. The air conditioning needed to be turned on in the apartment. She added calls to Jilly and Peggy to set up a powwow. Her plans included returning to Arlington after rush hour Tuesday evening. In her mind she began writing the article for the newspaper, jotting down key words as thoughts tumbled about. She would transfer the article to a disk and leave it with Mille with instructions not to open it until Wednesday evening in time to get it into the Thursday issue even though the paper might be late. She could always call and cancel those instructions if her plans did not work out.

After she finished her list, Cassie opened each drawer of the desk and carefully went through the contents. She found a stack of five-by-seven notebooks that she had used for her college classes. She pitched them in the trash can with the exception of the one marked "Political Science." Old shopping receipts, calendars, and canceled checkbooks followed the notebooks. The bottom drawer contained a collection of pens and pencils garnered from hotels and conventions. She sorted and wrapped them in rubber bands. She would give them to Jilly, who sent boxes of such items overseas to African schools from time to time. Satisfied that there was nothing in the desk that would interest their prowler, she turned toward the rest of the room. There was still time to go through a few dresser drawers. She shook out each of her panties and bras, unrolled every sock, and unfolded every T-shirt.

When she reached in the bottom drawer and pulled out a bunch of scarves, a box fell to the floor. Since her early childhood, Cliff had occasionally hidden small gifts in her dresser drawers. Would he have disguised evidence in a gift box, Cassie thought? She hesitated for a moment and then carefully untied the package. It contained a beautiful handmade silver necklace with stones of blue. Cassie had admired it when she and her father had passed Joseph's Jewelers on the way to lunch one day early in the year.

As tears streamed down her face, she heard Pearl's familiar voice coming from the foot of the steps.

"Good night, Cassie, sleep tight. I love you. I'll see you bright and early in the morning," Pearl called up the stairwell.

Pearl had stopped tucking her in after her thirteenth birthday but she never failed to say good night with the same predictable words. Cassie wished that this once she had climbed the stairs to tuck her in. Tears flowed freely as she thought of her dad, wondering what future he had really envisioned for her.

Monday morning, she rose earlier than usual, stashed her list in her tote bag, and dashed out the door with a coffee mug and a bagel, much to Pearl's dismay.

She left a message with Ross Larson's secretary at NBC for him to call her posthaste on her cell phone. Margie said he would be at a meeting all morning and not to expect a call before early afternoon. Cassie proceeded down her list.

Carol Morgan, a local writer, agreed to work as a stringer as long as she could do most of her writing at home. "Your timing is perfect. My youngest started school this past fall and I'm bored beyond measure," she said when Cassie called.

When she called the editor of the *Marion County News*, Doug Norris didn't immediately connect her name to Cliff's or the *Clayton Landing Weekly*.

"Pardon my lapse, a million things on my mind. All of us here at the paper were sorry to hear of your father's death. He was a stalwart among us editors, not afraid to chide the state politicians or take on Washington now and then. Now, you say you would like to talk with me. I can't imagine why, but it just so happens that I will be speaking at a Virginia Press Women's Conference at the Sheraton in Norfolk in a week, the tenth to be exact. Would meeting there suit you?"

"That's perfect, how about lunch on me at the hotel—one o'clock?"

"I never pass up a good meal. I'll wait for you in the lobby."

Midmorning, having overheard bits and pieces of Cassie's conversations, the ever-curious Mille could stand it no longer. She crossed the room and plopped down in the chair beside Cassie's desk and in a whispery voice asked, "What the hell is going on?"

Cassie looked up at the office clock before she answered. "I tell you what, I'm going to call Pearl and ask her to pack a lunch for two and meet us on the Green with it at noon. We'll sit on a bench while we eat and I'll fill you in. There are too many ears around here. Ace and the girls can cover at the office for a while. Meantime, I'll zero in on this week's editorial and write up the story of the wreck on Rt. 17 that happened over the weekend."

During lunch, Cassie shared most of the events of the past few days with Mille, including suspicions that one or more of the local politicians might be involved with the newspaper break-in. She did not disclose Cooper and Martin's relationship, merely saying that the disk contained a breaking story that would explain itself when she opened it and that she hoped to be breaking the same story on national TV.

"Does all this mean that you have made up your mind to return to NBC?"

"I've thought it over, Mille. I don't believe Dad meant for me to give up my career. He wanted me to try the paper and listen to an alternative within the year's time. But now I can see that running the paper is not for me. So I need to explore the alternative route and then decide. Meantime, I need to see that the paper is in good hands. With you doing the steering, I'm sure it will be."

"Thanks for the vote of confidence, at least it's something," Mille said with a shrug.

Cassie and Mille gathered their lunch trash and were walking back to the office when Cassie's cell phone rang.

"This is Jed. Can you tell me who bought Cliff's old Buick?"

"I sold it to Mary Clemmons for her son, Eric. Why are you asking?"

"Mrs. Clemmons reported it stolen a few days ago. Tully happened to be wandering down one of the dirt roads off Bay View Road and spotted it pushed off into the woods. When he investigated, he found that the kid's books and cell phone were strewn around on the ground along with the car manual and whatever else was loose in the car. But the thing is, the front seats were ripped and the back seat had been pulled out. The spare tire in the trunk had been thrown out and the mat pulled back."

"You're saying someone searched the car?" Cassie asked.

"Looks that way; it looks like they were after something specific."

Cassie frowned. "Jed, I've been meaning to tell you that Pearl feels sure that someone has been in the house searching too. Whoever it is doesn't want us to know. It's done carefully, but Pearl has an eagle eye for anything disturbed the least bit."

"Have you got any ideas about what they may be looking for?"

"Nothing concrete. I'll get back to you if I think of anything."

"Be careful, looks like someone is getting mighty anxious about something," Jed cautioned.

"Pearl and I have decided to keep the house locked. That's a big step for us."

Cassie ended her conversation and turned to Mille. "We need to get back to work. Carol Morgan is coming in at two this afternoon, and I'll give her some assignments. After I see her, I have to run over to Ed's office. I'll work with Carol tomorrow and then take off in the afternoon for Washington."

While going over story assignments with Carol, Cassie's phone rang.

"Ross Larson here."

"Hold on a minute, Ross."

Cassie excused herself and made her way to the back door. She leaned against the back wall as she talked to Ross. "Thanks for holding, too many ears around. Did I give you enough information on the phone Friday to warrant giving me a spot on the news this week?"

"I'll trust you, Cassie. We're giving you an interview spot on Wednesday night's evening news. I'll pull it if what you have is not as sensational as you indicate—so see me Wednesday morning, nine o'clock sharp."

"I'll be there," Cassie replied.

While still in the alley, Cassie rang Cooper's cell phone.

"Where are you?" Cassie asked.

"I'm on my way to Washington," Cooper said. "I spent the weekend with my mother to bring her up to speed on all that's happened."

"Good. I'm leaving tomorrow around noon. Barring a major holdup on I-95, I should reach my apartment in Arlington by five o'clock. How about coming over around seven for dinner? It'll be simple. That way we can go over some pre-interview notes. Ross says he'll put me on the air Wednesday night and hopes that you will do a follow-up exclusive interview on Saturday morning at my regular time."

"That sounds good—a little unethical, but welcome. Give me directions via my e-mail and I'll see you at your apartment Tuesday evening. If you're running late, just buzz me."

CHAPTER 32

Cassie glanced at the dashboard clock as she approached Dale City and made a decision to exit I-95. Luckily she spotted a convenient parking spot as she pulled into the lot at Wegman's Groceries. She hurriedly scoured the aisles, selecting a stuffed chicken breast entrée, salad fixings, and an apple pie. She plucked four bottles of wine from the shelves, hoping that Cooper would like at least one of them. On the way to checkout, she picked up several flower bouquets.

Traffic became brutal as she approached I-395 in Springfield just outside Washington. While at the King Street stop light, with her Glebe Road exit almost in sight, she dialed Cooper's phone and left a message that she had made it in time for their dinner appointment.

By the time the doorbell rang, Cassie had aired out the apartment, showered, made the salad, and distributed flowers.

Cooper's arms were laden with flowers and wine. "How did you find this place?" he asked. "As I crossed the Potomac River, the Crystal City high-rises loomed, but then as I turned onto Twenty-third Street and then Hayes, I felt I was slowly entering a time warp—back to the early nineteen hundreds."

"That's what I love about Arlington County's Virginia Highlands. The residents have managed to thumb their noses at developers who would love to crush every house and extend Crystal City. The houses have been renovated and upgraded, but they kept the flavor of Washington when it was a small town a hundred years ago. It grounds me amid all the superficial hoopla of political Washington. I've thought of buying one of the houses. I might yet now that I know I can afford one."

The addition of Cooper's flowers lent the apartment a garden atmosphere. After lighting the two candles on her small dining table,

Cassie thought the atmosphere entirely too romantic for an evening she hoped to keep strictly business.

During dinner, Cooper told Cassie of his visit with Madalaine, who had been anxious about his trip to Clayton Landing and the meeting with his father.

"She's bracing herself for the rapidly approaching publicity and all that it will entail," Cooper said.

"She will be hounded for interviews by all the talk shows, you know," Cassie said.

"She's well aware of that and is visualizing in her mind as to just how she will handle it. At the same time, she welcomes coming to rights with her past, as she puts it."

"Speaking of talk shows, shall we get down to business?"

"Sure," Cooper replied.

"Mainly I want to know if there is a subject that you wish to avoid. Nothing upsets an interviewer more than having an interviewee continually saying they prefer not to answer questions on some subject. On the other hand, we want spontaneity rather than seemingly rehearsed responses."

Cooper nodded. "I've always known that when I took the political path there would be nothing I might care to hide that couldn't be dug into and discovered. The Connecticut press has pretty much covered everything in my background as they know it up to the present. At this point, I imagine that just revealing my true heritage will be enough fodder for the press to chew on for some time."

"You're right," said Cassie, "and I don't plan to stray much beyond that, since we have just ninety seconds to cover that revelation." She paused to refill Cooper's wineglass, which was empty. "However, I do want to be sure that I'm clear on all the facts. I've developed an outline that I will tie my questions to, and we'll let it go at that. I won't reveal my questions until the actual interview, of course, but at least you can be assured that I will be asking pertinent questions. I just want to make sure that the facts of my outline are correct."

For the next half hour, Cooper went over his story while Cassie rechecked her notes.

Cooper rose and stretched. "I've been sitting too much these past few weeks."

"Then let's take a walk around my neighborhood. Even though I live in an apartment rather than one of the older homes, I feel a part of the past. This apartment building was here long before the park and the new library were built, and of course long before Crystal City."

"Sounds good. But before we go, I want to make sure that you did confirm your appointment with Jordan Mitchell at the Pinnacle Seven office for Thursday morning."

"I did. And Sunday afternoon I have a powwow appointment with Jilly and Peggy. I need their common-sense opinions about where all this is taking me. We've always weighed in on one another's quandaries. They will be furious that I didn't let them in on your news."

The evening was pleasant, a confirmation that spring had come to stay. Occasionally someone called out to Cassie from a porch. "Where've you been? We missed you." She had developed a porch-stop rapport over the months that she had been jogging and walking in the neighborhood.

As they left Grant Street and turned onto Twentieth, heading back toward Cassie's apartment, a familiar voice called out. "Hey there! The lemonade is free, and if you don't mind the dark, we're bug-free too."

Cassie turned inquiringly toward Cooper and quietly said, "That's Congressman Jake Miller from Iowa. Care to join him and his wife, Judy?"

"By all means," Cooper replied.

Introductions were made, lemonade handed out, and then the four settled into comfortable porch chairs. Jake recognized Cooper's name even though it would have been impossible to recognize his face; the porch was lit by only the remnants of light from the corner lamppost.

"Well now, I would have thought you would be running around all over Connecticut shaking hands this time of year. Personally, I should be out in Iowa doing just that. But fortunately I have only token opposition, and I'll be returning next weekend. During sessions, Judy, Connor, and Missy remain in Iowa in a stable environment for the children. We're taking advantage of the home here to give them a few extra history lessons during their spring break. And we want them to look upon this house as another family home where they can come and spend time with Daddy now and then."

Judy spoke up. "This home keeps us all grounded; it's a lot like our home back in Iowa."

Jake continued. "You see, actually this house has been handed off from Iowa congressman to congressman as retirements and reelections occur—always with the stipulation that it be sold without profit except for upgrades made by each interim owner. It's just a handshake agreement, but thus far it has worked."

"Now that sounds like a sensible arrangement," Cooper said. "I've read about the problems some of our lawmakers have with high rents and relatively low salaries, considering what's expected of them. In fact, I've often wondered when I read such articles why it is that states don't own housing for their elected state representatives in Congress—sort of like state embassies."

Jake laughed. "The majority of my constituents have modest incomes. They think my salary quite adequate, having never tried living dually in our nation's capital and at home. Furnishing me with a home might seem over-the-top, so to speak. So, what brings you to Washington this time of year?"

"Cassie here asked me for an interview. I thought I would accommodate her."

Judy said, "We've missed seeing you on your program, Cassie. What happened?"

"It's a long story, but when I lost my dad, circumstances at home caused me to ask for a leave of absence."

"Well, it's good to have you back—I hope for good. I watch back home and it helps me keep abreast of Washington doings," Judy said.

"At this point, I'm not quite sure what road my future is taking, but I really do like my job with NBC. I have some heady decisions to make in the next few weeks," Cassie said as she rose from her chair.

On that signal, Cooper also rose, glancing at his watch as he did so. "It's getting late," he said. "I'd better walk Cassie home and return downtown to my hotel. It's been great meeting you."

As Jake rose to say goodbye, he said to Cooper, "It looks like you are the popular candidate, even running as an independent. If you are elected, give me a call. I'll have two extra rooms after elections. Sometimes I take in a roommate, although from what I've heard of your glamorous parents, I doubt you need a helping hand."

"Thanks, that's kind of you. I'll keep the offer in mind."

Cooper did not enter Cassie's apartment when they returned. He leaned against the door frame for a moment, looking steadily into Cassie's eyes. Then he lightly brushed her cheek with a kiss and left her standing in the doorway.

Cassie found herself short of breath as she closed and locked the door.

CHAPTER 33

At last the office was quiet. His office manager had left minutes ago. It had seemed to take forever for her to straighten her desk and water her blasted potted plants. He should have thrown the infernal things out long ago, he thought. He was highly irritated, having just returned from the *Clayton Landing Weekly* office. He had stopped by on the pretense of making sure that the paper planned to cover the upcoming fishing contest the Lions Club was sponsoring over the weekend. Of course he knew the question was superfluous, but he had to have some reason to stop by Mille's desk and inquire as to Cassie's whereabouts. Mille seemed evasive. Tully's reports had been mighty disturbing lately. Until the packet of pictures was found, he had to keep Cassie under surveillance as much as possible.

He sat at his manager's desk and waited a few minutes before locking the door. She sometimes flew back in to grab something she left behind. It was an irritating habit and just one more reason he would like to get rid of her. He couldn't, he reasoned; her father was too influential. After a few minutes he rose, locked the door, and proceeded toward the back of the building to his own office. He locked his office door.

"Can't be too careful," he said aloud as he glanced into the large mirror that covered more than half his office wall. As was his habit, he paused a moment to study his reflection. He pulled in his stomach and straightened his belt buckle. He pushed back a stray strand of hair, noticing that he needed a haircut. His eyes squinted as he studied his face. He worried that his nose was showing too many veins and turning a shade darker than his ruddy facial skin. Maybe he would try a little makeup. I must keep up appearances, he thought.

He moved from the mirror to the closet door beside it. With one swipe, he pushed a couple of jackets and a sweater aside and began to twirl the dial of a small safe set into the closet wall. From it, he removed a large manila envelope. His hands were shaking as he proceeded to the couch opposite the mirror, where he spread the pictures out on the coffee table.

Two of his partners had repeatedly warned about the pictures. They didn't understand. The pictures were a titillating source, bringing back memories of experiences he could relive. Magazines and Internet sources could not give him that high.

He shuffled through the pictures hurriedly at first, just to make sure the missing five had not magically reappeared.

"They simply aren't here," he said aloud to his reflection in the mirror. How many times had he checked just to make sure? He sat staring at the remaining pictures for only moments before his arousal, and then his release from tension.

CHAPTER 34

It was not often that the boss stood by watching the evening news. Ross Larson remained anchored to the old-school philosophy that the evening news should be hard news.

The core of viewers of the same mind grew smaller and smaller each year. If the network expected to remain at the top of the ratings, the worthwhile celebrity news bites made sense. Exclusives rarely happened in this area. Cassie's exclusive had the mixture of glamour and political intrigue that had been prevalent in the Kennedy era. Ross was prepared to give the signal to expand the interview, dropping a segment hitherto agreed upon with Benny Long, the New York producer. The crew was unusually curious. There was no teleprompter in use for this segment. Cassie had the only script—her own interview notes.

Anchor Brian Williams stated that the network would be switching to its Washington affiliate for an exclusive interview following a brief commercial break.

Cassie and Cooper were seated opposite each other in an interview setting comprising two comfortable chairs—between them a small table bedecked with a vase of flowers. The background consisted of a bookcase filled with books and bric-a-brac. It was designed to give a relaxed intimate atmosphere.

When the tech gave the on-air signal, Cassie began by saying, "Lieutenant Governor Canaday, you have agreed to this interview today in order to reveal heretofore unknown facts relating to your birth. As far as the public is concerned, you are the son of the well-known couple, the actress Madalaine and the late Broadway producer Sam Canaday. I understand these are not the true facts of your birth."

"That's right, Cassie. I am here today to set the record straight."

Cooper had practiced his response to this obvious interview question so as to keep it concise and within the time constraints. He stated just the facts of his birth. Cassie added details regarding Martin Lansfield's position in Clayton Landing and revealed that she was in fact from that very town.

Cooper was surprised when he glanced at the monitor and saw pictures of Martin and Wahala Hall that appeared on the screen immediately following his revelation of his father's identity. There were pictures of Madalaine as well. He should have realized that Cassie had archives readily available. It threw him off balance for the last question, which he wasn't expecting.

"Lieutenant Governor Canaday, will you tell us why you are choosing to run as an independent in your bid for a seat in the United States Senate?"

Cooper hesitated for a moment. "Our country has functioned since the Civil War as a two-party system, and it has been the best government in the world to this date. However, we have been stumbling headlong into the abysmal state of governmental stalemate, entangled in a quagmire of powerful and demanding corporations and special interest groups who spoon-feed millions of dollars into our system in exchange for passage of legislation that gives little thought as to the effect on the people of this country. We do not have time for me to expound on this subject, but the premise of my candidacy is to take a large step in a new direction for our country."

Cassie became aware of frantic windup signals, so she was forced to call a halt to her interview. In New York, Brian Williams smoothly picked up halfway through his script for the next segment.

In Connecticut, Madalaine sat back and nervously drummed her fingers on the arm of her chair. Her private cell phone rang immediately following Cooper's interview. Without even glancing at the incoming number, she knew it was Brenda Scofield, her publicist. She would be understandably furious. Madalaine chose to let the phone ring.

In Clayton Landing, Martin watched the evening news with apprehension, knowing full well his life was about to change. The apprehension turned to pride and tears halfway through the interview.

Having been summoned to a get-together by Cassie, Jilly, Peggy, and Pearl watched the television together on the back veranda. When the interview ended, all three reacted at the same time.

"Wow, now that is soap opera news," Peggy said.

"Lord have mercy!" Pearl exclaimed.

"That ought to shake up this old town. I can hear the buzzing already. I wish I could see Mavis's face right now." Jilly chuckled as she spoke.

Their gab-fest afterward lasted until after dark.

Mavis and a group of friends were having drinks in the country club bar when someone held up a hand for silence and pointed. All eyes turned toward the television. At the end of the interview, all eyes turned at once to Mavis. She seemed to have turned to stone.

Across town, Mille picked up her phone and called the printer to release the *Clayton Landing Weekly*. She had been prepared to hold the paper and rush a new front page if anything went wrong with the interview. In the town office, Mayor Gordon Everly turned the television on to catch the evening news before moving the meeting to the Sound Side Restaurant. Charles Masengood, John Masengood, and Mason Langdon retrieved a bottle and glasses from the mayor's bottom desk drawer and helped themselves to a scotch and then settled down to watch the news before their monthly seafood dinner. "If that don't beat all," one of them said following Cassie's interview. Two of the men glanced at each other, brows furrowed, wondering how this news might affect them—each having a deep feeling that it would.

In his comfortable home in Potomac in the suburbs of Washington, Jordan Mitchell, coordinator of the Pinnacle Seven, raised his glass toward the television in salute. He would be seeing Cooper and Cassie in his office the next morning.

In Charlottesville, Linwood Johnson sat with his feet on his desk, hands behind his head, reflecting on the salvo that had just been fired at politics as usual.

CHAPTER 35

Cassie had been sitting at a window table for ten minutes waiting for Cooper at the coffee shop just down from the Pinnacle offices. She was beginning to get concerned when she saw him alight from a taxi and dash through the rain. As he entered the coffee shop vestibule he flicked spots of water off his jacket and looked around. He saw Cassie wave just as the hostess approached. He nodded toward Cassie, indicating that he was joining someone, and made his way to Cassie's table.

"Sorry, when it rains in Washington, taxis become scarce as snow on the Fourth of July," he said as he slid into the seat opposite Cassie.

"Don't I know," she replied. "But we need these spring rains for the cherry blossoms. It's a good thing we allowed a little extra time before our meeting with Jordan Mitchell."

Cooper turned his cup over and a waitress soon filled it with coffee. "I hope you brought an umbrella."

"As a matter of fact, I did. It was a short walk from the parking garage."

"It's lucky that you found a parking spot."

"It's one of the perks I allow myself; I rent it by the month. If you noticed, we aren't far from NBC, just far enough to get in my morning exercise when I was working there. Tell me a little about Jordan Mitchell's personality. I looked up his background—impressive."

"He's sharp, seems to have an uncanny ability to read people. He cannot abide those who wax flamboyantly to cover their incompetence or those whose competence is worn like a medal of distinction to set them apart."

"Thanks for the warning. In other words, don't try to impress him with rhetoric."

Cooper laughed. "I'm sure that you agreed to this meeting out of curiosity. It will be up to Mitchell to impress you."

Cassie thought this a peculiar remark but let it pass. She glanced at her watch. "It's time to make a dash. We'll share my umbrella."

The building that housed the Pinnacle office had been refurbished some years ago. It was not plush; the foyer was utilitarian. There was no reception desk. Cassie deposited her umbrella in the wrought-iron stand just inside the door as Cooper moved toward one of the four elevators. While they waited, Cassie glanced through the directory list mounted on the wall near the elevators. From the names listed, it would be hard to decipher what kind of business went on behind those office doors. As they entered the elevator, Cooper pushed the button for the fourth floor, and the elevator slowly rose.

Cooper pointed toward the right as they left the elevator. He stopped in front of the office numbered 404.

The room they stepped into was not large. It held a reception desk, a few file cabinets, a coffee table in front of a plain beige sofa, and a matching side chair. Mocha-colored carpeting covered the floor. Except for the original oil paintings that adorned the walls, the office was nondescript. There was no one at the reception desk. The inner door was open.

It was just moments before a tall, broad-shouldered man appeared at the inner office door, his hand held out in welcome as he came forward to greet Cassie and Cooper. Judging by the attractive gray streaks in his dark brown hair, Cassie guessed that he was in his early sixties. His brown eyes looked deeply into Cassie's as if he were reading brain waves. He clasped both of his large hands over hers as he said, "I'm so pleased to meet you, Cassie."

They moved into the inner office. It was only slightly larger than the reception area, furnished simply and with good taste. The walls were also adorned with impressive paintings. The one behind the small conference table where Jordan motioned them to sit was particularly impressive.

"I'm surprised that we haven't met previously," Cassie said. "I've read a few articles about the Pinnacle Seven studies, but I've never seen you around the Washington circuit."

"We recently moved the offices to Washington. If you are planning to attack the lion's den, then you must move your campsite close to the lion."

Cassie decided to be straightforward. "I'm here out of curiosity. Cooper has made a vague reference to my being programmed for some sort of political role or something along those lines. I'm just plain offended by such a notion. The very idea that my father raised me to be some sort of guinea pig is repugnant. He tells me that you will be the one to explain what he means by this."

Jordan's dark eyes sparkled in amusement; a slight smile creased his lips. He swiveled his chair toward Cooper, leaned back with his hands clasped behind his head, and studied Cooper for a few seconds before he said, "Seems we have to work on your diplomacy, Cooper. You've got the lady's ire up."

Cooper chuckled. "Seems I have, but we're here for you to tell the story, Jordan."

"So you are. Well, let me begin some sixty years ago. Your father was in his last year of college at the university in Durham. During that year, he formed a friendship with several young men who were serious thinkers. They had each served in World War II in one capacity or another. Like so many who had returned to take advantage of the G.I. Bill, they were older than the youth on campus who had not gone to war. They took their studies seriously and were at odds with the carefree attitude of the young men who were relieved of the burden of facing enemy guns. I recall there were seven young men in the group. It was from this small nucleus that the Pinnacle Seven group grew. The seven spread out into different professions and attracted like-minded men. They really had no specific mission in the beginning other than to have an interchange of ideas as related to the condition of the country. They stayed in close contact, and some fifteen years or so after they graduated, they decided to meet yearly to exchange ideas, share experiences, and dissect the current political scene and its impact on the country. A number of prominent women joined their ranks."

Cassie broke in. "That would be the yearly sabbatical Dad went on. He was always off-handed about it. He said he was getting together with a bunch of college buddies to solve the problems of the world. I always pictured a bunch of old guys sitting around a wood stove in a forest somewhere."

Jordan chuckled and then continued. "For purposes of cohesion, and to be both abstract and symbolic to honor their founders, they continued to call themselves the Pinnacle Seven. It remained merely an altruistic group dedicated to the country and to world peace until the assassination of Kennedy and the rise of the Nixon era. Then they began to get serious. They formed a blueprint for the future of the country based on mutual experiences and growing apprehension about the stalemated political process developing in the United States. They inched forward with plans for a third party. The election fiasco of 2000 and the ensuing years of corporate greed, presidential ineptitude, and a gridlocked Congress have created an emergency mandate for the group. We have stood as a nation watching an avalanche of catastrophic events barrel toward us, and we seem to be watching in a helpless state, waiting to be swallowed in its path."

Cassie found that she was holding her breath. Jordan Mitchell's words came from deep in his diaphragm with resounding force, as if he were speaking to a large gathering. She glanced at Cooper. Undoubtedly he had been privy to the man's oratorical presentations previously, but nonetheless, he too seemed mesmerized.

"We now have the momentum of purpose under way and enough restlessness and discouragement with the political process among our country's citizens to expedite the launching of a third party," said Jordan. "The time is nearing for the introduction of a viable third party into the mire of Washington's political swamp. A party founded on the sound principles of our forefathers and by men and women of purpose, vision, and knowledge seeking not prestige for themselves but the prestige of being at the forefront of a movement to put principle and expertise back into politics. Our dream is to launch a movement so forceful in its effort to bring fairness, hope, and prosperity back to our citizens that our success will eventually inspire the citizens of all nations to demand that their leaders respect human dignity and progress for all mankind."

For a moment no one spoke. Jordan took a sip of water.

After seconds of silence, Cassie said, "At the risk of sounding negative, historically the eloquence of oratory has projected a few men to great heights, but unfortunately too many of them have succumbed to the very frailties of human nature that they proposed to eradicate."

"Ah ha! There you have it in a nutshell, that creeping parasite, power paralysis—power that gets under the skin and erupts as pus-filled fissures of greed, arrogance, and self-indulgence, eventually eradicating judgment and reason. This pernicious vermin has infected, in epidemic proportions, far too many leaders in every walk of life throughout the history of mankind. A man drunk from a bottle intellectually knows the depths to which over-indulgence will take him and cares little for the unintentional destruction he causes in his path. The man drunk on power is far more dangerous, for he sees only glory ahead and employs destruction to clear his pathway."

"I don't understand," Cassie said. "Are you insinuating that the Pinnacle Seven group has some magic formula that will do away with this problem?"

Cassie glanced from Jordan to Cooper as she spoke, noticing that both men had raised their eyes to the painting above the conference table.

CHAPTER 36

Jilly poked her head in the veranda screen door and said, "Anybody home?"

Pearl responded from the kitchen, "Just me and Muffin."

"I came by Thursday to drop off that recipe I promised you, and the door was locked. What gives?"

"I guess Cassie forgot to tell you," said Pearl. "We're suspicious that someone has been sneaking around the house looking for something when we're not here. So we decided we have to lock up when no one's at home."

Jilly made her way to the kitchen, pausing briefly to scratch Muffin behind the ears. "What's happened to our sleepy old town? It's been one thing after another for the past few months, and now we've made the national news. I saw Doc Lansfield at the drugstore yesterday, and he looked ten years younger. There was pep in his step, and he was just beaming."

"Well, the man deserves some happiness in his life. And that Mavis deserves some come-uppance. I'll bet she wet her pants when she heard the news. That girl hasn't done a lick of work in her whole life, and I expect she thought she'd inherit the whole works one of these days."

"Speaking of things happening, after much debate, we have decided to have a small ceremony by the flagpole in honor of Matty Jasman on spring break day at the elementary school. He would have moved up to fifth grade this year. It was hard to decide whether to remind the kids of his death or honor his memory. We decided it was best to remember him so the children would know that he is missed and not forgotten so quickly."

"I can't believe such a thing could happen in Clayton Landing. When was it—back in January sometime? I guess with Cliff's death and all, it just slipped my mind. Poor child! It would have to be a monster to do something like that," Pearl said.

"As president of the PTA, I insisted that Sheriff Ryan give a safety talk to the whole elementary school."

"That was a smart thing, I'd say."

"Anyway, the reason I stopped in is to let you know that I'll be by about seven-thirty Monday morning to pick up those cookies you've been baking and freezing for me. And before I forget, here's the copy of the cookie recipe you wanted."

As a stocking gift one Christmas, Cassie bought several plastic boxes for Pearl that just fit her recipe cards. She then helped her organize a drawer in the kitchen cabinets. Pearl walked over to the cabinet and filed the new recipe in the desserts box.

"I hear you'll be over Saturday night? Cassie says you girls are having a powwow. It's been a long time since you had a powwow," she said to Jilly as she filed.

"That's right, too long. It seems Cassie is in a whirlwind these days."

"She'll be all right. She's her father's daughter. She just needs to get her head wrapped around all these changes going on," Pearl replied.

"Yeah, I know. My future is pretty much set in concrete with John, Johna, and Mary Sue at the center of it. Lord knows what Peggy will get into along the way. But Cassie, now that girl was meant for big time."

Pearl nodded her head in agreement. "That's true, but don't sell yourself short, young lady. You dabble all over the state in one cause or another."

"That's stuff anybody can do. Gotta go. Will I see you Saturday night?"

"I'll set supper out for you ladies, and then I'm going off for barbecue, and then over to Corley's to watch a DVD with her mother, who is mostly confined to a wheelchair these days. I'll see you Monday for sure."

CHAPTER 37

While he relied on Tully to filter information to him, now and again he felt compelled to check on the status of investigations himself. He knew that if he didn't keep his inquiries casual, even that thick-headed Tully might get curious. Luckily, Shirley Forester, the receptionist/dispatcher, seemed to be the only one in the sheriff's office as he stepped inside.

"Good morning. I just stopped by to see if the sheriff had suggestions about how to keep tourists from clogging up my parking lot. Signs don't seem to be working. You know I've been trying to get a town parking lot down by the docks for some time."

The phone rang before Shirley had a chance to reply.

He ambled over to the bulletin board and studied the posters. He noticed that the reward for information leading to Matty Jasman's killer had been upped by five hundred dollars to two thousand. The thought occurred to him that he should also contribute to that reward. There was also a small reward posted for information leading to the arrest of the person responsible for the break-ins at the *Clayton Landing Weekly*. He glanced over the remaining miscellaneous posters and found a new poster had been added to the car theft section of the bulletin board. A one hundred dollar reward was being offered for information about the theft of a 1998 Buick Century. Another thought crossed his mind. Wouldn't the sheriff have a hissy fit if he knew all three of those posters were related? He was startled to find that he had laughed out loud at that thought.

"Something funny?" Shirley asked as she hung up the phone.

"No, just remembering a joke I was told just before I came in."

"Well, I can always use a good joke to brighten my day."

He was saved from racking his brain when the sheriff came in the back door.

"I just stopped by to complain again about the tourists clogging up my parking lot, Jed. You need to testify at the next town meeting in favor of that dock parking lot we've been trying to push through."

"You might be right. We just don't seem to have enough parking spaces in the summer. But we hardly need a parking lot in the winter months. I just don't know whether the money spent will be worth it."

Jed's caveat annoyed him. He motioned toward the bulletin board. "I see you aren't making any progress on the crime going on around here."

"Actually, we're making more progress than you might think. I've got the FBI lab working on some evidence on one of the cases. I hope there will be a breakthrough soon."

"On which case?"

"Well, I can't rightly say. It's confidential information right now. I've said too much already."

"Certainly you can share that information with me. After all, I'm on the town council, and we pay your salary."

"Oh. I thought the taxpayers paid my salary. Anyway, that's all I'm going to say for now."

He felt flushed and knew he was turning visibly red-faced. He started to say something but thought better of it. "Have a nice day," he said as he left the office, slamming the door behind him.

He was rattled. He walked over to the Green and sat down on a shaded bench to cool off. After a few minutes, he fumbled for the cell phone hooked to his belt and dialed.

"Something is up," he said into the phone. "The sheriff has some new evidence … No, I don't know what kind of evidence. He refused to say … Well, how in the hell do you think I'm going to make him tell me? I tried throwing my position on the town council at him. He didn't take the bait."

He listened to the person on the other end of the line for a few moments before continuing. "I don't like the sound of it either, and I don't see what more we can do. I've looked everywhere for the packet. Until it's found, neither of us is safe … Now don't go blaming it all on me. You're in this thing as much as I am, and don't you forget it … Okay. We'll meet tonight, usual place. I'll see if I can get anything out of Tully in the meantime, although I doubt the sheriff lets Tully in on anything of importance if he's smart."

The party on the other end of the line hung up. He sat looking at the phone for a minute or so and then slowly put it back in its holster.

CHAPTER 38

Cassie, following the lead of the two men, studied the painting hanging on the wall above the conference table. Shafts of morning sun highlighted tall pines and the waterfall in a deep valley that divided twin mountains. Barely visible on one mountain, a glassed enclosure hung suspended out over the valley. Across from the enclosure, the morning sun lent a pink hue to pockets of snow on the bald mountain top. She wondered what the peaceful scene had to do with their conversation concerning a third political party. Her attention returned to Jordan Mitchell as he began to speak.

"When I was still a young whippersnapper in my late twenties, I went to New York to visit a well-known relative of mine who had made it big in the stock market. His office was on the thirty-fifth floor, high above the streets. In the process of giving me advice, he took me over to the window. We stood looking down on the street below where pedestrians went about their daily lives. They looked like mere specks as we stood high above them."

"'See those folks down there?' he said. 'You don't want to be one of them. You've got to set your sights to reach the top floors, my man. Leave the peons to scramble about in their nickel jobs. Set your goal and stick with it, my man. It takes guts, some smarts, and I think you have both.'

"I couldn't help it. I almost laughed in his face. The thought suddenly struck me that there was no way I could avoid descending from the thirty-fifth floor and onto that sidewalk among the so-called peons. And even funnier, neither could he."

"Meaning of course that no matter how high the office, no one can ever escape the fact that he or she is part of the masses of humanity," Cassie said. "Sitting here listening to you is like hearing the voice of my father. How did this melding of philosophies come about?"

Cooper interjected, "This is a fascinating story, and one I wouldn't mind hearing once more."

"Our small group had begun to study the politically powerful, dissecting the personalities of those who made quick descents from power due to their own narcissistic personalities. What was the common denominator? Then, some months into our study, Michael Stone joined our group. He taught philosophy at a Midwestern college. He seems to have an aura about him that no one can explain. His mere presence is calming; his few words added to a discussion are profound; his ability to take pieces and mold them to a whole is uncanny."

"I've heard of him," said Cassie. "I read one of his books years ago; it's in my dad's office library. Stone seems to have dropped from sight. I assume he is still living."

"Very much so," Cooper said. "In fact, I was with him a few months ago before I announced my candidacy for the Senate."

"Yes, we are fortunate," said Jordan. "He became intrigued with some of our ideas. He also became fascinated with the idea of controlling the debilitating effects of power. He believes his methodology could produce a new breed of politician."

Cassie shifted uncomfortably in her chair, which squeaked. "Don't tell me this is some kind of new religion?"

"No, not at all. He believes that deep down inside of us we are constantly fighting our demons, demons implanted within our genes, and that our real purpose in life is to overcome those demons."

"Isn't that what religion is all about?"

"To a certain degree, of course, but Michael has concluded, as a result of the Pinnacle Seven group's many discussions and research, that power is the foremost demon of them all, as far as politics is concerned. We also know that power affects many lives. Tyrant power creates criminals. Tyrant power over a family or a community infects and spreads, sometimes from one generation to another. We know from history what misuse of power can do to nations. Hitler, Stalin, and certainly to a much lesser extent our own Senator McCarthy and yes, President Nixon, are prime examples, as well as many others. In the last few years, misuse of power by politicians and corporate heads has had disastrous results on our country's economy."

Cassie raised an eyebrow. "Are you saying that Michael Stone has some magical solution to the abuse of power?"

"I wish. However, he has developed a methodology for reducing excessive power—combating its destructive forces through periodic removal of the person from the scene of his or her power. Nothing deflates the egotist so much as being shown that the world, the country, or the organization can function without him or her at the helm. The Pinnacle group has decided that all of our third-party leaders, as they rise to the top, will be periodically required to take a sabbatical. That means total disappearance and hands off the reins, much as if he or she had suddenly died. The real mark of a good leader is to be surrounded by the equally capable. The maestro is nothing without the orchestra, but a cohesive, well-practiced orchestra can manage to perform without the maestro."

"Simple in theory, but has it been tried?" Cassie asked.

Both men spoke at the same time. "Yes."

Jordan motioned toward the painting. "We've called our first sanctuary the Pinnacle, a hidden paradise for restoring humanity to power. The name suited both our group and our sanctuary. Cooper here jokingly calls it the battery store."

Cooper interjected. "Joking aside, something happens when you get off the world, so to speak. The seclusion humbles one's soul and at the same time recharges the energy sources of the mind."

Jordan smiled and went on. "Michael oversaw the building of the Pinnacle on an abandoned plateau carved out of a mountainside by a mining company west of Denver. It's very secluded, reachable by a Jeep trail up the mountain or by helicopter only." Jordan paused to study the painting once more. "As you can see in the painting, the glass atrium is cantilevered from the side of the mountain. When sequestered in that room, one is enshrouded in silence, nestled in the majesty of nature. Hours can go by while the soul feeds. Across the deep valley, a waterfall continuously flows—symbolic of life's constant flow."

For a few moments, the three were quiet as they studied the painting.

Cassie broke the reverie. "I presume Michael Stone acts as the guru of the Pinnacle. Is it his responsibility to keep the party leaders in line?"

"No, not really," said Jordan. He leaned back in his chair as he continued, apparently not at all put off by her skeptical response. "The purpose of the sabbatical is the restorative value—the setting aside of ego supplanted by examination of one's inner self, one's value to life. The atrium is attached to a two-story building on the plateau. In the painting, that part of the building is hidden by tall pines. Guest rooms, two small apartments—one being Michael's, a large common room with a well-stocked library, a kitchen, storage, and utility space are located in that area. Michael is available to those on sabbatical, but only by request. No one is required to examine his or her life, only to withdraw from it. Each guest on sabbatical is given a schedule for use of the common room and the atrium sanctum. By use of a schedule, several guests can be in the facility, rarely crossing paths. If you join our movement, you will be asked to spend a few days at the Pinnacle."

"A test run, I presume. This is all very interesting, but where do I fit into this picture? Cooper and Linwood seem convinced that I am somehow destined to become a part of this movement. Apparently my father did also. But historically, third parties have never worked. I'm not convinced this one will be successful or that I should be a part of such a movement."

"Third parties are successful in western Europe and in Canada," Jordan reminded her. "A government frozen by stalemate is a dangerous government. A government blocked by obdurate personalities unwilling to compromise is a stagnant government open to an undertow of creeping paralysis."

Cooper said, "People are frightened. They want to know if the foundation our forefathers gave us will survive the onslaught of rampant corruption and greed that has swept this nation like a tsunami. Some of the antics of both our political leaders and corporate heads in the past few years are tantamount to treason."

"Those are strong words, Cooper," said Cassie. "Gentlemen, I have a great deal of thinking to do. What exactly are you asking of me?"

"That you consider joining our third party at the ground floor in your state legislature, that you run temporarily as an independent, and that you agree to spend five days at the Pinnacle prior to making your final decision," said Jordan.

"Very cut-and-dry," said Cassie wryly. "You are only asking that I change my career path, figure a way to supplant an incumbent, become a member of a party that I don't even know the name of while calling myself an independent, and take a week out of a busy life to examine my inner soul."

Cooper laughed. "You do have a way of reducing the seemingly sublime to the ridiculous!"

"And it is not ridiculous, even though it may sound so at first light," said Jordan. "The name of the new party will be decided shortly. In the meantime, like Cooper, those who expect to eventually become members of a third party are running as independents. Time spent at the Pinnacle will test your mettle. We know that the incumbent that you may replace is a man made of slimy morals—we just need the way to prove it. Somehow we will!" His fist hit the table for emphasis as he spoke the last words.

Cassie was a little taken aback by Jordan's vehemence. She spoke deliberately. "Well, right now I have to get back to my roots. I realize timing is critical at this point, but surely you don't expect me to make a snap decision here and now. I'm returning to Clayton Landing tomorrow. Perhaps from that vantage point, I can begin to sort through all that has happened in the past couple of months and make sense of it."

"And I return to Connecticut," Cooper said. "Dare I ask if you are free for dinner tonight?"

Cassie laughed. "I do sound rather antagonistic, don't I? Yes, I will join you for dinner."

"Good, I'll pick you up around seven."

CHAPTER 39

"Pork chops, collard greens, cheesy grits, and corn bread, how can you beat that?" Jilly said as she pushed her chair from the table and started collecting plates.

"Pearl always cooks *your* favorites when she gets a chance," Peggy said.

"Now ladies, no pouting! Pearl spoils us all when she gets the opportunity. I know for a fact that she made a strawberry pie for you, Peggy," Cassie said. "We'll have that later."

"Come on, let's get the dishwasher going. I'm on pins and needles waiting to hear all the latest news out of you, Miss Cassie Danforth," Jilly said impatiently.

"Shall we adjourn to the back veranda? It's a nice night," said Cassie.

"Heck, no! If we're going to have a powwow, it has to be in the middle of your bed like always," Jilly replied.

They settled into their customary places on Cassie's bed. Jilly and Cassie sat among the pillows, resting against the headboard. Peggy lay at the foot of the bed, Muffin in the middle.

"Give," Peggy said.

"I don't know exactly where to begin. Of course, you know it all began when Dad asked me to return to Clayton Landing in his last moments. He told me to be a brick—funny expression for him, and I've been anything but since then. I thought I knew exactly where I was going, and I was making darn good progress. Now I'm confused. You need to help me sort it out."

Cassie took them through the sequence of events: coping with the newspaper, the break-ins, Cooper and Linwood's involvement in her life,

146

the interview with Jordan Mitchell. She also shared the information about her newfound wealth, eliciting a whistle from Peggy.

"All this and not even a mention of dealing with my problems and tornadoes," Peggy said.

"Wow, girl. I don't think I've been so excited since John asked me to marry him," Jilly said.

"So I had dinner with Cooper and came home to sort it all out with you two and Pearl," Cassie finished.

"Whoa. Don't skip over the dinner with Cooper. Seems to me you've been seeing that handsome gent quite a bit lately. Anything going on?"

"Jilly Rogers, you've been expecting a romantic relationship with every man I shake hands with for years now." Cassie threw a pillow at her friend, who caught it, unperturbed.

"Well, have you done more than shake hands with Cooper?"

"You are incorrigible. As a matter of fact, he kissed me on the cheek after our first dinner. Thursday night when we parted he lifted my chin and just brushed my lips with his. I will admit it gave me chills."

"Jeez, girl! That's romance, the kind I read about in my books. The dudes I see every day at the diner think they have the right to grab my ass after the first howdy," Peggy said.

For moments all three were quiet.

Jilly said, "You know, we sound like we've reverted back to high school days. We're way beyond that. Maybe this is the right time for you to consider stepping into politics, Cassie. You'd be a natural. Life for all three of us has changed significantly. These are serious times. Thank goodness John's job with the electric company seems pretty safe. Folks will always need electricity. Even so, the budget is getting tight. I've thought about taking a part-time job to help out now that the girls are older."

"She's right, Cassie," said Peggy. "Times are tight. I hear it all the time at the diner. It seems like the hard-working patriotic folks have been taken for a ride by the greedy folks. And it seems like all those bigwigs in Washington do is bicker with each other while everything in the country goes to pot."

Jilly nodded. "She's right. If this consortium or whatever you call it means what they say about wanting to set this country back on the path that our forefathers meant for us, then I say go for it. You certainly have the background."

"It's not that simple, Jilly," Cassie said. "First, if I am going to run this fall in the state legislature, Mason has to step aside. And second, a zillion signatures will be needed to put me on the ballot."

"The zillion signatures is no problem. Anyway, I know it only takes a few hundred. I can get to work on that immediately," Jilly said.

Cassie sighed. "I have to admit I've always been fascinated by politics. That's why I wrangled my way into assignments in that direction wherever I worked. But I never gave any thought to diving in myself."

"Heck, Cassie, you've never shied away from advising me, so I say go for it, kiddo," Peggy interjected.

Cassie looked from Peggy to Jilly and back again. "Of course, you know none of this will happen any time soon if we don't solve the mystery of my dad's missing evidence. I can't think of anywhere else to look, and apparently our culprit can't either."

"I wish I could help," said Jilly, "but you certainly know more about where your dad might have hidden evidence than anyone else except maybe Pearl. But if the plan comes about and you do decide to jump into the monkey cage, I'll be ready to help with the campaign."

"Thanks, Jilly. As a matter of fact, your talent for getting involved in all sorts of volunteer jobs will come in handy. You are certainly well known in our district. We'll be using some professional staff and some local staff. So maybe it could work into a part-time job for you."

"I've worked with those professional types before, and I'm not so sure I can cope with them, but I would try for your sake. I just know that Larry Ferguson lost his election because I couldn't convince the young men in charge that you just can't call people around here three or four times during a campaign and not expect a backlash. You should have heard some of the irate comments from a few I called. One man said he was for Ferguson, but if he got one more phone call he would vote for Mark Kearney. I finally just refused to follow the schedule."

"Well, I am hoping a new breed of politicians means a new way of soliciting votes, too. But all of this conversation is moot until something breaks."

Peggy rose from the bed. "If I'm going to have any of that strawberry pie, it's now or never. It's time for me to go. I'm on the late shift tonight, and I just begged off for a few hours. It gets real busy at the diner around this time until we close. The place will be rocking by now."

The three went down to the kitchen and ate their dessert with relish. Cassie saw Jilly and Peggy out the back door and waited by the screen door until she saw Pearl arriving home from Corley's. She gave her a hug and said, "How was your evening?"

"It was all right, I guess. The barbecue was delicious. But as for the DVD, I don't rightly see how a person could believe someone could be born old and die a baby. It doesn't make sense. I've got to say though, some acting."

Cassie locked the door and they made their way to their respective bedrooms. Muffin was already fast asleep in her kitchen bed.

CHAPTER 40

Suddenly, Cassie sat straight up in bed. Light from the corner lamppost seeped through the thin drapes and cast shadows around her room. She felt disoriented, having awakened from a strange dream. Slowly her thoughts reached back, trying to remember the dream. She did remember that it was about her father and then slowly the hospital scene repeated in her mind. That was it! She was back in the hospital reliving those last moments, a place she did not want to be. Somehow she seemed to have felt his grip on her arm and heard again those last words, "Be a brick." No. That wasn't it. She lay back on her pillow and closed her eyes, hoping to recapture her dream.

Had she drifted off to sleep? She wasn't sure. She rose up on her elbow and looked at the clock. The red figures read 2:32. She lay back on her pillow again, staring up at the shadowy ceiling. The last words of the dream kept nagging at her. "Be a brick—Be a brick." They just weren't right. Her father had never used that expression in their lifetime together. She drifted off again.

Again, she sat straight up in bed. The red figures on the clock read 3:43. This time she was alert. This time she knew! The dream had come back to her or had she merely dreamed again? Was her father trying to contact her through a dream? No matter. She knew. His last words were *"Behind* a brick." He had been gasping for breath as he spoke, so the word must have been slurred.

Cassie rose from the bed and reached into her bedside table for her flashlight. She retrieved her letter opener from her desk. Barefooted, she quietly made her way across the room and opened the door as silently as she could. She did not want to wake Pearl. She felt apprehensive as she approached the attic door at the end of the hallway. The door had a tendency to stick, and she had to give it a sharp tug to get it open. She winced at the noise and listened for a moment, but there was no sign that she had disturbed Pearl. She left it open and quietly made her way up the flight of steps. It had been so long, she couldn't even remember the last time she'd been in the attic. At the top of the steps, she paused, casting her light over the expansive space. It really could have served as a third floor. At one time, this had been her indoor playground. A large cleared space had held her dollhouse and tea-time table, complete with a miniature set of china from France that had been her mother's. Along one wall close to the chimney that ran through the attic stood her bookcase, still filled with children's books. Now everything was covered with old white sheets, and nothing had been touched for years.

She paused to remember. She must have been around five when, on one rainy afternoon, her father had followed her up to the attic to attend a tea party with her assorted dolls and teddy bears. If she recalled correctly, Pearl had made her father's favorite oatmeal cookies for the occasion. He had patiently gone through her ritual and admired the costume of dress-up clothes that she had rummaged from several trunks.

"That was absolutely delicious," she recalled him saying. "And now I have a surprise for you."

He rose and went over to the chimney. Then with his pocket knife, he loosened two bricks and set them on top of the bookcase. He reached his hand inside a cavity and drew out a small box that he handed to her. Inside was a charm bracelet with a single charm. It was a tea cup. During the ensuing years, she frequently found little treasures, more charms, and as she got a little older, small sums of money hidden there. Not even Pearl, Jilly, or Peggy knew about the secret hiding place. It was a covenant between father and daughter long forgotten after she reached her late teens.

Cassie made her way over to the chimney. She laid the flashlight on top of the bookcase so that it shone on a particular section of the chimney. She did not want to turn on the attic lights in case someone might be watching the house. There were small diamond-shaped windows on all sides of the attic. Using her letter opener, she carefully loosened a brick, then another, setting each one carefully on the bookcase. She reached her hand inside.

The envelope was a standard five by seven with a clasp. Cassie retrieved the flashlight and made her way to her grandmother's sheet-covered rocking chair. She laid the flashlight on her lap so that it shone away from her. She held the envelope in front of the light and carefully opened it.

She gasped, hardly believing what she was seeing. Her heart was racing. She felt like retching.

The shadows seemed to close in around her. Suddenly out of the darkness something leaped at her. She screamed. Muffin landed in her lap, purring her request for petting time.

Cassie sat shaking, trying to control herself while automatically stroking Muffin. She willed herself to calm down, listening for sounds that would indicate that Pearl had heard her scream. All remained quiet in the house.

Finally, she whispered to Muffin, "Now I have to think this through."

First she would have to call the sheriff. But not right now, she thought. I'll do that early in the morning. How can I meet with him tomorrow without raising suspicions if anyone is watching? Weekdays I frequently consult with Jed, but tomorrow is Sunday. I don't normally consult with the sheriff on Sundays. Church—I'll see him in church. Maybe he'll have a suggestion when I call. I have to act natural. I have to avoid Tully. I can't talk to anyone.

Cassie felt overwhelmed by her own thoughts as she slowly made her way back to her bedroom with Muffin. The red figures on the clock now read 5:45. She watched every minute change on the clock until it finally flashed 6:00. She couldn't wait any longer. She reached for her cell phone and called Sheriff Ryan.

"Hello. This had better be important," an irritated Jed Ryan responded to the call.

"It's Cassie, Jed. I found a packet of pictures that apparently someone has been looking for. It was in a secret hiding place in the chimney that Dad and I had up in the attic. It's no wonder that someone is desperate to find it. I really haven't closely examined the pictures, but they are sickening. The packet is dangerous for me to have around. How can I get it to you without raising any suspicions? It's Sunday, you know. We don't normally cross paths except at church. I want to be particularly cautious. You'll understand when you see this packet. Would it be all right to slip it to you at church?"

"I don't think so, there's way too many eyes watching there. You always sit up front in your family's usual place, and I sit in back so I can scurry out if needed. If either of us changed that arrangement, it would cause as much gossip as the morning Miss Maime lost her bloomers going down the aisle. If we meet outside, someone might get nervous over that. Tell you what; let me call you back shortly. I'll think of something."

When she made her way downstairs for breakfast, Cassie was visibly jumpy to the point that Pearl noticed.

"What's the matter? Didn't you sleep well last night?"

"No, as a matter of fact, I didn't. Maybe I need a cup of coffee."

Cassie took the coffee to the veranda. She had just unfolded the morning paper when her cell phone rang.

"I understand. Yes, I can arrange that, let's say one-thirty. Pearl gets home from church around twelve-thirty, and that should give her time to whip something together. It won't be fancy, but we'll make Selma's and your visit legit. Besides, it's been a while since we had you over. It's only natural that I would have one of Dad's best friends and my godfather over for Sunday dinner."

It was time to level with Pearl, who stood in the doorway listening.

"We're having company. I'll explain."

Although uncharacteristically flustered by all that Cassie told her, Pearl immediately set about making plans for dinner. By the time she left for church, she had the veranda table set, a pot roast surrounded by vegetables roasting on low heat in the oven, and the iced tea made.

After church, Cassie mingled outside among the parishioners—a Sunday ritual. As she moved about chatting and giving hugs, she deliberately avoided Sheriff Ryan. But at one point, he moved closer to her while walking toward his car with his friend Ned.

"I won't be meeting you at Starkey's today, Ned; Selma and I got us an invite over for one of Pearl's Sunday dinners." He moved a few feet closer. "Well, hi there, Cassie. I was just telling Ned here that Selma and I will be seeing you later today for dinner. It's been a while since we were over."

"Yes, much too long," Cassie responded. She realized Jed was saying this for the benefit of anyone who might be keeping an eye on her.

Jed then headed for his car with Selma on his arm.

CHAPTER 41

"It's all right, Tully. I already know that the sheriff is going over to Cassie's today. I heard him say so after church. If it were anything but a social visit, he wouldn't be broadcasting it around like that. You're taking this detective business a little too seriously, although I'm grateful for your reports."

He used his cell phone and spoke quietly even though he was alone in his upstairs home office.

"No, I don't think you should stick around and keep a watch. You're off this Sunday and the sheriff is no dummy. You might arouse his suspicions. You just continue to keep track of Cassie's whereabouts when she's in town and any information coming through the sheriff's office about any case he's working on. We both know where Cassie is today, so lay off. And yes, your envelope will be in the usual place Monday morning."

He hung up the phone and sat thinking. He was not as confident as he let on to Tully. And another thing, Tully was getting a little too curious. It was not unusual for the Danforths to have folks over for Sunday dinner, but since Cliff died there hadn't been many. Why the sheriff and Selma? Why now? Well, why not now. Jed and Cliff had been good friends for years. Cassie is just trying to show her appreciation toward old friends. That's it, of course. Or is it? I'm getting paranoid, too jumpy. I can't let that happen. I have to stay sharp. I've got to find that packet. Where else is there to look? Searching the house is proving difficult. Send a burglar? That's easy enough to arrange, but too risky. Besides, I can't take a chance on anyone else seeing those photographs; you always have to think about blackmail. Damn! Where the hell is that packet?

Sunday meant dinner with friends at two o'clock at the Waterfront Restaurant at the permanently reserved table upstairs overlooking Main

Street. He was not in the mood for the small talk and gossip that the wives always relished. Maybe he could claim a bellyache. No. At church he had said he'd be there. I've got to get a grip, he thought.

On the way out to the car, he decided to mosey on over to his office after dinner and finish up a little work. He needed to be ready for an early meeting on Monday.

And maybe I'll just mosey by Cassie's and see if there's anything unusual going on, he thought.

CHAPTER 42

Jed habitually used Selma's car any time he was off duty. He avoided any use of county property that might warrant criticism. The truth was, however, that as a small county sheriff, he was on duty twenty-four hours a day, seven days a week. He parked along the side of Cassie's garage in the alley, and he and Selma made their way along the brick walk to the back veranda door.

Cassie opened the screen door as they started up the steps. "It's so good to see you, Selma. I see plenty of Jed, but I have missed your visits."

Jed knew Cassie was being especially cautious and speaking for the benefit of anyone who might be in the yard or at the windows in the homes across the alleyway. He was surprised, however, when he entered the veranda to see Miss Maime Sanderson seated in the most comfortable of the wicker chairs.

Cassie knew this was cause for bewilderment and quickly said, "I haven't had Miss Maime over in ages, and I knew Selma hadn't had a chance to visit with her for a while, so I thought it would be great if we all got together today."

Jed caught Cassie's eye and nodded slightly, an indication that he trusted her to handle the situation.

Pearl busied herself serving sweet iced tea while Miss Maime started the conversation by complaining. "We've interviewed three candidates for our new pastor, and every one of them is too young and too radical. One of them, that red-haired one, Lewis Crane I think his name is, he just plain said he would welcome homosexuals into the church openly as God's children. Can you imagine that! I never heard of such tripe before from a man claiming to be a pastor."

Selma said, "Times are changing too fast and too much for me. I hardly read the *Raleigh News & Observer* anymore. It's just full of crime, and we get enough of that at our house."

While the rest were talking, Pearl was bustling about between the kitchen and the veranda dining table. She interrupted the conversation by announcing that all the food was on the table and going to get cold if they didn't come on to dinner. Pearl took her place at the table after the others were seated, and Miss Maime asked the blessing.

Dinner conversation included compliments for Pearl's dinner, comments on the weather being just right for spring planting, and a few questions for Cassie about the mysterious stranger who had turned out to be the son of that famous actress and their own Dr. Lansfield.

Cassie pushed her chair back as they finished the meal. "Why don't you ladies sit a spell before Pearl serves one of her famous desserts? I have a couple of Dad's things that I would like to share with Jed. We'll go see what he would like."

Pearl refilled the tea glasses and sat down with Miss Maime and Selma. She had been instructed by Cassie and was about to do her duty.

"Corley has been filling me in on what that Mavis is up to and how Dr. Lansfield is handling that young lady these days. Well, you wouldn't believe …"

Pearl had their attention as they made mental notes as to what they would repeat and to whom they would repeat it. The absence of Cassie and Jed was hardly noticed.

Cassie led Jed upstairs to the hiding place in the chimney, where she carefully removed the bricks with her letter opener as she had done during the night. Then she stepped back. "I'm afraid I carelessly handled the envelope, and I expect Dad did too, but maybe there are discernable prints left."

Jed reached into his pants pocket and took out thin rubber gloves and put them on. He reached for the packet and then carefully opened it and examined the contents. There were five photographs.

"God Almighty!" Jed exclaimed.

Jed shuffled through the pictures again. "Never in a million years would I have connected any these men with Matty Jasman's murder. It's no wonder they were so desperate to find them."

"It's so sickening." Cassie voice choked as she quietly spoke.

"Even I find this hard to believe after all these years in law enforcement. I wonder how long Cliff had been holding on to these."

"Not long, I can assure you, knowing my father. In fact, I have been thinking that perhaps this discovery brought on his fatal heart attack since he was already having some problems. I confess that it does seem a little strange that he didn't immediately call you."

Jed examined the pictures once more, repulsed by what he saw.

"Maybe he wanted to implicate the whole bunch. These pictures don't do that. I'll have to examine them with my magnifying lens. There are shadows that might give us more evidence if enhanced by a lab. This is going to take some work before we can move. That was probably Cliff's conclusion, too."

"I have another envelope for you. I have included some newspaper clippings from both our paper and the *News & Observer*. They were in a secret shelf in Dad's office. I'm not sure how they connect with these pictures, but Dad was apparently on to something."

"I've thought about where I will keep this information. Too many have access to the office safe, and they would be too curious if I denied them that access. There is a file case in my office where we hold cold cases. No one has looked at them for years. There is a key that's on the ring with the rest of the file cabinet keys. I'm going to take the key off that ring and put it on my personal key ring. I'll put the unmarked packet in the back of that file. I just want you to know where it is in case anything should happen to me."

"Don't talk like that, Jed. I'm getting jittery as it is."

"Okay, Cassie, but we can't be too cautious. I have a hunch we're on to something really big. Now we're pretty sure we're dealing with a murderer. Let's pick up the other envelope on the way back to the veranda. Do you have something you can give me as a cover for our absence from the ladies?"

"Yes, I've already thought of that. Dad's favorite fishing rod and his tackle box are in his office. We can put the envelopes in the tackle box."

As Cassie and Jed returned to the veranda, Jed said, "Hey, Selma, take a look at this. Cassie has given me Cliff's favorite fishing rod! I can't count the times we sat on the river bank together and compared our rods—each of us declaring he had the best. Now I know I have the best. Lordy! I do miss that man!"

Pearl served dessert, a creamy chocolate pie that she knew was one of the sheriff's favorites. When they finished, Jed offered to escort Miss Maime across the Green to her house. Shortly after his return, he and Selma said their good-byes. Selma carried a doggie bag that Pearl had packed for them, and Jed carried the fishing rod and tackle box.

CHAPTER 43

Cooper was sitting on the patio by the pool at his mother's Connecticut estate enjoying an infrequent lazy Sunday evening when his cell phone rang.

"Good evening, Cassie, I was just wondering when I might hear from you."

"I don't want to go into the details over the phone, but a great deal has happened over the weekend. The situation in Clayton Landing is changing dramatically and dangerously. While I can't say that I've come to any definite decision yet, I do need to talk with Jordan Mitchell again, this week if possible. I was hoping you could be there when we meet."

"My schedule is pretty heavy, but I'll certainly try. Hold on a second." Cooper roamed through his BlackBerry. "It looks like the week coming up is frantic. Unless Jordan is willing to meet next Saturday, I don't think I can manage it this week."

"I'll call him. Saturday might be good if he is willing. I hope to have a good deal more information on the situation here by that time."

"You're being mysterious, and I don't like that dangerous part."

"I'm being cautious. The situation I'm referring to may escalate rapidly and if so it could be explosive."

Cooper sat up straight. "What do you mean? Are you personally in danger?"

"I don't really think so, although I have to admit I'm a bit jumpy and watching shadows rather closely."

Cooper glanced at his schedule again. "There is a meeting with my election staff on Wednesday that I could cancel, although they'll howl mightily if I do so."

"No. Let's aim for Saturday, perhaps by then something more concrete may have developed."

Cooper looked up and saw that across the table, his mother was signaling with an imaginary phone up to her ear.

"I think my mother is using her acting ability to signal that she would like to talk with you. Are you up to speaking with Madalaine?"

"Yes, of course."

Madalaine took the phone. "Cassie, dear, I've been sitting here listening to a one-sided conversation. I would so like to meet you once more after so many years of watching you grow through pictures and conversations with your father. I've even watched your show a time or two. I'm sorry to be such an eavesdropper, but if you and Cooper make arrangements for a meeting on Saturday, do you think I could hitch along?"

Madalaine caught the hesitation on the other end.

"Oh, I don't mean for your meeting, dear. I would love to have you and Cooper as my guests for dinner Friday evening. I am really free of obligations right now and have much too much time on my hands for reminiscing. I usually stay at the Willard when I'm in Washington, and they will arrange dinner for us."

"That would be delightful. Thank you. I'll let Cooper know if I make arrangements with Jordan Mitchell."

Cooper took the phone back.

"Would you like me to call Jordan?"

"No, he gave me his home phone number. I'll call right now and I'll let you know if he can manage a meeting."

Cooper laid his phone on the table and quizzically studied his mother's face.

"What? You don't approve?" Madalaine asked. "There can't possibly be any harm in my meeting with Cassie now. It's all out in the open. I would love to see the child again."

"She is no child, as you well know. In fact she is quite a remarkable young woman. I don't think she has the slightest idea how remarkable. She's well educated, level-headed, independent, talented, and mature way beyond her years. Besides that, she is damn good looking."

Madalaine smiled. "Listen to you. That's quite a litany."

"Cut it out. I was just making a point."

"Hmmm. I got the point."

Cooper's phone rang. It was Cassie again.

"Jordan says he can meet with us at eleven o'clock Saturday morning. Are you all right with that?"

"Yes, Mother and I will make our way down Friday afternoon and check in at the Willard. Let's plan on dinner around seven-thirty. We'll have cocktails at seven.

"Great. I'll see you at seven then."

The two by the pool were quiet for a few minutes. Then Cooper spoke. "I think we're on our way. The pieces are falling into place, and so are the participants."

"Yes, I gathered as much."

The tone of her voice conveyed a double meaning. Cooper rose and dove into the pool, retorting by splashing his mother as he did so.

CHAPTER 44

Cassie did not want to appear to be rushing off to the sheriff's office. She went about her regular Monday routine of doling out assignments and checking stories submitted by the stringers and the local gossip columnists.

She glanced at the clock and decided she could now reasonably justify a trip across the alley.

"Mille, I'll be over at the sheriff's office for a bit if you need me. I need to check on the weekend happenings."

Mille did not even bother to reply, just gave a quick wave to indicate that she had heard while she kept her eyes glued to the work before her.

Cassie found the front reception area unusually deserted. The door to Jed's office was partway open. She poked her head inside.

"I figured you'd be over about now," said Jed. "I sent Shirley off to Walmart for some supplies. The rest of the deputies are on duty around the county or over at the courthouse. I'm holding the fort for a little while. Leave the door ajar, I'll have to keep one ear on the radio calls."

Cassie noticed the pictures laid out on Jed's desk.

"Is it safe to do that?" she said as she pointed.

"Only for a short time while you are here. I have a problem though. These are dynamite, but they are standard 4x6 pictures. I need them enlarged right away, and of course I can't take them to the drugstore. It's highly unorthodox for me to ask you, but do you think you can scan and enlarge them without anyone knowing? I can't take any chances on leaks around here right now before I have my investigation nailed down. You are an integral part of all this already."

"Sure, let me have them and I'll go over to the office right now."

"No, wait until Shirley comes back." He glanced at the clock on the wall. "She should be back any minute. I'll go with you. I don't want to take any chances on your safety."

"If you go with me, someone is bound to get curious. They'll think we have a big news story. It's not unusual for me to play around with the scanner, particularly if Ace isn't in the office. Fortunately, he's over at the courthouse on an assignment this morning. It won't take long."

"Maybe you're right. Okay, but come right back as quickly as you can."

Cassie casually walked across the alley with the envelope.

No one seemed to take notice of what Cassie was doing. Mille did glance her way but returned to her work unperturbed.

Fifteen minutes passed before Cassie walked back across the alley with a somewhat larger envelope.

"I haven't examined the enlargements. I made the prints and got back as quickly as I could."

"Okay, let's take a look one by one and see if details show up any better."

Cassie felt an urge to retch. "These are even more sickening enlarged. I had difficulty sleeping last night, and when I did drift off, I had terrible nightmares," Cassie said.

Jed nodded as if he understood from experience. He pointed a finger. "I think that nails a third one. I thought I saw that in the smaller prints, but I wasn't sure. I spent half the night going over the newspaper articles. There's got to be some connection, but I haven't quite figured it out yet, although I have a theory. I left the articles at home. I'll go over them again tonight. I may need some help. I have a good friend down Atlanta way, Tom Slattery. He used to be with the FBI, retired about two years ago. He's set up his own shop now, the Slattery Agency. He bought himself some fancy equipment and works as a private sleuth, sometimes helping out local police. I think I'll feed him all this information. I've got a little money in my budget for outside help. This takes priority over everything. Obviously, I have to keep this information as confidential as I can."

They heard Shirley come in. Her hands were laden with plastic bags. She pushed Jed's door open with her foot enough to poke her head in and say, "I'll take over, sheriff." She dumped bags full of paper goods for the jail behind the reception counter.

Jed got up from his desk and closed the door.

They reviewed the pictures for a few more minutes, talking softly.

"I'd better get back to the paper," Cassie said. "Mille will get antsy if I'm gone too long on a Monday. I'm glad these are safely in your hands now."

Jed gathered the pictures and put them in the cold file cabinet.

Shirley was busy at the dispatch radio when Jed went into the reception area. He took a piece of scrap paper from the basket on her desk and wrote a note. She read it, nodded, and kept right on with her radio conversation. "Gotcha," she said into her microphone, "You're at Ford's corner helping a little old lady with a flat tire. Do you reckon she ever heard of AAA?"

Shirley rolled her chair back to her desk just as Tully came in.

Tully asked, "Anything happening?

"Nah. Morris is out by Ford's corner helping a little old lady with a flat. The sheriff just went over to the courthouse. Sadar Miles is being sentenced today. Hank just took Sadar to the courthouse. They're probably in the holding room right now. I'd say it's pretty quiet around here even for a Monday. Cassie did come in earlier for her usual news briefing."

"I guess Jed didn't have much for her," Tully said.

"There must have been something. Jed had pictures strewn all over his desk and Cassie and he were looking them over when I came back from Walmart. He shut the door when I came in. I couldn't hear what they were talking about."

"Pictures, you say. Did he give them to you for filing before he left?"

"No, as a matter of fact, he didn't. Maybe they're still on his desk. He didn't have them with him when he left. Come to think of it, neither did Cassie. If they'd had anything to do with Sadar's case, Jed would have taken them with him."

Jed's office door was closed. Tully walked over, opened the door, and looked around. There was nothing on the desk but the blotter, the phone, a picture of Selma, a pad, and a pencil holder. Jed was noted for being orderly.

"He must have put them in his drawer. I'm kinda curious, have you got a spare key to his desk drawers?"

"Tully Reese, you know perfectly well I haven't. He keeps his keys on his ring. Even if I had, I wouldn't be giving it to you. Sometimes you get too curious for your own good."

"It can't hurt to keep in the know, especially when you are dealing with criminals. I guess I'll just get on with my rounds. I just stopped by to see if anything was happening."

"You could have called me, that's what I'm here for."

"Well, I'm on town duty today, just as easy to stop by."

Shirley studied Tully's back as he left. His questions about the keys made her a little uneasy. She reminded herself once again to be more careful about unnecessarily sharing information with him.

CHAPTER 45

He was on the way to the post office when he saw Tully sitting in his squad car in the library parking lot under the shade of a large maple tree, apparently just people watching.

He walked across the street to the car, and in a deliberately loud voice for the benefit of anyone passing by, he said, "Well, Tully, I see you're keeping crime down." In a whisper he added, "Anything new to report?"

"Nope, everything is as still as pond water on a full moon night," Tully whispered back.

He slapped his hand down on the hood of the car and again in a loud voice said, "Good work, Tully."

As he came out of the post office and started up the street, his phone rang. He answered and then glanced across the street at the squad car still sitting under the shade tree.

"I forgot to mention a small thing that did seem kinda queer. I don't reckon it's of much importance, but when I reported in a while ago, Shirley told me Cassie had been over to the office to see Jed."

"That's not unusual, especially on Monday."

"I reckon not, but Shirley said the two of them were looking at a bunch of pictures when she came back from Walmart."

He stopped walking. "That's not too unusual either. Cassie uses a lot of pictures in the paper. Maybe she was just checking out some facts."

"Maybe so, but they shut the door when Shirley came in, and then Cassie didn't take the pictures with her and neither did Jed when he went over to the courthouse, and he didn't give them to Shirley to file."

"Is that unusual?"

"Well, sorta. Shirley usually makes up our file and gives it to whoever is assigned if it's a domestic case or a fight or something where we take pictures at the scene for evidence when the court case comes up."

He knew all this. Each officer had to report to the court when his case was on the docket. He kept fishing.

"You have any idea what might have become of the pictures?"

"More than likely they are in Jed's desk. His bottom drawer is a hanging file drawer. Once in a while he'll put a case file in there if he's mulling it over."

"What do you mean by mulling it over?"

"Well, you know, when he's trying to decide how to go about doing something about a problem case."

For seconds neither man spoke. One of them was thinking.

"Are the keys to the sheriff's desk in that wall rack of keys? If so, is the rack key available anywhere?"

"Funny you ask, because I asked Shirley the same question. She said he keeps the only desk key on his key ring."

He shifted his thoughts.

"Tully, do you happen to know the schedule for this week? Is the sheriff on patrol duty any night?"

"Wait a minute while I take a look. Shirley printed out a copy for us early this morning like she always does. Yeah, looks like he's doing rounds tomorrow night, as a matter of fact. We're short of deputies. Mark has the flu, and Ray went off to Missouri for his mother's funeral. The sheriff is filling in on weeknights because the rest of us trade around weekend duty covering the rowdies."

"Will Jed be covering the usual places on Tuesday?"

"Well, that's up to him. There's no set schedule as long as we keep our eye on the heavy drinking bars. You know, the usual; Kelly's, the River Bend, Jerry's."

"Tuesday would normally be a quiet night, I'd guess."

"Mostly, that is unless someone speaks sideways out of their mouth at somebody that takes offense. It doesn't take much to gin up a ruckus."

He was breaking out in a cold sweat. What if the pictures were the missing packet? His life, his career, everything is in jeopardy, he thought. Desperation and imagination began to color his reasoning powers. He tried to shake it off, dismiss his presumptions. He couldn't. Deep down intuition told him that his fears were true. He began to walk hurriedly back to his office.

Without speaking to his assistant, he dashed into his office and closed the door. He fumbled in his pocket for his key ring and selected one. He unlocked his center drawer and reached far back until he found a small address book. He thumbed clumsily through the pages until he got to the right page. The phone number he was seeking was identified by initials only. It had been months since he called the number. He dialed. No answer. He glanced at his watch. He had a little over an hour to spare.

As he dashed through his outer office, he told his assistant that he would be back shortly.

"You know you have to be back by eleven," she said to his back as he shut the door behind him.

He went down Main and turned onto Bay View Road. A few miles farther up the road, he stopped at a ramshackle shed-like building identified by a sign: Slim's Auto and Motorcycle Repair Shop. He was quite aware that the sign was a front for its owner, who was involved in many other business arrangements. He carefully pulled his car into a space between two rusty old pickups sitting on the side lot.

No one was in the small office at the front of the building. When he stepped into the back area, a space for two work bays, a man he'd never seen before rolled out from under a blue Ford that had seen better days. He was wearing grease-covered jeans and a shirt open to his waist, revealing a hairy chest. He pointed to the back door when asked about Slim's whereabouts.

He found Slim poking around in the engine of an old car. True to his name, his gaunt frame supported a scar-faced head bedecked with greasy brown hair.

"Surely you don't expect to get that pile of junk to run again," he said as he approached Slim.

Slim glanced around, raised his hand in acknowledgement then continued what he was doing. "Well now, what brings Mr. High-and-Mighty to these parts? I'd shake your hand, but I'm a mite dirty. I thought you made a point of contact by phone only."

"You didn't answer. Anyway, this is too important. I've got a job for you."

Slim stood and took a puff on the cigarette hanging out of the side of his mouth and wiped his hands on a dirty cloth that he took out of his pocket. "Well, let's go inside and talk a bit; I got a bottle in my office."

"What about your helper? I haven't seen him before, and I don't want any big ears."

"Mac, nice dude, he's helping out. He's pretty good with motorcycles, and he comes cheap. He showed up a few weeks ago. He's got no home, so I fixed up that shed out back a little for him to sleep in as part of his salary. So, I got me a watchman for the same price as a mechanic. I always like a deal, you know."

"That's what I'm here for, a deal."

"Let's go inside. I'll send Mac out to hunt for the part I'm looking for."

He would rather have stayed outside. Slim's office reeked— the mixture tobacco and grease smells being primary. The chair behind Slim's beat up desk looked as though it had not been cleaned in years. The chair Slim pointed him to was no better.

After he explained the job, Slim just sat and looked at him for a few moments.

"Now let's get this straight. You're *only* asking that I get a hold of Sheriff Jed Ryan's keys and deliver them to you. That's a hell of a risk—not to mention a felony offense if I get caught. It's going to take some fancy doing and a little help. I must say there will be a certain amount of pleasure in the job. The sheriff and I have had a few run-ins."

"There are five big ones in it for you."

"Man, there you go, underestimating the job as usual. I'll be taking on all the risks. I'm thinking twenty big ones."

"Come on, Slim, you know I don't have that kind of money to throw around."

"And I know for a fact that you throw money around in some mighty peculiar places. So now, let's get real here. Besides, I've got to round up a couple of fellas to help on this one." Slim took another pull on his cigarette and licked a stray fleck of tobacco from his lips.

He thought for a few seconds. He didn't have much choice. He wasn't the only one in trouble. They'd have to pool the money.

"All right. I think I can arrange it."

"In advance."

"Come on. That's not good business. How about half in advance?"

"Okay, but if anything goes wrong, you'll regret it if I don't get the other half."

"Deal! I'll come around before suppertime with half. The job has to be done tomorrow night."

"Leave the details to me," Slim said as he rose.

He returned to his car and waited until there was no traffic on the road before he pulled out. He checked the dashboard clock. He was running close to the time he had to appear. Speed dialing, he called three numbers to arrange an emergency meeting for later in the afternoon.

CHAPTER 46

Cassie nestled among the cushions on the front veranda swing, trying to read a magazine despite Muffin's determination to have her sole attention.

"All right, settle down," she said to Muffin as she turned off the floor lamp and nuzzled the cat in her arms. "A little quiet time before bedtime will do us both good."

She was beginning to doze when her cell phone rang, breaking the silence. It was Ace.

"I just heard on my police radio. There's been a hell of a fight out at Jerry's place. I'm on the way out there to take some pictures. From what I gather, the sheriff got hurt in the fracas."

Cassie sat up abruptly, dumping Muffin on the floor.

"I'll go over to the sheriff's office and see what I can learn."

Cassie retrieved Muffin and went inside. Glancing at the kitchen clock, she saw that it was close to eleven. Pearl would be sound asleep. She put Muffin in her bed by the stove and quietly closed and locked the back door as she left. In minutes she was at the county jail.

A few off-duty deputies had reported in for information and assignment if needed. Others were gathering as the news spread. All were milling about waiting for word. Shirley dashed in and took over the radio from Clarence, the night duty clerk.

She spoke as she listened to the radio. "No news on Jed's condition yet. We can expect a few drunks that were rounded up in here before too long." She pointed to one of the deputies. "Lou, take Clarence and go over to Jerry's and retrieve Jed's car. Get back here pronto. Tully is already at the hospital." Shirley was not officially in charge, but that didn't seem to matter to anyone.

Cassie made a few notes. She noticed that the room was getting crowded. There was a good deal of speculation as they waited for word of Jed's condition. Her phone rang. It was Ace again.

"I passed the ambulance on my way. I found out when I got here that the sheriff was inside the ambulance. Luckily, I managed to get a picture of the destruction in the bar before they routed everyone outside and taped off the building. There's not much more I can do here. Do you want me to go to the hospital?"

"No, come here to the sheriff's office. They're bringing in the drunks that caused the fight soon. If you hurry, maybe you can get pictures. I'll go over to the hospital and see what I can learn."

"They've been getting names and questioning a bunch at the scene here. I can get there before they arrive with the guys they're bringing in."

"Good. There are a good many people milling around here waiting for word on Jed's condition. Get some pictures. I'll let you know if I need you at the hospital later."

A deputy Cassie recognized as Matt Townsend was escorting Selma into the hospital emergency entrance as Cassie arrived. She scurried in and joined them at the reception desk.

"I'm so sorry, Mrs. Ryan," the night clerk at the desk said as Selma identified herself. "They are evaluating the sheriff's condition right now. It shouldn't be long before I can escort you back to his cubicle. I really don't have any information right now."

"Then he's alive. Thank God," Selma said.

"Oh yes, that much I can tell you."

Cassie found Selma a vacant seat close to the desk. "Can I get you anything?" she asked.

"No thanks, dear, I'm as nervous as an old mother hen. I do wish I'd thought to bring a sweater. It's freezing in here."

"I keep a jacket in my car. I'll go get it for you."

On her way back with the jacket, she passed Tully going toward his car.

"I didn't see you inside, Tully. Do you know any more about Jed's condition?"

"No. I stationed myself at the nurse's desk in the emergency room just so's I could keep an eye on everything in case of any trouble. Matt just took over for me. I'm heading back to the jail to help with the rowdies."

Cassie helped Selma into the jacket and settled into the seat beside her. Both watched the clock on the wall above the reception desk. Thirty minutes passed before a nurse came through a door from the inner area.

"I can take you back to see the sheriff now, Mrs. Ryan."

"Please go with me, dear," she said to Cassie.

"Is it all right?" Cassie asked the nurse.

"I don't see why not. You might have to wait outside the cubicle though."

As they arrived at cubicle five, a doctor stepped out. Cassie glanced at the name embroidered on his white jacket. She had never seen him before but did know that the hospital had hired new personnel recently.

"Mrs. Ryan," he said in a questioning tone as he glanced at both women.

"I'm Mrs. Ryan," Selma identified herself.

He took her hand. "I'm Jeffrey Larimore. The sheriff is going to be all right. He was knocked out for a time. He took a very nasty blow to the head, apparently from a heavy bottle. There are also deep cut marks on his back where he fell on broken glass. We've extracted a few pieces of the bottle."

"Oh! What a relief," Selma said.

"We will be keeping him overnight for observation and some tests. It's standard procedure. If all goes well, he can go home tomorrow but should remain quiet and rest for a few days."

"May I see him?"

"Yes, for a few minutes. We'll be taking him upstairs shortly. If you like you may stay the night with him, but we expect him to sleep the rest of the night. We've given him something to assure that he does."

Cassie said to Selma, "I'll be back. I'm going outside to use my phone for a few minutes."

She reached Ace but could barely hear him. The background noise was loud. Then the connection cleared.

"I stepped outside. It's packed in there. I'm going around back to the jail door. The deputies are on their way here with several men that were involved in the fight."

"Okay. Give Shirley the word that the sheriff is going to be all right but will be staying in the hospital overnight. After you take your pictures, call it a night. There's not much else we can do tonight."

"I just think I'll mosey on over to the paper and transfer the pictures to my computer. You know me. I always like to see what I've got."

"All right, I'll see you in the morning."

Cassie returned inside and leaned against the nurse's station counter, chatting with Matt.

When Selma stepped out of the cubicle with Dr. Larimore she said, "I guess I'll do as he says and go on home. I'll be back early tomorrow morning, if that's all right?"

"Sure. Like I said, what he needs right now is rest and some observation on our part," Dr. Larimore said.

A nurse approached Selma with a small bag in her hand. "Mrs. Ryan, please take these personal items, we really don't want to be responsible."

"Of course, dear, thank you."

Matt said, "I'll take Mrs. Ryan home, and then I'll come back and sit outside Jed's door. I'll get someone to relieve me early tomorrow morning. Somehow I'd just feel better doing that."

And I'd feel better if you did that too, Cassie thought to herself.

She slept for a few hours and arrived downstairs for breakfast earlier than usual.

"You're an early bird. Have you got a lot to do today to get the paper out?" Pearl asked.

Cassie told her of the night's events.

"Lordy! I never heard you going or coming. That's kind of scary what with folks nosing around here. Anybody could be roaming about and I wouldn't hear them."

"Anyway, I've got to gather all the facts and get over to the hospital and see Jed if I can."

"Just give me a few minutes; I'll have breakfast ready in a jiffy."

Cassie was the first one to arrive at the paper, so she made the coffee before settling in front of her computer. She was intently working on the article about the night fracas when Mille appeared beside her desk.

Cassie looked up. "You startled me. I didn't hear you come in."

"I know. What's up?"

Cassie filled Mille in on the news and then added, "Ace may be late. I'm sure he worked until all hours last night."

"Something mighty strange is going on around this town. Do you remember the time, must have been around 1965, when the county treasurer was siphoning off all that money and took off on fancy trips, and bought a new Cadillac?"

"No, I don't, Mille. I wasn't born then."

"You're right. Anyway, your father got real suspicious and did some digging on his own. It took a while, but he figured it out. You will too," Mille said as she returned to her desk.

Cassie finished the article except for a few additional facts that she needed to fill in the blanks. Just as she was about to leave for the hospital, Ace arrived.

"Sorry, I'm a little late, but I didn't get much sleep last night. I have a bunch of pictures. Do you want to look through them now or later?"

"I'll look them over when I get back. I'm going to run over to the hospital and see Jed if I'm allowed. I don't think I'll be long. I'd like to hear his version so I can finish my article."

"Meantime, I'll just get the pictures in some sort of sequence for you."

Cassie noticed that there was no deputy sitting in the hallway. When she inquired at the nurse's desk, Cassie was told that Sheriff Ryan was not receiving any visitors.

"Would you mind just checking to see if he will see me?" Cassie asked.

The nurse frowned. "I have to go in and check his vital signs right now anyway, so I'll ask, but I wouldn't be too hopeful."

Cassie followed the nurse down the hallway and stood outside the door. Several minutes passed before the door to Room 411 opened again.

"He says you are to go right in. He seemed anxious to see you."

Cassie was surprised to see Jed sitting in a chair and dressed except for a shirt. He had a hospital gown thrown over his shoulders.

"Good morning, Cassie. If that doc doesn't show up with my release papers before too long, I'm out of here," he said. "I had to go downstairs for a test a while ago. He claims I have to wait for the results."

"Well, good morning to you, too. Considering you got a pretty nasty blow, you're looking pretty good, but don't you think you should take it easy for a couple of days?"

"Selma is already harassing me; I don't need you to add to it. She's been here since dawn. She went down to the cafeteria to get a bite to eat when I went for the test. She'll be back shortly. I sent Matt away to get a little sleep when she came in. I'm going to call for a deputy to pick me up. I've got to get to my office."

"I can take you to your office. What's the hurry?"

"Something is bugging me. Selma brought a bag with my wallet, change, pocketknife, and cell phone in it, but my keys were not there. I thought maybe Matt had them, but when I came back from the test, they were right there on the bedside table." He pointed to the right side of his bed.

"Maybe Selma put them there, or Matt."

"I don't think so. Selma dug in her purse and handed me the bag when I insisted on getting dressed and ready to go the minute the doc gives me the word. The bag was tied in a knot just the way it was given to her. Matt wouldn't have left them on the table. He knows better."

"What are you getting at?"

"As far as I know, you and I are the only ones who know about those pictures. But just suppose someone found out that we had them. How far do you think they would go to get them back?"

"Are you saying that you might have been deliberately bushwhacked?"

"Well, there's something else. When Doc Larimore was telling me what all they had patched up, he mentioned that the deep cuts on my upper back had glass pieces in them and gritty material like sand."

"That's not surprising; Jerry's isn't the cleanest place in the world."

"Dirt I can understand, but sand is another thing." Jed looked up at the wall clock. "I'll give him just ten more minutes."

Selma came in the door and right behind her came Dr. Larimore.

"The tests are looking good, so I'll let you go. However, you will have some pain for a few days. Those back wounds are deep, and no doubt you will also have a mild headache. So I advise rest and no driving until I check you at the end of the week."

"I'll see that he behaves," Selma said.

Dr. Larimore removed the gown from Jed's shoulders and examined the bandages on his back. "No bleeding, that's good." He handed Selma a prescription. "The nurse will make an appointment at my office for you, Jed. I'll see you Friday."

Jed quickly rose, grabbed his shirt off the bed and began struggling to put it on.

"Here, let me help you with that," Selma said.

"I guess I am a little stiff. Selma, Cassie here is going to run me over to the office. Then I'll pick up a deputy to drive me out to Jerry's. I've got to check on something. After that I'll come on home and rest a while."

Cassie was taken by surprise, and Selma was livid.

"You'll do no such thing, Jed Ryan. Didn't you hear a word the doctor said? You are to rest until you see him Friday."

"He's a nice young man, but he doesn't know who he's dealing with," said Jed. "Doc Lansfield would have known better than to tell me that. I've had these little scrapes before. Now you just get on home and I'll be along directly."

"Jed Ryan, don't you dare patronize me! Get on home indeed. I've a good mind to find Dr. Larimore and tell him not to let you out of here. You are darn near retirement age and not nearly as tough as you think you are."

"Selma, just shush. I'm leaving right now. Let's go, Cassie."

Cassie wasn't quite sure what to do. In a quandary, she looked at Selma, who just shrugged her shoulders. Cassie took this as resignation and followed Jed out the door.

A nurse escorted the sheriff to the hospital's front door while Cassie went to get her Mustang. The nurse left them with a warning that Jed should go right home and rest.

"With a slight detour," Jed said as the nurse closed the car door.

"I'm not sure I should be enabling you to circumvent doctor's orders," said Cassie. "Suppose you pass out on me."

"I'm not likely to pass out between here and the office. After we confer a few minutes about my suspicions, you are free to get back to your job. I'm only involving you to a certain point. Remember, everything is off the record, and you are involved only because of your help and personal connection to the case."

"I'm aware of that, Jed. I know we're dealing with a highly volatile situation right now. So, you think someone deliberately threw that bottle at you?"

"It looks that way. I need to take a look at the spot where I fell before Jerry is allowed to clean the place. I called in orders to keep everyone out of there until I give the word."

Cassie pulled her Mustang up to the back door of the jail and let Jed out. He was met by Deputy Matt Townsend.

"I'll just take my car home and walk back. It's easier than trying to find a parking place this time of the morning. I'll just be a few minutes."

When Cassie returned, Shirley waved her into Jed's office.

Jed was sitting at his desk. The file cabinet drawer was open.

"It's just as I thought. The envelope containing the pictures is gone. Whoever did this is a fool to think we don't have copies. "

"The blown-up copies weren't in with the originals?" Cassie asked.

"No, I took them home to study. Good thing. I need copies made. I need to get them to Tom Slattery post haste. There is a shadow bouncing off that mirror in the room, and I believe he can enhance the picture enough to identify a person. I want copies of the news articles as well. His trained mind may be able to tie some loose ends together."

"I can scan the pictures and e-mail them for you."

"No, Cassie, I can't send child pornography via the Internet. You should know that. But I do need your copy help one more time. I know I'm out of line in involving you, but I hope the subject of how I handled copies never comes up. If Matt has had a few hours sleep, I'll have him run them down to Atlanta to Tom in a sealed envelope. It's just an eight hour drive, and in an official car he can push the speed limit. I believe Matt's completely trustworthy. I've known him since he was an eagle scout. As you know, I'm worried about leaks in my office right now, and I can't take any chances with curiosity."

"After you get settled at home, I'll drive out and pick up the pictures and articles and make copies for you."

"Good."

"By the way, we're finishing up the article on Sadar. I understand his charges include drugs, rape, attacking an officer when being arrested, and possibly manslaughter of Peggy's baby."

"That's right, all of the above, so to speak. The plea bargain that Larry Stillman offered Sadar was accepted. That saves the county a trial. Tomorrow he'll be on the way to Pasquotank prison. He'll be out of our hair for years."

Jed tapped his pencil on the desk for a few seconds while clearing his thoughts. "Cassie, I'm appreciative of all your help. Some of it we need to keep just between the two of us. Right now I'm feeling uneasy about this case and need to keep evidence as close to the chest as possible."

"I understand. I know that my involvement is out of line. Now, to get back to you. Are you going home now like you promised Selma?"

"Only after Lou Morgan and I go over to Jerry's bar. I need to check out the scene. After that, I'll have him drive me on home; I have to admit I'm a little shaky."

Cassie returned to the newspaper office. She sent Ace over to the courthouse to pick up Sadar's court record.

"I'll review your pictures from last night while you're gone. We'll settle on a couple when you get back," she told Ace.

CHAPTER 47

"What the hell do you mean you don't have the rest of the money right now?" Slim yelled into his cell phone. "You were supposed to be here over an hour ago. That was our damn agreement."

"Now don't get excited. I'm just getting it together, that's all. It will just be a delay of a couple of hours."

"A couple of hours to raise a thousand—don't play around with me, mister. I saw that the job was done proper. Nobody got killed, and there is no evidence that the job was set up."

"I know. I appreciate your efforts. I'll have it for you shortly."

"Damn right, you'd better. If I don't see you by noon there's gonna be trouble, mister. I got enough on you to send you away, and you'd better believe I will."

"Don't threaten me. Likewise, I have enough on you to send you away too, Slim. I keep accounts."

"You don't scare me, Mr. High–and–Mighty. Just see that you're here by noon."

Slim sat fuming for a few minutes and then looked around to locate Mac. He was under a car fooling around with an exhaust. Good, Slim thought, no chance he overheard the call.

The man on the other end of the line sat for a few minutes rethinking the conversation. He didn't like the counter-threats at all. He didn't like any of the recent events. He picked up his cell phone and speed-dialed a number.

"Get over here with your damn part of the money," he said. "No reason for you to delay, and now I have a deadline of noon."

He tapped his pen nervously as he listened to the reply.

"What do you mean by that remark? What choice do I have but to let Slim push me around? I'm taking all the chances, the only one to show his face, so to speak. If you want to be covered, you'll play the game like I say. Now get your ass over here. I may have to go out for a few minutes. If I'm not here, leave the money on my desk. I won't be long."

He came near to slamming his cell phone down on the desk. Things were not going right. I've got the pictures, he thought, but just suppose Jed had time to copy them. That thought sent chills through his body. No, he reasoned. If they were put in that file on Monday more than likely Jed was studying them like he tends to do before he acts on something. He obviously had not shared them with personnel, or they wouldn't have been in that dead file cabinet. Lucky I tried that small key on his chain. The fight on Tuesday night probably saved the day. Yes, that's it, he thought, comforting himself. But then, where did he get them? Did he find them somehow, or is Cassie involved?

Once again he dialed a number.

"Tully, I need you to keep an eye on Cassie's goings and comings, particularly when she is in contact with the sheriff."

"Well, that will be a little tricky today, as a matter of fact. I've been assigned to Route 17 duty today. I think Matt is getting some sleep. Route 17 is normally his duty roster on Wednesdays."

"Where's the sheriff?"

"He's gone home. Lou drove him. He's supposed to rest for a couple of days."

"Good. His home isn't too far off your beat. Just drop past there once in a while and let me know if you see anything of Cassie's car. I'll drop by the newspaper and see if she's working. She's usually pretty busy on Wednesdays."

He took a short walk over to the *Clayton Landing Weekly* office.

Mille got up from her desk and walked over to the front counter.

"I'm thinking about putting one of those fancy ads in the paper, with a picture maybe. How much will that cost me?"

"It depends on the size, of course, as you well know. Here, take this price list and think about it. Your assistant can probably work up a layout. If you want a picture, that's extra and noted on the price list," Mille said.

"Thanks, Mille, it's been a while since I placed an ad. I thought maybe you had changed some prices. I'll get back to you." He waved to Cassie, who was busy working in her cubicle. She did not respond.

He left.

Mille shrugged her shoulders, wondering what that was all about. He knew the routine, and his assistant usually handled his ads.

His cell phone rang as he stepped out onto the sidewalk.

"I dropped down by the sheriff's house like you said. Lou was just pulling in the driveway with Jed. I guess they got a later start for home than I thought. Anyway, he is at home and no sign of Cassie being around."

"I know. She's at the newspaper churning out stuff for Thursday's edition. Nevertheless, just keep a check now and then."

He'd done all he could do. He checked his watch. It was about time to take the money to Slim. The rest of it had better be on his desk as he had instructed when he got back.

CHAPTER 48

After Cassie left the sheriff's office, she wrapped up the article about Sadar's sentence and wrote about the attack on the sheriff. By noon, the layout for the weekly edition was finished. Cassie congratulated herself; everything was running smoothly. Hiring Carol Morgan was already proving to be a godsend. She handled all the school board proceedings, the county fair planning meeting—all the mundane but necessary information important to a local newspaper. Cassie left her cubicle and walked over to Mille's desk.

"I'm planning on leaving around ten o'clock Friday morning. I'll check in with you first to set assignments. I'm going to meet Doug Norris, the editor of the *Marion County News*, in Norfolk for lunch, and then I'm off to Arlington for the weekend."

"So you're mulling over giving up as editor."

"Not so loud, I don't want anyone to be upset about changes until they are firm."

"Hey, they are already speculating over lunch. They don't seem to think you were cut out for the job despite your abilities. You have to have your heart in it too, you know," Mille said in almost a whisper.

"Well, I think I have tried my best to fill my dad's shoes, but it's not easy when you've already set your sails for another port. Luckily, the news around here has been so explosive of late it makes me look good."

"That it does. Don't sell yourself short, however. You're learning fast."

"I'll be in for most of the day tomorrow."

Cassie returned to her desk and picked up the pile of pictures that Ace had given her earlier to review. Together they had selected a picture of Sadar and the ones most suited to her story of Jed's attack. However, something was bugging her about the pictures related to Jed's attack. She began examining them once more. Ace had taken a series of pictures of Jerry's bar, the men being rounded up by deputies, their arrival at the jail, and the crowd milling around in the sheriff's office waiting for news. As she browsed back through them, several pictures caught her attention. She got out her magnifying glass and studied them.

She tucked several of the pictures into her bag along with the magnifying glass, grabbed her cell phone, and made her way to Mille's desk once more.

"I'll be out for a while. I'm going over to the sheriff's house. Call if you need me for anything."

Cassie walked home, checked in with Pearl, and then backed her Mustang out of the garage into the alley. She headed up to Court Way, took a right on Court Street, and then a left on Bay View Road. While driving she made a call to let Jed know she was on the way. He told her to just come on in when she arrived.

She stuck her head in the door and announced her arrival. Selma stepped into the hallway. She was wiping her hands on her apron.

"Come on in, Cassie. Jed is expecting you. I've just finished making a pie for supper. If you stay long enough, you can have a piece. It should be done in about thirty minutes."

"Thanks, I don't think I'll be long. Where's Jed?"

"He's back in the family room in his lounge chair. Would you like some iced tea?"

"No thanks, I'll just go on back."

Jed greeted her, then motioned to a nearby chair. "I'm glad you got here so soon. I know you're busy on Wednesdays, and I have already interrupted your morning routine."

"I have some new pictures to show you. These are the ones that Ace took in your office while we all awaited news."

Cassie pulled up a chair closer to Jed. She handed him the magnifying glass and presented the pictures in a series for him to examine.

"Ace was standing on Shirley's stool, the one she uses when she files in top drawers. He wanted to get a view above shoulder height so he could see faces and expressions."

"I see. So what's your point? I guess I am not picking up on what you see in the pictures."

Cassie took the pictures and then returned them one at a time.

"See, in this one, your office door is closed. Look who's standing near it. In the next one, the door is slightly ajar, in the next closed again. Then this one clearly shows the door opening, and look who's edging out of it and seemingly looking around to see if he was noticed. Also notice the time lapse by the clock on the wall near your office."

"Danged if you're not right. Well, I got some new evidence at Jerry's. If Tom Slattery gets back to me pronto, I think I can move on this case quickly. The evidence is mounting."

"By the way, I didn't see Matt outside when I arrived. Wasn't he supposed to stay with you?"

"Remember, I sent him home to get a little sleep. We're short right now, but I have a deputy driving by now and then. I have my phone handy, and my gun is in reach, as you can see. Besides, Tully has also been checking. Selma has seen him driving by a couple of times. My house is not too far off his beat today. Lou Morgan is coming back in a few hours to take me to the jail. Seems one of those guys we rounded up has asked to speak to me in private. Funny thing, he slipped a note to the deputy on duty. We're about to release most of them, so I'd better check it out."

"Selma won't be happy about that. I'll be on my way then. I'll leave these new pictures with you. Ace has copies, of course." You'll let me know when you're moving in I presume. We'll want pictures along with the story when you release the details."

"You deserve that much. It looks like the *Clayton Landing Weekly* is being read lately by some Associated Press people. I hear *People* magazine has been nosing around. That story about Cooper Canaday caught enough attention that our tourists have already increased, and it isn't even summer yet."

"I'm planning on being in Norfolk most of Friday and in the DC area Saturday. I'll be back sometime on Sunday."

"Think you'll be back in time for church?"

"I hadn't planned on it, why?"

"I'd be back if I were you."

Cassie looked at Jed quizzically and then made a mental note to leave in time Sunday morning to be back for church services. She also made a mental note to be sure that Ace would be attending church with cameras.

"Let me have everything you want copied. I'll make up a packet and get it back to you later this afternoon," she said.

"Good, I'm sending Matt off to Atlanta tonight."

~ ~ ~

Thursday was uneventful, although Cassie had a feeling she was being watched. She was glad to be leaving town for unannounced destinations.

She was early Friday for her luncheon appointment with the editor Doug Norris. After pulling into the parking garage across from the Sheraton, she elected to take a walk along the waterfront near where the Spirit of Norfolk tour boat docked. For a little while, she sat on a bench and enjoyed the fresh breeze coming off the water. Pigeons hung around her feet hoping for a handout. She relaxed for the first time in a long time. Reluctantly checking her watch, she found that she would have to hurry for her meeting.

Doug Norris was near the hotel reception desk as they had arranged. He recognized her and approached as she entered the hotel.

"You're right on time, Cassie. I occasionally watched you on Richmond's Channel 12. I recognized you immediately. Shall we go in to lunch?"

"I'm so glad to meet you," Cassie said after they were seated. "I've heard a great deal about you from my father. It seems you two were of one mind about a great many things."

"Yes, I suppose that's true. I'm a watchdog when it comes to legislation, and so was your dad. He and I stumbled across many a shady bit of political maneuvers."

"And you're still at it, from what I hear."

"I guess that would be so."

When the waitress approached, Cassie quickly ordered.

While Doug ordered, Cassie had a moment to observe him. She noticed that his dark hair was speckled with gray; white accented his temples. His eyes were dark brown; his tan complexion made him seem younger than the sixty-odd years she knew him to be. His smile for the waitress was warm and gracious when he finished ordering.

"Now, just what can I do for you, Cassie?"

Cassie explained her mission. Morris was a bit taken aback.

"Taking over as editor of the *Clayton Landing Weekly* is the last thing I would have thought of when you called. I'm fairly well set where I am. I figured to retire from the *Marion County News.*"

"I knew this proposal would come as a surprise. I am aware of your compensation, and I'm offering considerably more per month. You will have complete control of the paper as you do now. Your editorials will be welcomed; my father's have been missed. I will remain as owner/publisher out of respect for my father's wishes, but it will be strictly hands-off. You see, I may have plans to go in another direction. The estate that my mother left me includes some property. There is a very well-kept home on Church Street close to the newspaper office that has been vacant for a few months. It needs a tenant. I promise the rent will be most attractive."

"I see you have covered all the bases. I can't answer you today, of course, but I will promise to think it over. As a matter of fact, the offer comes at a good time. It seems that the owners of the *Marion County News* would like to see their son move up to my position. He's only been out of Western University for a few years, but they feel he is ready. I've been getting hints to that effect along with assurances that they are in no way dissatisfied with my work and that there will always be a position for me at the paper. Too, my wife is a teacher, and the county is pushing some of the staff to retire for budget reasons. I'll talk with her and get back to you before too long with my answer."

"That's all I can ask."

CHAPTER 49

As she had hoped, Cassie moved along I-64 smoothly just ahead of the swarm of traffic that would soon make the sixty-five-miles-an-hour speed limit a joke. She relaxed a bit and began to turn her thoughts from the events in Clayton Landing to the quandary of her future.

She admitted to herself that life in the nation's capital had seduced her for a time. She had let herself become mesmerized by the glamorous who fed at Washington's trough. Thus far, she had admitted to no one that the enchantment had slowly eroded over the past couple of years as she dealt with powerful unelected congressional aides, wrangled for inside information, and dallied at local cocktail bars with vainglorious lobbyists who seemed unable to help themselves as they bragged about the hold they had over this congressman or that senator. She realized that her father's admonitions had resulted in her increased wariness. While he seemed proud when she told him of her offer with the NBC Washington division, he warned of the powerful web surrounding the city that sucked the unsuspecting into its tangle of silken strands woven by manipulators of reality and truth.

Many of her colleagues who dealt in investigative journalism were turning cynical, frequently frustrated from trying to untangle raging political rhetoric, unable to siphon off meaningful dialogue leading to solutions. Rarely could they pass along unqualified hope to their readers and listeners. Far too much time seemed allotted to reporting vicious rants in congress that filtered down to the nations' citizenry. Civility appeared lost in a swamp of greed and hypocrisy. It seemed as if there was a countrywide rope-pulling contest underway, with more and more joining the pull on one side or the other without a pause for thought

and reason. The result was tearing apart a great nation. Grecian and
Roman history appeared to be repeating itself like some baffling and
unstoppable hereditary disease. Arrogance, avarice, and extended wars
brought down those great nations. Could her beloved country be next?
Were her forefather's visions of freedom and the pursuit of happiness
just a dream after all—overwhelmed by the greed of human nature? An
involuntary frown creased Cassie's brow.

Cassie glanced up at the large directional sign ahead, startled to see
that exit ramp 200 was a short distance away. She maneuvered to the right
lane and merged into traffic on I-295, skirting Richmond. The traffic was
still fairly light. She returned to her thoughts.

Over the past few weeks, Cassie had realized how removed she had
become from the reality of life in her own hometown. Somehow, during
her career years, she had let the comfort of nostalgia color her thoughts of
home so that they had taken on a rainbow aura. Forgotten were her father's
treatises that vigilance must begin at one's own hearth, where rot begins in
small crevices. Cassie shuddered to think how far that rot may have spread.
On the surface, Clayton Landing appeared lost to change and bowed only
to a smattering of technical progress. The several ghosts that townspeople
claimed still lived among them remained perfectly comfortable with their
unchanged familiar surroundings, according to those who reported on
their antics. And yet, unbidden, the rot had crawled its way into the
heart of the town, sanctioned by benign complacency that shook off any
forewarnings to the contrary.

Cassie tried to concentrate on the heavy Friday traffic as she merged
into the center lane of I-95 for the last lap. With any kind of luck, she
could count on being at her apartment in a little over two hours. Even a
car stopped on the shoulder to change drivers could alter that estimate.

She kept her eyes on the road, careful of the traffic around her, until
she saw the striking steel emblem that symbolized the raising of the Iwo
Jima flag towering over the tree tops. It rose from the rooftop of the
National Museum of the Marine Corps just off I-95 at exit 150. For
the next few moments, her mind conjured up rows and rows of tattered
marching Marines disappearing from the vicinity of Quantico and into
the darkening clouds. Will there ever be an end to war? Will there ever be
a monument to peace? Is mankind capable of living in peace? Strange, she
thought, that the citizenry of the world professes to want peace while its
leaders continually find reasons to execute war.

Cassie's reverie was interrupted by a sudden stop in traffic as she neared exit 160. From that point she concentrated on inching forward and avoiding jockeying drivers. She finally arrived at her apartment an hour behind her anticipated schedule.

CHAPTER 50

Cassie elected to park in her garage space and take a short taxi ride to the Willard Hotel on Pennsylvania Avenue in downtown Washington. Any other time, she might have considered walking, but the shoes she had chosen to wear were not made for walking. After mulling over the clothes in her closet, she had selected a simple navy blue and white sheath dress with a short navy jacket for the evening dinner with Cooper and Madalaine. She fussed over jewelry—nervous about meeting Madalaine—but finally decided on her mother's large pearl earrings, which picked up the white accents of her dress. No other jewelry seemed necessary. Her navy blue heels were high, but not outrageous.

Cassie rarely had an opportunity to visit the Willard Hotel. Most of the professional friends that she mingled with in Washington preferred a myriad of bars and restaurants around the city and in Georgetown. Lobbyists, lawyers, and the Hollywood elite preferred the newer, more modern hotels for their visits and meetings. Cassie still had a soft spot for the Willard. In 1850, the Willard brothers took over the property determined to develop a grand hotel. They succeeded. At one time or another, the Willard had hosted nearly all of the presidents of the United States and had been the place to be seen for more than a hundred years. During and after World War II, the city expanded. Visionaries erected grand developments that included the infamous Watergate Hotel complex. The Willard was forced to renovate at an astronomical cost. Recently, the hotel seemed to be enjoying a guest revival among the more affluent visitors to Washington, the location being ideal and the historic atmosphere a bonus.

As Cassie paid the taxi driver, the uniformed doorman hurried over to assist her. She thanked him and made her way under the portico and up the steps, the doorman a stride ahead of her to open the door. Once inside, she turned toward the reception desk to the left of the entrance. The highly polished marble counter fronted equally polished dark wooden cabinets. The large center cabinet contained the message slots; above it and blending into the wood, the clock read 6:55. An attractive young lady with light brown hair asked if she could be of assistance. The nameplate on her jacket identified her as Katie Moreland.

"Yes, thank you Katie, Miss Madalaine is expecting me."

"Yes, of course. I'll call and let her know that you have arrived." As she phoned, she wrote Lincoln Suite, sixth floor on a slip of paper and handed it to Cassie. "I'll have someone escort you if you wish."

"That won't be necessary, Katie. I'll escort Miss Danforth," Cooper said as he touched Cassie's elbow.

"You're timely, as usual," he said as he took her arm to escort her toward the elevators at the opposite end of the marbled lobby. He was casually dressed in a dark sport coat, open-necked white shirt, and khaki slacks.

"I'm bunking in an adjoining room to Mother's suite for tonight," he said as the elevator began its rise.

Cooper opened the door to the Lincoln Suite with his key. Cassie couldn't help being impressed. The lovely suite was decorated in hues of Prussian blue, smartly blended in Persian carpeting, drapes, and sofa. The room was elegant yet restful. Gold accent chairs drawn up to the sofa coffee table invited conversation. She noticed a full-sized dining room adjacent to the sitting room. The table was adorned with a beautiful floral arrangement. Place settings indicated that dinner would be served in the suite.

"Mother will be with us in just a moment. She's putting on the final touches—as if she needed them."

The words were barely out of Cooper's mouth when Madalaine quietly entered the room, her arms outstretched.

"Cassie Danforth, welcome," Madalaine said as she swept Cassie into her arms. "You don't know how I have longed to see you again after all these years. It's been almost your whole lifetime since I last saw you."

As Cassie stepped back from the hug, she studied Madalaine. She knew the famous actress to be in her mid-seventies. Her famous blonde hair had not changed over the years other than perhaps being a little thinner. Her skin reflected years of care; her makeup was impeccable. Her mauve silk sheath, worn just below the knee, flattered her slim figure, which bordered on frail.

"I am delighted to meet you. It's an honor. I did catch your one-woman show a few years back at the National and attended the press reception you held here at the Willard, but I didn't really meet you. Of course, I did not know then of our connection through my father."

"Please forget the actress Madalaine for the evening, Cassie. That's the working half of me. For this evening, I'm Cooper's mom and a dear friend of your father's. We've so much to talk about."

Madalaine motioned Cassie toward a gold chair beside the sofa and then took her place in the middle of the sofa.

Cooper busied himself at the wet bar mixing Cosmopolitans while Cassie and Madalaine got acquainted. He soon returned with cocktails and canapés.

"Although I remember your home on the Green from my few years in Clayton Landing, I was never in it. Tell me, have there been many changes in town over the years? I never really talked about Clayton Landing with your father. Our conversations took other avenues."

"Very few changes actually, and that's the reason we have our share of tourists during season. People are intrigued by our carefully preserved architecture, which dates from the mid-seventeen hundreds. However, nearby Route 17 has become a mecca for the typical chain restaurants and of course the inevitable Walmart."

"I'm happy to hear the uniqueness has been preserved. It seems that so many towns are difficult to identify from one another with all the same chains moving into them," said Madalaine.

"Many of our Connecticut towns have managed to keep their distinctive identities, and I hope that remains so," Cooper added to the conversation.

"Now tell me, Cassie," said Madalaine. "Cooper informs me you just may become involved in the Pinnacle plans. I think that would have pleased Cliff immensely."

"I haven't made any commitment as yet. Perhaps after the meeting with Jordan Mitchell tomorrow I will have more facts on which to make a decision. There are also events developing in Clayton Landing that may have some influence. I'll know more about that aspect early next week. Then perhaps I'll be considering a change in my career path. I'm finding that I'm not cut out to be a newspaper editor like my father."

As they were talking, Cassie noticed that two uniformed waitresses were busy in the dining room. They must have entered from a different door, she thought.

When a waitress approached to announce dinner, Cooper rose first.

"May I have the pleasure of escorting my two beautiful blonde ladies to the table?"

Madalaine and Cassie each took a positioned arm as they made their way to the dining room. Cooper seated Madalaine at the head of the table and Cassie to Madalaine's right, opposite his chair.

"Most of the time I dine next door at the Occidental since the Willard no longer serves in the dining room. But this catered arrangement is cozier and a better setting for conversation," Madalaine said.

Their discussion took a turn to Cooper's campaign and to Madalaine's latest project, a cameo appearance in an HBO production. Cassie brought them up-to-date with some of the events in Clayton Landing. They were so engrossed in conversation through dinner, dessert, and coffee that Cassie failed to notice that it was getting late until she glanced at her watch.

"I didn't realize the time. I've enjoyed the evening so much, but I really think I should be going," Cassie said as she rose from the table.

"Time does have a way of slipping by in good company," Madalaine replied.

"Please, let me see you to your car," Cooper said.

"I parked in my own space at the garage and took a taxi. It's just a short taxi run but a convenience for me."

"Then I will call the concierge to have one waiting for you. I will see you to the taxi, of course. And I'll be meeting you tomorrow morning in Jordan's office at eleven o'clock. Shall we plan on lunch afterward? Mother has a lunch date with a senator, I understand."

"Just an old friend," Madalaine explained. "We catch up with one another now and then."

"Then that's a plan," Cassie said.

Cooper slipped his arm around her waist as he and Cassie waited for the taxi to pull up. Then he brushed her cheek with a kiss as he helped her into the car. He leaned across the front seat as she settled in and handed the driver a twenty dollar bill.

"Be careful with her," he said to the driver.

Cassie rose just past dawn the next morning. She took a plate of fruit, toast, and jelly out to her small balcony. As she sipped coffee and read the paper, she occasionally interrupted her reading to watch a tennis game in progress. Despite the early hour, several mothers and fathers strolled past the courts, pushing carriages with toddlers in tow. Joggers stretched and chatted among themselves before taking off for their runs.

Cassie leisurely spent some time watching and gathering her thoughts for the meeting with Jordan Mitchell. She tarried on the balcony longer than she meant to and then had to rush to shower, dry her hair, and select something to wear. She was ready by ten-fifteen, figuring that there would be a Saturday morning lull in traffic about that time.

It did not surprise Cassie to find Cooper waiting on the bench just inside the parking garage. Rather, she was amused. As she slowed to wait for the entrance bar to rise, he opened the passenger door and slipped in beside her.

Cassie laughed. "I suppose you think I can't find my way to the Pinnacle office?"

"Not at all, it's a beautiful morning and I thought we could enjoy the walk together." He looked down at his watch. "As a matter of fact, we have a little time for an extra cup of morning coffee."

"That sounds good, but only if we make my order tea. One jolt in the morning is usually all I need although I find myself drinking more just to be polite these days."

"Don't tell me you're not one of those journalists seldom seen without a coffee mug at hand?"

"Generalizations are the hallmark of poor research and faulty statistics—the times are a changing with us health-conscious mavericks. If you want to impress the political reporters that will be on your trail, you might want to hand out fruity health bars instead of sugar-pill doughnuts."

Cooper took an imaginary notebook out of his coat pocket and wrote an imaginary note to himself. "So noted, thanks for the update."

Cassie pulled into her slot close to the elevator.

It was between breakfast and lunch hours in the coffee shop.

"We can actually hear ourselves talking," Cooper remarked as they found a small table for two after picking up their order from the counter.

"So, did you catch me early to coach me, or what?"

"Coach you—hardly! I think I know you well enough to know you are an independent lady with a strong mind of your own. Actually, I wanted to know what you thought of my mother after meeting her."

"She's lovely, but somehow more gracious than I pictured. She has a natural warmth about her that is not always found in the famous."

"There you go—generalizations. And you just warned me about such."

Cassie laughed, "You're right. I guess I'm not expressing myself well. Touché."

They discussed Madalaine's contacts in Washington and her love for the Willard Hotel as they sipped their drinks.

"Mother loves the Lincoln Suite. Due to her long relationship with the Willard, if the suite is not occupied for her spur of the moment visits, she gets a much reduced price," Cooper explained.

Soon after they left the coffee shop, Cooper said sheepishly, "I must confess that I was hoping you might give me a hint as to what's on your mind before we see Jordan. You must be giving some thought to what Linwood and I discussed with you back in Clayton Landing."

"Some, yes. There's been a lot going on back home that has me in a whirlwind and very troubled. I'll fill you and Jordan in on that. As I said last night, I think recent events in Clayton Landing may shape my decisions for the future."

"I can't wait to hear more. But I'll have to wait—here we are."

CHAPTER 51

Sheriff Ryan sat at his desk sipping his coffee—his third cup since arriving at six o'clock on Saturday morning. He stared at the rough chart he had sketched, a series of circles with arrows to connect clues and evidence. While some of it was clear-cut, there remained a great deal of investigation ahead. In one circle, a small stick figure depicted the murder of that poor child, Matty Jasman. Which of the men they were investigating had actually committed the murder? Were the others also implicated? He thought he knew the answer, but could it be proved? Money flowed freely on trips to Mexico. Who was financing their trysts? Who paid for the private planes? While all of the men were well-off by Clayton Landing standards, none were really wealthy.

Jed rolled back his swivel chair and propped his feet on the desk. He rubbed his sore head. The headache was not as severe today, but it reminded him that he could have been another victim. They must have been getting desperate when they contracted with Slim. Was the contract for murder or just the whack on the head? Most likely they wanted him out of the way, since they naively thought they had the pictures back.

Could the taped conversation that agent Paul Ruddick had obtained at Slim's garage be used as evidence? Jed admitted to himself that he had been shocked when he got the note from one of the men picked up at Jerry's Bar. Posing as a mechanic working for Slim and going by the name of Mac Turner, he turned out to be FBI agent Paul Ruddick. In his note, he asked to be processed last. Could the sheriff arrange a private meeting?

Although still shaky from his attack, Jed had managed his time so that he was in the office during the processing of the men brought in from the bar. He had a deputy bring Mac to his office.

"I know all those men, except that mechanic guy. I'd like to question him a little before we release him."

The request did not seem unusual to the deputy. Jed often questioned those who weren't the regular Saturday night drunks. He liked to profile anyone who might be a continual troublemaker.

When the man known as Mac entered his office, Jed dismissed the deputy and told Mac to sit down. The sheriff observed that he had long stringy hair, wore a washed-out denim shirt and baggy ragged jeans, and smelled of booze.

"What's on your mind?" he asked.

That's when Ruddick introduced himself. He explained that he had no identity on him but could furnish it when necessary and would have someone call the sheriff in the meantime.

He explained. "I work undercover at Slim's garage investigating drug runners using Routes 1 and 17 along the east coast. The I-95 corridor has become too risky for them. They drive old jalopies stashed with drugs to dealers at specific destinations. So that the old cars appear to be local, the drivers stop and change tags state by state. Despite their appearance, the engines are well maintained. They drop the drug-loaded car off and pick up another for the return trip. Slim moves the rusty jalopies to the back of his lot among the many such wrecks. He's free to take his time distributing to small-time dealers around this area."

"Danged if I haven't had my eye on Slim, too. It seemed strange that he mostly worked on beat-up cars. He turns away folks by saying he's too busy most times. He's only had the business a couple of years. He just appeared about the time old Ross Snyder gave up on the shop."

Ruddick nodded. "Seems like this cartel out of Mexico watches for the right situations and zeros in. Now and then Slim takes a legit repair just for appearances. He made no explanations to me about any of his business. I'm playing it like I'm homeless, uneducated, and willing to work for cigarettes, beer, and a roof. I stay out back in a shed. For appearances, I splash beer on my clothes now and then. I reek with a purpose."

"Well, I'd have to say you are doing a yeoman's job of that," the sheriff acknowledged.

"I have a tape of Slim's calls. No names were mentioned by the caller that arranged for your attack, but it should be easy to identify the guy through a trace. I also got a glimpse of him when he brought in the payoff. We are about to close in up and down Routes 1 and 17 but need a little more time. So this can't get out right now."

"The tape will be needed down the road. Right now I have to turn all the evidence I have over to our district attorney, Larry Stillman. It's going to take a lot of sorting. How come you were at Jerry's Bar?"

"Slim sometimes invites me along when he goes bar-hopping. The pseudo fight caught me off guard. I'm glad you weren't seriously hurt. You'd better get me back out front for processing, Sheriff. We don't want this to look like anything special."

"Right you are," Jed said as he rose and ushered Agent Ruddick out to the front desk. For effect, he patted the man's shoulder and said, "Make sure you keep your nose clean from here on, Mac. You're welcome in Clayton Landing if you don't cause us any trouble."

"Don't worry, Sheriff. I don't aim to be a boarder at your jail."

Jed's thoughts returned to his chart, and once again he connected the dots. He picked up the five enlarged pictures and studied them. Then he studied the pictures that Ace had taken in the front office when word got out about the attack at Jerry's place. Tom Slattery's quick work and his phone report clarified the information Jed needed—his written report would be in hand the next day. He was satisfied that he had enough evidence. He began to think about his plan for Sunday.

CHAPTER 52

Almost as if in meditation, Jordan Mitchell sat quietly studying the portrait on the wall opposite his desk. If George Washington was known as the father of our country, then the man in the portrait certainly deserved to be known as the architect of our country, he thought, as he had many times. And many times he had studied that high Jefferson forehead while his thoughts reflected on the mystery of birth. Why is it that some men and women seem to be born with an innate sense of destiny, advancing through life toward their *terminus ad quem*, leaving behind trails to be followed for generations?

Jordan took a small box from his desk drawer, tapped a button on his desk, and then swirled his chair toward the wall behind his desk. He watched as a landscape painting slowly rose toward the ceiling, revealing a wall map of the United States beneath it. He studied the pins dotting the map. The yellow markers identified the location of each potential candidate. There were many scattered all over the United States. The blue markers identified active Pinnacle political participants temporarily publicly recognized as independents. The green markers identified those on the cusp of becoming blue markers. From the box, he took a blue marker and exchanged it for a green one in Virginia. Linwood Johnson had officially entered the political field as an independent candidate. There were still far too many yellow pins, but he took solace in knowing that some of those would soon change to blue, bypassing green altogether.

Jordan closed his eyes in order to visualize some of the faces behind the many yellow markers. They were not just markers; they were men and women indoctrinated from birth toward curious minds and sound political principles. They were thinkers all.

Reluctantly he turned back to his desk and again tapped the button that lowered the landscape painting to cover the map. It would not do for Pinnacle's candidates to associate themselves with a stick pin on a map. The map was merely his personal tool, a way of tracking the progress toward a restructured vision fashioned from the remnants of the vision the forefathers had for their country.

Jordan moved to the front reception office. He was sitting at the reception desk when Cassie and Cooper entered. "Good morning. Punctual as usual, I see," he said as he rose from the desk chair. "I'm taking advantage of the Saturday morning quiet to compare my schedule with my secretary's. She has a problem with me. I frequently make commitments without telling her."

"Scheduling is an irritant in my existence also," Cooper said as he shook Jordan's hand.

"Let's go into my office. I have a carafe of coffee ready on the conference table," Jordan said as he shook Cassie's hand.

After pouring coffee, Jordan sat at the head of the table with Cooper and Cassie on each side.

"By the way, I took the liberty of inviting Linwood to join us a little later. He's in town for a meeting at Howard University. Now tell me, Cassie, what has changed in your life that brought you back here today?" Jordan asked.

"Not any one event, but several. First, while I love journalism, I realize that I am not cut out to be a newspaper editor. I think my dad knew that, because I have always enjoyed rooting out the news, delving into cause and effect, following rumor to its source. All too frequently, that has led me to discover corruption in government and in private industry. That has resulted in a good deal of frustration and the feeling of helplessness on my part. My dad effectively fought his way, with words, editorials, and personal influence. So far, I haven't found a path that suits me."

"Cliff had a respectable amount of success in combating unfair legislation," Jordan said.

"True, but that is not my forte. Because of events in my own small town, I am coming to realize that corruption exists in every corner of the world. People continue to eat around the rotten core, hoping the rot will not affect them personally. Before they know it, there is little left but rot."

"And at that point," said Jordan, "the people feel powerless and perplexed by their own naiveté."

"Exactly! Now I am finding that I too am guilty," Cassie replied. "I haven't paid attention to the signs of corruption close to me even though my father expressed concern before his death. Lately I've been selfishly involved in my own woe-is-me agenda."

"That's being a little hard on yourself, Cassie," Cooper protested.

Cassie continued. "I've been thinking about The Pinnacle group's movement toward a third party, but I need to know more. As you proposed, it's quite possible that I may have the opportunity to slip into a state position. However, decisions have to be made quickly in order to make filing deadlines. I'm not fully comfortable as to my qualifications as a politician."

Jordan took a sip of his coffee, deliberately pausing before commenting. "Cassie, first let me say that we are not asking you to become a politician. The public, and even Webster's dictionary, designate a politician as one more concerned about winning favor and retaining power than about maintaining principles. Those who join our third-party movement must think of themselves as statesmen, men and women who apply wisdom, common sense, and ability to governing without thought of personal gain."

Cassie turned to Cooper. "Do you think of yourself as a statesman?"

"Let's just say I'm a work in progress. Someday I hope to truly deserve that designation."

"Ah yes," Jordan said, nodding his head. "We are all works in progress. The premise of our entire movement goes back to that ancient philosopher, Socrates. Socrates admonished those concerned with fame or political accolades. According to Plato, Socrates summed up his philosophy in a few words, the necessity of man to know himself, gain intelligence, seek truth, and develop character. He is reputed to have said, 'to know oneself, that is to know oneself completely, one's conscious self and unconscious self, makes for power, self-control, and success.'"

Just then they heard the outer door open. Jordan rose to greet Linwood as he entered the office. Linwood shook hands with each in turn and then took an empty chair at the table.

"We've been discussing some of Cassie's concerns regarding our third-party movement," said Jordan.

"I'm glad you've joined us, Linwood," Cassie said. "I'm particularly concerned that the public will see this movement as an attempt by a wealthy group to control the United States. I'd like to hear your viewpoint on this."

Linwood addressed her concern. "That's an assumption that we must be careful to be up-front about. We will be counterpointing that premise with the fact that the United States is already being bought by wealthy corporations and self-interest groups. We will be publishing books, writing editorials, and using electronic pathways to explain that our party intends to buy back this country, regain its respect, and reinstate its middle class—those Americans who have been losing ground steadily."

Cooper added, "It's a well-known fact that China has been building up its middle class. The executive greed of Wall Street, as well as corporate executives in the past decade, has smothered our middle class to the point of asphyxiation. In the book *Ideas of the Great Philosophers,* William S. and Mabel Lewis Sahakian state, based on Aristotle's philosophy, 'A middle-class majority together with a middle-class rule is the healthiest condition for a nation.'"

"A new party must from the beginning rise above the fray of bickering, obstinate Democrats and Republicans bent on their own agendas, even fragmenting among themselves, to the detriment of their country. We cannot be seen as having any other agenda than the welfare of these United States," said Jordan.

"That's a tall order," said Cassie. "I'm not so sure it will work."

In a cautionary tone, Jordan replied, "Our preliminary function is to fund the fledgling party, assure the values of its foundation, and encourage patriotic citizens to hop on board toward a renewed pride in their country. Our citizens are tired of asking the ultimate sacrifice of our young men and women in the name of democracy while mercenaries mask their greed by flying the banner of capitalism rather than the stars and stripes. We do not have to abandon capitalism, but we must rein in the runaways."

"You gentlemen have given me much to think about. This is heady material. I'll be back in touch next week after I determine if this is the right time for me to think about such a proposition, even if it proves feasible."

Cooper asked Jordan and Linwood if they would like to join Cassie and him for lunch.

"Thanks, another time," Jordan replied. "I promised my wife, Linda, that I would be home in time to help with a dinner party."

"Another time for me too," Linwood said. "I have to get back to Howard University for a late-afternoon session, and traffic time, even on Saturday, is not dependable around here."

CHAPTER 53

The grandfather clock in the hall was just striking eight when Cassie descended the stairs Sunday morning. The aroma of bacon frying wafted through the hallway.

"Smells good," she said to Pearl as she entered the kitchen.

"What time did you get home, child? I tried to stay awake but gave up around ten o'clock."

"It was after midnight. I hoped I hadn't awakened you. I got caught in a construction traffic jam on I-95. I kept thinking it would break up. Then it got too late to call you."

"It's never too late when I'm worried. But I didn't hear you come in. Maybe it would have been better if you'd driven down this morning."

"Before I left, Jed hinted that I should be sure to attend church today. I didn't want to take a chance on being late, so I decided to drive down last night."

"That's really strange. What do you reckon is going on?"

"I'm not privy to Jed's plans, but I am sure that I will be in church on time. I don't promise to have my mind on the sermon."

"Like I've been saying, mighty mysterious goings-on around here," Pearl remarked as she dished up breakfast.

Muffin appeared and jumped up on a spare chair, staring in deep concentration at the bacon on Cassie's plate. She was rewarded with tiny pieces that Cassie laid on the edge of the table for her.

"She doesn't get that kind of spoiling when you're not here," Pearl noted.

"That's because you seldom fry bacon when I'm not here. Don't pretend to be so hard-hearted. I know whose lap she curls up in when I'm not home."

"Shush. Now tell me what happened up in Washington at your meeting."

"I asked a lot of questions, and there was a great deal of discussion. I'm definitely at a crossroads."

The two talked on as Cassie brought Pearl up-to-date. Neither realized how long they had talked until Cassie glanced at the kitchen clock.

"Oops. Let's get these dishes in the dishwasher and get going."

At church, Cassie greeted friends as she walked from the parking lot. Sheriff Ryan stepped up beside her as she neared the front door of the church.

"Morning, Cassie," he said rather loudly. Then, almost in a whisper, he said, "Go to the courthouse parking lot immediately after church."

He moved on and greeted others. On the surface, everything appeared normal.

Cassie took her usual place in church, as did all the regular parishioners. Now and then she glanced toward the back. She saw Jed and Selma come in, taking their regular seats in a back pew. Nothing appeared to be amiss.

She could not concentrate on the sermon. It seemed to go on forever. Finally she heard the closing words. She was jittery as she made her way slowly down the aisle toward the front door. Instead of standing in line to greet Reverend Michaels in the vestibule, she scooted around the line and stood on the top step observing for a few minutes. She saw Ace at the street curb waiting in his car. He rolled down the side window as she approached.

"Jed told me to go to the courthouse parking lot after church. You go on over. Park toward the back of the lot near the jail entrance. I'll get my car and be there shortly."

Cassie made her way to the church parking lot, trying not to be rude to those whom she would normally have stopped for a chat. When she neared her car, she noticed four of the sheriff's deputies in the parking lot in uniform. They were standing at various spots in the lot. She had just reached her Mustang when she observed Deputy Matt Townsend stepping up to her cousin Mason's Buick just as Mason opened the door. They spoke and Mason shook his head. The deputy said something else. It must have made an impression, because Mason gave his wife, Adele, his car keys and started walking with Deputy Townsend to his squad car. Mason stopped for a moment to watch Deputy Lou Morgan approaching John Masengood's Cadillac. Mason looked shaken as Matt Townsend opened the passenger door for him. The two other deputies were waiting near their assigned cars.

Cassie quickly started her engine and drove out the exit, turning left on Main toward the courthouse. When she pulled into the parking lot, Sheriff Ryan was standing at the back of the lot near the rear jail entrance. Ace was parked close by. One by one, four deputy-driven squad cars pulled into the courthouse lot and made their way to the back, where the sheriff was waiting. Ace got out of his car with his camera ready for action.

John was the first to get out of a squad car. He began yelling at Sheriff Ryan. "What is the meaning of this? How dare you? I'll sue for false arrest."

He turned toward Ace, who was busy snapping pictures. "Shut that goddamn camera off."

He lunged toward Ace, but Deputy Morgan quickly restrained him.

In seconds, Charles Masengood joined his brother in castigating Jed Ryan.

Mason Langdon, equally verbose, began a tirade directed at the sheriff.

Mayor Gordon Everly stepped forward. Red-faced, he stood on tiptoe as he asked, "Are you out of your mind? What do you mean embarrassing all of us on the Lord's Day? You've got a hell of a lot of explaining to do. I'll have your job for this outrage."

The sheriff held up a hand to stop the melee as a deputy stepped behind each man and snapped on handcuffs. One at a time, he looked each man in the eye as he read their rights, repeating the spiel four times. Then he told the group that he had search warrants for their homes and offices. "The warrants are signed by Judge Crandall," he said.

John Masengood began yelling again. "Crandall hates me. I know more about the law than he does, and he knows it. This is a conspiracy!"

Cassie heard every word from her car as she busily took notes. She did not get out of the car so that she would not be too visible. She had every right to be there but felt discretion was called for at the moment. She looked around the parking lot while the sheriff read the rights. Several more deputies were in parked vehicles watching. Strange, she thought. Tully, who normally put himself in the middle of everything, was missing.

The suspects' wives began arriving as did others. The sheriff, noting the new arrivals, signaled the deputies to take the prisoners inside. He followed them in. No one else was allowed through the back door.

Cassie joined the group as they walked through the alley toward the Green and the front of the sheriff's office. Tacked to the door was a notice. It said, "Sheriff Jed Ryan will be available at 4 PM." The door was locked.

As she reached her car, her phone rang. "Cassie, because of your involvement, I gave you a head start, but at four o'clock I'll hold a quick press conference open to all. I have no way of telling how quickly the word will get out about the arrests, but with the speed of a bullet, I'd imagine. Of course I'll see you Monday morning for our usual briefing."

He hung up before she could ask any questions.

Cassie and Ace arrived well before the designated hour. Townspeople, wives, relatives, and two out-of-town reporters that she recognized were milling around. Some gathered in small groups where they speculated among themselves. From conversations she overheard, although a few were incredulous at the arrests, there were also a few who thought it was about time.

Promptly at four o'clock, Sheriff Jed Ryan stepped across the street onto the Green and called for attention.

He named the four and then explained that they were arrested on suspicion of Matty Jasman's murder, robbery, illegal use of public funds, and attacking an officer of the law.

Collectively the crowd drew in their breaths and then began shouting questions.

Jed raised his hand for silence.

"Further investigation is under way, and we may ask the assistance of the FBI. At this time, I will not answer any further questions. There will be another news briefing at 2:00 pm Monday." With this he turned and reentered the jail office.

Around the Green, relatives gathered in groups. Disbelief prevailed as well as tears. They slowly began to make their way back to their cars. Other bystanders walked toward Main Street, where they would quickly spread the word among the restaurants, coffee shop, and drugstore.

The out-of-town reporters rushed over to Cassie. They both told her they had gotten text messages from a news junkie in town and had made a mad dash to Clayton Landing. Cassie knew the junkie, whose reports amounted to electronic gossip most of the time. With a straight face, she assured them that she had no more knowledge than they did.

She spent most of Sunday evening writing and rewriting the lead story of the arrests on her home computer.

Cassie arrived at the *Clayton Landing Weekly* office before dawn Monday morning. She put a disk in her office computer and began reworking her article. She watched the clock as she worked until time for her morning briefing with Jed.

Prudently, she crossed the alley toward the back of the jail, where she rang a bell. Deputy Lou Morgan let her in. She made her way to the front.

"Good morning, Cassie. I promised you some excitement," Jed said as he motioned her into his office.

"I thought it best if I came in the back way this morning. You have this town abuzzin.' I know I have to wait for your afternoon briefing like the rest of the reporters, but there are a few questions I can't ask then. It would lead to too much speculation."

"I'll answer only those that won't compromise the arrests. You are entitled to some leeway, but it's off the record. You can only print information released to the press. So, fire away."

"Did you find out if the attack on you was premeditated, and was it connected to the arrests? Where was Tully while all this was going on? He's usually in the thick of things. I couldn't help but notice his absence. Did you hear from Slattery? And if possible, I need to know if Mason is involved. My plans for the future may depend on knowing."

"Whoa. I'll answer what I can. The attack was premeditated. When I went back to inspect at Jerry's, I found a pile of sand around the broken bottle. I never heard tell of a bar selling a bottle of sand. I'll just say I have a little more evidence than that. As for Tully—he's been talking of late like he was some kind of big-time detective. I've seen his car in some peculiar places and watched him follow you a couple of times. Then too, I went over those pictures that Ace took of the office when the pictures were stolen. There was Tully in most of them hanging about my office door as if he was watching out.

Jed hesitated for a breath and to think out his next words. "Yes, I did hear from Tom. Matt insisted on driving all night when I asked for his assistance. I don't think anyone really missed him. I covered for him by saying he'd been on duty too long and needed some sleep. Tom called me with some vital information. And for now, it remains confidential."

"I understand. Why did you choose Sunday morning for their arrest?"

"When else would I find all four together for sure? I couldn't risk any slip-ups or time for warnings. Nobody knew about these arrests until I called deputies out early Sunday. Saturday, I sent Tully over to Washington County, ostensibly to help Sheriff Nelson with a big motorcycle rally. I took no chances on leaks. Orders were given to my deputies just as church began."

"I noticed Tully following me a time or two, but I didn't think much of it. He seems to be all over the place. Do you think he's involved? He doesn't seem that smart."

"It's hard to say about Tully at this point. As for your cousin Mason, I'd say his political career is over. There's not going to be a lot of folks around here sorry about that. He and his cohorts have treated Clayton Landing like a private fiefdom long enough. Anyway, I've got to send you out the door to stand with the rest of the reporters." He looked up at his office clock. "I'll be out on the Green as announced in a few hours."

"Ace and I will be there, along with probably half the town."

Larry Stillman joined Sheriff Ryan for the press conference, which followed normal procedure. There was little new information other than the date for arraignment and a repeat of the various charges. Crime and political reporters scattered, each making a mental list of resources to contact. Someone somewhere must know something, they surmised.

CHAPTER 54

The following Saturday morning, Cassie sat in the roomy leather chair in her father's office. She reflected on the many times in her life that she had curled up in the chair talking with him. Often their conversations started with a question, "What do you think about …?" Cassie recalled that in the past ten years, most of those questions had had to do with actions under consideration by the state legislature or on the national level in the Senate or House of Representatives. Or sometimes they had concerned a particular individual who seemed to be off-base. Now she realized that her father had led her by questions into thinking and analyzing both sides of any situation. As they talked, he had frequently taken a book down from a shelf, suggesting that she read about the history of a situation similar to the one occurring in the present. "It seems to be human nature to repeat mistakes rather than learn from them," he had often said. Had he really been grooming her for a political future? She would never know for sure, but on reflection, the odds were that he had been.

Pearl interrupted her thoughts. "Jilly and Peggy are here. Lunch will be ready soon."

When her friends arrived, there were hugs all around. "I dropped Johna and Mary Sue off at the movies. They'll walk over later," Jilly said when Cassie asked about the girls.

Conversation at lunch naturally revolved around the recent events in Clayton Landing.

As Pearl got up to clear and serve peach cobbler, Jilly said, "Come on, Cassie, give. You must know more than the sheriff is telling us."

"Honestly, I can say that I don't know any more about who is charged with what than you do. I'm sure Jed will release more information when he has it all nailed down. But I have come to a decision. As soon as we finish dessert and the table is cleared, I have an announcement to make."

That statement enticed everyone to quickly finish their cobbler. Peggy helped Pearl clear and stack the rest of the dishes on the counter.

"Remember our last powwow when I told you about the Pinnacle Seven and their interest in me? Well, despite many qualms, I have come to a decision. I've decided to test my toe in the shallower waters of the state legislature. Perhaps from there I will be able to launch a career on the national level. I called Jordan Mitchell and told him my decision yesterday. All of you must promise to keep this to yourselves until I announce my decision publicly. I'm telling you this now because we've shared too much for you three to read about my decision in the paper. The time for the announcement will depend on what indictments come about from Jed's arrests. He did hint that Mason's political career is over, but I have no idea in what way he is involved in this mess."

"All right, it's high time to forget about those qualms," Jilly said. "I can't think of anyone with more natural ability to lead. Don't forget we saw this ability all through high school. We observed your rise to class president in college and we know your uncanny ability to analyze, organize, and delegate. You've never considered yourself special in any way, but truth is, Cassie, you are."

"And I say amen to that," Pearl said.

"Do you know how hard it is to wait tables and carry beer mugs with your fingers crossed? Well, mine have been crossed ever since you hinted at changing careers," Peggy said as she held up her crossed fingers.

Jilly became serious. "I know enough about election rules to know that you don't have too long before your announcement is necessary to meet deadlines."

"You're right, Jilly. The Pinnacle group is aware of this and is prepared to make quick moves once I make the announcement. This week several things fell into place that will help free me to concentrate on an election. Doug Norris has agreed to take the position of editor of the *Clayton Landing Weekly* beginning next month. I will remain as publisher. I let the crew at the paper know this at the end of the day yesterday. I know it didn't surprise Mille. The rest were just glad I didn't decide to sell or shut down."

"How can we help move things along?" Jilly asked.

"I'm leaving town for four or five days in connection with Pinnacle training. It's sort of a retreat, and I can't be reached. Yesterday, I got the key to the bakery that closed on Main Street. It seems I own the building. It will be satisfactory for a campaign headquarters. The front display cabinets have to go. The kitchen will come in handy, and upstairs, where there used to be a rental apartment, there is plenty of storage and office space. If anybody has an uncanny ability to organize, it's you, Jilly. So can you quietly arrange for the minor renovations, a battery of phones, and office equipment while I'm gone?"

"Sure, if anybody questions me, and they will, I'll just say I'm going into business. I think you did say you'll be using my services."

"Absolutely. I don't know how far this path will take me, but I'm going to depend on you being there for me all the way. I've arranged to open a credit card account jointly with you. Just keep a careful account of expenses for the record. Everything has to be on the up and up. We'll talk about your compensation later, but rest assured it will be fair."

Pearl, who had been busy loading the dishwasher, sat back down and joined the conversation.

"Lordy, this is exciting!" Pearl exclaimed. "I'll be in charge of seeing that your volunteers eat properly."

"Everybody talks about change and nothing happens. I'm counting on you, girl," Peggy said. "If there's any way I can help, count me in too. I do have a way with those who haven't exactly made top grade but somehow plug along."

"That includes too many folks right now, Peggy. Of course I will need your help. And while I appreciate all of your confidence, I'm going to have to convince this whole district that I have some political skills. That is going to take a great deal of work. Pearl, you are my rock. Your main job is to keep my head on straight."

Pearl smiled. "Your father and I have been doing that for thirty-two years, and I reckon I have a few more in me."

They became quiet for a few moments. Each lost in their own thoughts about the many recent events in Clayton Landing.

Jilly was the first to give voice to their collective thoughts. She frowned as she said, "I can't believe all that's happened in our small town recently. It's as if undesirable vermin were crawling out from under every rock."

Cassie sounded a little defensive as she said, "I'm sure now that Dad started his own investigation shortly before he died. I know that he never trusted those four men, but I doubt that even he would believe the extent of their degradation."

Johna and Mary Sue bounded through the door, hugging their mother and both adopted aunts.

"So, what's up?" Johna asked.

They all laughed. This was the normalcy that they all needed at the moment.

"A couple of jean jackets jumped into my bags on my way through Macy's while I was in Washington last weekend," said Cassie. "I wonder if you two could use them."

"A customer gave me some passes to that country western concert at the high school next weekend. Do you suppose you two might be available to go with me?" asked Peggy.

"And I need a favor," Pearl declared. "I tried a new cookie recipe yesterday and I just can't decide whether I like them or not."

Cassie leaned back in her chair, observing the girls' exuberance as they accepted all offers. I have an opportunity to contribute to the enrichment of their future, she thought. Really, how could I consider doing otherwise?

CHAPTER 55

Sheriff Jed Ryan sat in his wife's car, which he had parked in a spot with a view of an old willow tree near the bank of the Pasqua River. Enabled by a strong breeze, some of its greening branches continually swept the ground as if trying to erase the scene that Jed could not get out of his mind.

~ ~ ~

Around noon on a Saturday during an unusually warm spell in late January, Deputy Lou Morgan had radioed for the sheriff to drive out River Road to the makeshift parking area near Ford's Crossing. When he arrived, he walked down to where Lou was standing. A red bicycle stood leaning against the willow; a fishing pole lay on the ground beside it. Half in, half out of the water, the body of a young black boy lay face down, arms extended as if he had crawled from the river. Jed turned the body over and recognized the child.

"My God!" Jed felt bile racing to his throat. He gagged. "This is Celia Jasman's boy."

Celia helped Selma out now and then. She worked the early morning shift down at Ruby's Laundromat, and afternoons she did some housecleaning. Back before Christmas, the boy had shown up at Jed and Selma's house one day looking for Celia. Jed had asked him then about his new bike. He had earned it. "A couple of dollars here and there," he'd said with his impish grin.

Jed shook his head and knelt next to the boy's lifeless body. "Nice kid. I'm going to hate telling Celia. How did you find him?"

"I stopped in the parking area to eat my lunch and watch the river go by. That's when I noticed the red bicycle and thought it a little strange that I saw no one around. I walked over to check it out, and that's when I found the boy. Do you suppose he drowned?"

"His body wouldn't have washed up right by his bicycle. It would come up downstream. Put in a call to the medical examiner and rope off the area. Something's not right. This kind of thing just doesn't happen in Clayton Landing."

~ ~ ~

And now he knew what was not right—the whole sickening story.

At first all four took the total innocence and injustice stance until confronted by mounting evidence—some of it, like the pictures, gleaned from egotistical stupidity. John and Charles Masengood refused to talk. Mayor Gordon Everly and Mason Langdon began to talk only when confronted with the medical examiner's report. It concluded that Matty had died of asphyxiation, not drowning. In addition, there was evidence of molestation. The latter two men, who wanted nothing to do with a murder indictment, clarified some of the details of Matty's smothering. With enhancement, one of the enlarged pictures placed all four men in John's office with Matty. Faced with that evidence, Mason and Gordon began to fill in the blanks.

They had gathered as usual that Friday evening for drinks and supper together in John's law office, where they normally played poker until early morning. Two of their usual poker partners were absent, having gone hunting out west. They usually ordered out for their supper, either fried chicken or Chinese. That night Mason's wife, Adele, had offered to send chili over since she was making a big batch for her bridge group anyway. Around supper time, Matty had arrived with a carefully boxed chili dinner in his bicycle basket.

Earlier that evening, Matty had gone to the Langdons' to check with Celia about spending the weekend with his cousin, Willie. Celia had finished her cleaning chores but was staying to help with Adele's bridge party. Matty and Willie often spent weekends at each other's homes. Celia readily gave permission. Adele asked Matty to drop the dinner off at John Masengood's office on his way. She gave him two dollars.

By the time Matty arrived at John's office, the men had already belted down several drinks. They invited him to stay a while and have some chili. John gave him a five-dollar bill and patted the seat beside him on the office couch. Charles got out his camera. The eccentric bachelor habitually chronicled every month of his life with pictures. The boy began to protest when John began petting him. John dug another five-dollar bill out of his pocket and told Matty they were just going to have a little fun.

At that point, Mason Langdon and Mayor Gordon Everly left. They knew full well what would happen, although murder did not occur to them. They weren't attracted to boys; they protested and did not want to be a party to that scene. They went downtown to the Waterfront Restaurant for dinner.

Saturday morning they got frantic calls from John. "It was just an accident," he said. "We didn't realize we were holding his head down in the couch pillow too long. He kept hollering even though we promised him a ten spot." Mayor Everly and Mason agreed to provide an alibi for the evening.

Charles deleted the pictures from his camera, but not before printing a set on his HP Photosmart. John insisted that Charles give him the pictures and checked the camera to make sure they were deleted. John placed the only set in his briefcase, meaning to put them in his office safe Monday morning. He overslept. He barely made it in time for the bank board meeting. In his office, after the meeting, he searched his briefcase, finally dumping it out on his desk. The pictures were gone. He could not account for their loss but concluded that he may have shuffled them out of his briefcase during the board meeting. Cliff Dansforth was a member of the board. John vaguely remembered Cliff leaning down at some point in the meeting and picking something up from the floor. By the end of that week, Cliff was dead of a heart attack. John momentarily relaxed, but then he realized the pictures could be somewhere in Cliff's office or home. They had not turned up anywhere else. He called Charles. He knew that Charles had kept a key to the newspaper office after the bank moved across the street years ago. His searches turned up nothing. He enlisted Mason to nose around Cassie's house. Because Mason couldn't be sure who had been photographed, he agreed. John had Tully keep an eye on Cassie and report. Pretending to be upset over parking problems at his law office, he also made excuses to visit the sheriff's office to keep up-to-date on the investigation.

As Jed puzzled over the various newspaper articles that Cliff Danforth had collected, he made some inquiries. He discovered that there was a quiet investigation underway, led by Mason Langdon's opposition party, into funds used for frequent chartered plane flights to Tucson, allegedly for state marketing opportunities. The fact that he took passengers with him unrelated to the project added to the charges. Art Turner, a member of the town council, told the sheriff that there were rumblings about funds that Mayor Gordon Everly had appropriated for travel to Tucson. "He claimed to be looking for tourist opportunities for the town," Turner said. Others came forth with tidbits of information that added to the mounting evidence.

Jed concluded that the four had become so addicted to their jaunts over the border south of Tucson that they began to get careless. One of the pictures was of the four posed in front of a notorious men's club in Nogales, Mexico. Tom Slattery, who at one time had worked undercover in Nogales, recognized it as a club frequented by men who preferred boys. The mayor and Mason became frantic. While the mayor and Mason were not interested in boys, in another move to distance themselves from murder, they admitted to enjoying "the young ladies" of Mexico and begged the sheriff not to reveal their indiscretions.

Two one-dollar bills and two five-dollar bills were found in Matty's pocket. One of them had a clear print outlined with chili. As the evidence mounted, Jed had no doubt about a grand jury indictment of Charles and John Masengood. All four were implicated in the attack on Jed. Gordon and Mason were charged with obstructing justice. With reputations tarnished beyond repair, both Mayor Everly and Mason Langdon announced their immediate retirement from politics.

Confronted with the incontrovertible enhanced pictures as well as other evidence found at their homes, the two Masengood brothers resorted to a popular excuse for immorality—childhood molestation. While Jed had not known their parents well, others proclaimed them a loving, law-abiding farming couple, who had struggled to send their boys to college.

~ ~ ~

Jed got out of the car and walked to the riverbank. Maybe I'm getting too old for the job, he thought as he stared into the meandering waters. After years of supervising law enforcement in a fairly peaceful county, it had all come crashing down. Fabricated veneers of respectability and power shouldn't have negated his growing suspicions. He'd missed some signs. He'd tolerated Tully's peculiarities as personality traits. He'd gotten wind of drug use increasing in the county but hadn't gotten a handle on the source. His small, mostly rural county didn't warrant the funds for sophisticated law enforcement, but degenerates existed everywhere.

Jed reached down to pick up a stone and skipped it along the water's surface. He took a deep breath as he turned back toward the car. He'd skipped church that morning. It was time to pick up Selma.

When Selma slid into the front seat, Jed said, "Let's go to dinner and talk about doing some traveling. I'm thinking about retiring."

Instinctively, Selma knew he didn't really mean it.

CHAPTER 56

Cassie felt the change in airspeed as the pilot began his descent into Denver International Airport. Checking her watch, she noted that she had an hour to spare before boarding a helicopter that would take her to the Pinnacle retreat.

Cooper and Linwood had filled her in on what to expect. However, never having experienced isolation, her thoughts mixed expectation with apprehension. Girl Scout camp had been her first separation from home, but that adventure included Jilly and Peggy, as well as other friends— hardly a test of fortitude. High school trips, college years, and her career had added adventure and exploration to her life but never detachment from society.

Passengers began gathering their belongings as the attendant announced connecting flights. Cassie put away her book and turned toward the window, observing the sprawling communities of Denver as the plane began its runway approach.

She gave the captain a thumbs-up as she left the plane and began her walk to the baggage area. She expected to be met. Cassie spotted several men and women waving signs. One of the signs had her name on it. She approached a tall thin blonde-headed young man wearing a flight jacket and cap. She identified herself.

"Hi, glad to meet you, Miss Danforth. I'm Danny with Western Colorado Helicopter. How was your flight from Washington? I'll be helping you with your luggage and escorting you to the helicopter pad. Your pilot today is Jake. He's the one that usually flies down to the Pinnacle. It can be tricky sometimes, but he's the best. Have you ever flown in a helicopter before?"

Not in the mood to encourage Danny in conversation, Cassie replied, "A few times. My luggage has a strap with my name on it. Will you hold on to my bag while I make a run to the ladies room?"

Jake proved to be Danny's opposite. He had little to say. Jake had a stocky build; a well-worn cracked leather cap topped his long brown hair. His ruddy complexion highlighted deep blue eyes and a well-creased forehead.

"Afternoon, ma'am. We'll take off in about ten minutes. We have freight to board. Just settle in and make yourself comfortable."

Danny helped her into the helicopter and gave her a salute as a goodbye. Cassie took the seat next to the pilot and watched the loading activity.

When Jake took his pilot's seat, he turned to her.

"We'll be in the air more than a half hour. We're flying southwest. Sometimes the flight is a little rocky, but that's normal, nothing to worry about."

Cassie became mesmerized by the unfolding snow-capped mountain scenery. She was caught by surprise as Jake descended, landing precisely onto a marked pad a short distance from a building she presumed to be their destination. From this approach, the building looked nothing like the painting in Jordan's office.

A man stood a short distance from the helicopter waiting for the blades to stop rotating. He advanced as Jake helped Cassie to the ground. Cassie noted that he appeared to be an Asian man of medium height and slender build. He had jet black hair slicked close to the scalp. He wore chino slacks and a flannel shirt. "Welcome, Miss Danforth. I'm Kelly, at your service during your stay with us. This way, please."

He took the handle of her rolling bag and preceded her into the building. She followed Kelly through an inconspicuous door that blended into the melon-colored stucco siding. Cassie realized that they had entered through the utilitarian section of the building. Inside they proceeded along a corridor lined with doors marked kitchen, storage, and electrical. She noticed a stairwell just before they entered into a very large room.

"This is our great room," Kelly said. He gave her a few moments to look around.

A large stone fireplace accommodating huge blazing logs dominated the room. Twin deep-cushioned red leather couches flanked the fireplace with a large square wood coffee table between them. Various chairs and small tables were scattered around the room. Bookcases lined every wall, interspersed with several doors, including double doors with stained-glass inserts at one end of the room. There were no windows in the great room.

Kelly opened one of the doors. "This is your room, Miss Danforth. I hope you will be comfortable during your stay with us. We will disturb you as little as possible. On the desk you will find a schedule that allows a great deal of privacy for each resident in the various areas. For meals you will proceed to the kitchen at the times noted on your schedule. In the large freezer you will find lunches and dinners marked with your name, each microwavable. For breakfast there are assorted cereals, buns, and fruit. The Pinnacle sanctum is located through the double stained-glass doors at the east end of the great room. It is best if you introduce yourself to the sanctum in order to appreciate its full effect. Your time to do so is noted on your schedule. Do you have questions?"

"Please call me Cassie. Kelly, what happens if I don't adhere to my schedule? Do I get forty lashes?"

Kelly saw no humor in the question. "You are fortunate, Miss Danforth. We have only one other guest, so your schedule for use of the various venues is generous. The less contact you have, the greater will be your experience."

Cassie realized that Kelly preferred his formal stance. "Is Michael Stone here?"

"Yes, he may join you from time to time if you wish. Just pick up the house phone and leave a message if you wish to see him."

After Kelly left, Cassie explored her room. The view was magnificent. From the wide double window she saw a stand of pine trees; towering above them, a rugged mountain terrain. Patches of snow glistened as the sun's rays swiped them. The walls of the room were painted a soft sea green. The double bed, covered with a coordinated comforter bed set, appeared comfortable. A wide upholstered chair, ottoman, floor lamp, and bookcase invited reading. The desk drawers held ample supplies of writing materials. A dorm-type refrigerator and microwave sat beside the desk. A small table and chair placed beneath the window completed the furnishings. The room lacked a TV, a radio, an outside phone, or any other form of distraction.

Cassie opened one of the two doors in her room to find a closet with shelves on one side. Assuming the other door led to a bathroom, she opened it to find a small but adequate facility, bigger than a cruise ship's but not by much.

She examined the contents of the bookcase in her room. The titles ranged from religion and philosophy to economics and politics. She presumed she was to select her own homework.

Cassie picked up her schedule from the desk and then glanced at the desk clock. She was due in the Pinnacle sanctum in a half-hour. Meantime the great room was hers to use.

She quietly opened her door and entered the windowless great room. Slowly she circled the room, stopping to explore book titles or touch an attractive piece of porcelain. Drawn to the blazing fire, she warmed her back while continuing to familiarize herself with the surroundings. As her eyes roamed, she saw the magnificent grandfather clock that blended with the polished mahogany paneling on the west wall, making it almost invisible. The clock began to chime. It must be there to keep the guests on time, she thought. With the validation of time, she approached the sanctum's stained-glass doors.

Cassie gasped as she stepped into the room. Suddenly she felt as if she were in space. Two stories tall, the glass-walled sanctum came to a vertex at its eastern-most point, giving the feeling of a ship floating beneath fleecy clouds. Scarcely breathing, she approached the vertex and found herself suspended over a valley of dark pines. Across the valley, water flowed from a deep crevice beneath a bare snow-capped mountain. Complete silence prevailed. She felt as if she was actually standing inside a painting—the one on the wall in Jordan Mitchell's office.

The soft Mediterranean blue carpeting blended with the sky. Two leather chairs and ottomans, upholstered in a hue closely matching the carpeting, generated a feeling that there were no furnishings at all. They were placed to one side of the vertex. Somewhat lightheaded and overwhelmed, Cassie crossed the room and sat in one of the chairs. A small cloud floated by. She reached out, longing to touch. A sense of euphoria enveloped her. She had no desire to move.

CHAPTER 57

"Anybody here?"

The call from downstairs startled Jilly. Her total concentration had been on the drawings laid out before her on the card table that served as a desk.

"I'm up here," she called back.

When her visitor stepped into the front room where she worked, Jilly expressed surprise.

"Dr. Lansfield. I haven't seen you in ages."

He chuckled. "Occasionally I get out of my routine. Hospital to home and back again can get monotonous at times. Rumor has it that you are going into some kind of business. This old building could use a new tenant."

"Well, sort of. I'm working on some small renovation plans right now. Please, have a seat."

He chuckled again. "I've been let in on your little secret, Jilly. I had a long conversation with my son yesterday. Previously he told me a little about the Pinnacle Seven and his affiliation with them. When I called to tell him of a proposition I had in mind, he felt obliged to fill me in on Cassie's plans, provided I kept her secret for a little while."

Jilly noticed that he used the term 'my son' instead of Cooper's name.

"In that case, have a look at my doodling. There's not a great deal to be done. My John has some buddies that agreed to help take out the display counters in the downstairs front room. They'll be recycled to the new butcher shop opening at the other end of town. Sid Olson has carpeting remnants in the storeroom out back of the salesroom. I found a perfect piece for that front room downstairs. The sofa and chair in this room were left by the former tenant of this upstairs apartment. I'll move them downstairs with a little help from John's friends. Voilà! That becomes our reception area. Up here we'll have a room for phones, and the former bedroom will be a conference/work area, plus we'll divide off a storage section. I've already bought three card tables with chairs. John drew up a plan for wood tops for the card tables to expand the work area. Casey Harlow, the shop teacher at the high school, agreed to make sound barrier section dividers, kind of like voting booths, so volunteers on phones can hear themselves talk. Pearl is coming over tomorrow to scrub the kitchen to her standards. That rounds out our work schedule."

"I knew I had delivered a prize when you came into the world. Now why haven't I had you over at the hospital all these years? We doctors really depend on someone to organize us."

Jilly laughed. "Up to now I haven't worried about a paycheck. But things are getting tight. I could use a little extra income. This job needed doing in a hurry, so I rolled up my sleeves. By the way, how is Mavis? I haven't seen her for ages, but then we don't travel in the same circles."

"Well, there's been quite a change for that young lady. She is well-educated, you know. I told her that she had to get a job. No one should go through life just playing tennis and sleeping. She nearly blew a gasket. I did help her though. We had a position open in the administrative department at the hospital, and I called in a few markers. She's been working for a couple of weeks."

"That is news," said Jilly. "I can just see her sashaying through the halls in those spiked heels she wears. Sorry, I didn't mean to be catty."

"That's all right, Jilly, no apologies needed. We all know Mavis and her ways. I fully expect that she will snag one of the freshmen doctors we have at the hospital. I really came over to ask you if you knew when Cassie is expected home. I want to make arrangements for a meeting."

"She was a bit vague about that, but I think sometime over the weekend."

"I was surprised she left in the midst of all this ruckus. What do you think of the sheriff's arrests?"

"Like a lot of people, I wasn't too fond of those pompous dolts, but it's hard to believe the depths of their depravity."

"Well, you can't fool all of the people all of the time, but some people sure come dang close to it."

"Now that you're mostly retired, why don't you run for mayor, Dr. Lansfield?"

Before he could respond, Peggy appeared carrying bolts of material in her arms. "I found the material to go with the carpeting," she said as she came through the door. Oh. Hi there, Dr. Lansfield, I certainly didn't expect to find you here."

"I'm about to take off and leave you two ladies to your work."

"Peggy is a great seamstress," Jilly said. "She'll add the finishing touch. We should be in business by the first of next week if everyone keeps to the schedule. It will all come together quickly."

"Then I'll expect to see a new sign out front shortly. Good day, ladies."

"I wonder what that was all about," Jilly said to Peggy after she heard the front door close.

"What do you mean?" Peggy asked.

"I don't know."

CHAPTER 58

By the third day Cassie had settled into her routine. She spent every waking hour reading or meditating. On the fourth morning, she added some exercises to her schedule. Her appetite for renewed knowledge grew as her appetite for food waned. Her quick trips to the kitchen triggered by the chiming clocks became a chore—an interruption to her refresher course among the great thinkers.

At the same time, there was an unearthly feel to her surroundings. Except for occasional footsteps overhead or an occasional door closing as she entered the great room, she saw or heard no one.

Unbidden thoughts also crept into her mind. Did Mille, Carol Morgan, and Ace cover the arrests properly without her? Had Jilly made any progress at the former bakery? Could Peggy keep mum about Cassie's plans? Was Pearl all right without Cassie's daily calls? What progress were Jordan, Cooper, and Linwood making on her behalf? What was happening at the sheriff's office? Could she really just get off the planet and expect her world to shuffle along without her? Did her father really endorse this ego-stripping methodology?

After her lunch that third day, she picked up the desk phone.

When Kelly answered, she asked, "Do you think Dr. Stone might join me in the sanctuary later today during my scheduled time?"

Kelly had her hold for a few moments. "Yes, he will be happy to join you."

As Cassie entered the sanctum, she found it enveloped in shades of gray. It was as if the skies wore a solemn cloak. Mists floated up from the valley, obscuring the view of the waterfall. Although the room was sufficiently warm, Cassie shivered as she wrapped herself in an afghan and settled down to read. She had trouble concentrating. She laid the book in her lap and closed her eyes, struggling to assimilate some of the profound wisdom of the great sages handed down through the ages.

He slipped into the chair opposite her. She had not heard him enter the sanctum.

"Excuse me for interrupting your thoughts, Cassie," he said as he reached across to shake her hand. "I'm Michael Stone."

Cassie studied Michael for a moment. She found him pleasant looking but not especially handsome. His black wool sweater hung on a tall slim frame. She suspected that he was much younger than his white hair might suggest.

"My thoughts are the reason I asked to talk with you. The wealth of reading material available challenges me. But most times when I am in this room, I seem to sit here in some kind of suspended animation."

He smiled. "This sanctum does have that effect. We've become so harassed in our daily lives with the proliferation of technology, the media, traffic, and tension that silence becomes a fascinating luxury. Beauty and silence together equates to tranquility, an elixir for the soul."

"The experience also leads you to ponder your very existence. It can be a bit deflating," Cassie replied.

"I know that you've been told the purpose of your retreat. You are not here for instruction or mind bending. Simply put, the purpose is to take you away from your own particular environment into a situation where you can evaluate life and the importance of your own contributions to life without the clutter."

"I believe Jordan mentioned one purpose being to 'power down'—allowing the world to function without your presence," Cassie said.

Michael laughed. "That's one way of putting it. We humans do have a way of becoming polluted with self-importance. I see you're reading Aristotle."

Cassie held up her book. "Yes, I've been traveling the cobble-stoned pathways the past philosophers have laid. I've concluded that we have covered them with thick asphalt subject to many potholes."

"And with the vagaries of human nature," Michael added.

"Yes, I've recently had a graphic demonstration of just how debauched our public leaders can become within my own home town. Their façade, while questioned by some, was enough to fool too many. I'm beginning to understand why my father wanted me to return to my roots for a while. I've probably lived in the rarified atmosphere in Washington too long. We need to understand that the subliminal life in small towns is in grave danger."

"Unfortunately, I think all those great thinkers and men of religion would have to agree that there will always be the greedy and evil among us, but we do not have to be crippled by them. At all times we must remain wary and alert to those who would bring us down," Michael responded.

Cassie sighed. "I've had many reservations about a third party bankrolled by those rich enough to buy their way into the political system of the United States—much like special interests have been doing for years. Yet I know that in order to save this great nation, something drastic must take place, and soon. I'm still not sure if people will believe or trust the message."

Michael leaned forward in his chair, resting his elbows on his knees, cupping his chin in his hands.

"That's understandable. It will take men and women of great fortitude and ethics to turn away the great economic tsunami ahead of us. And it will take men and women of great vision to accept their gift and join the mission. As you know, most of the fifty-six signers of the Declaration of Independence were men of means who put both their lives and their wealth on the line in order to create this country. Indeed, fourteen lost their lives during the Revolutionary War; most all lost their wealth. Their sacrifice was a great gift, as was the gift of those who trusted and stayed on the battlefield with General Washington at Valley Forge."

"This aspect has been drilled into me in the past few weeks. I'm just not sure that we have that kind of stamina today. Vietnam, Korea, Iraq, and Afghanistan—we patriotically send our sons and daughters off to war to fight for freedom. Then we order in Chinese or pizza and return to our computers and television sets as if our duty is done. For a time, even our President did not want us to see those flag-draped coffins come home," Cassie said.

"Perhaps you have been in journalism too long, Cassie. Disenchantment can lead to surrender—giving in if the problem seems insurmountable. If you recall, it was Aristotle who admitted that 'the man or group of men noble enough to govern solely for the best interests of the people at large is rare and hardly to be found.' Do you also remember that even before Aristotle's time it was Confucius who believed that only ethical leaders could effect a good government? He trained his group of disciples in ethics as well as other disciplines. Their honesty was highly valued."

"It is my understanding that the teaching of ethics will be one of the missions at the Americas World Academy?"

"Yes, of course. If our vision is successful, there will be more such academies."

Michael stretched his long legs and leaned back in his chair. For several minutes, he and Cassie were content to watch the darkening shadows. Even in silence, Cassie felt enriched by Michael's calming presence. The faint sound of chimes broke the silence. Cassie turned toward the niche in the back wall where long chimes hung.

"The mechanism is hidden in a panel above the chimes," said Michael, following her gaze. "As you've come to know, the chimes keep us on our schedules. So I'll bid you a good evening." He rose from his seat.

Cassie followed. She had two days left and much more to absorb.

CHAPTER 59

"The sheriff wants to see you," Shirley said as Tully signed in for duty.

Jed did not offer Tully a seat. "I have here a list of charges that I have drawn up that include passing confidential information to our current prisoners."

Tully studied the paper the sheriff handed him. A few beads of sweat appeared on his forehead, but he managed to keep his voice nonchalant. "I thought I was just helping out the town council—you know, just keeping them informed so they could do their job," Tully explained to the sheriff.

"That won't wash, Tully. You were actually aiding and abetting. Oh, I know, you certainly weren't involved in Matty's murder, and I don't think you even knew about their involvement, but you were in on the cover-up. As an officer of the law, your first duty is to report suspicious behavior, not become part of it."

Jed reached into his desk drawer for pictures. He spread them out on the desk. "How do you explain acting as a lookout while John Masengood rifled my office? And just how did he know where to look for those incriminating pictures? Before you answer that, Shirley told me you were asking about my keys."

Tully lost his cockiness and began to stutter. "I ... I just like to know what's going on, Sheriff. I ... I didn't mean no harm."

"Bullshit. The district attorney might cut you some slack if you turn state's evidence. Meantime, you'll remove your badge, give me your gun and car keys, and get out of my office."

A short time later, Jed left his office and said to Shirley on his way out, "Hold down the fort for a while. I'm going to walk around town and let off some steam."

"I'd say that's a good idea. You look like you could blow a gasket. I gather Tully is dust. Stormed out of here like hornets were after him."

Jed stopped by the drugstore, wandered into the bank to see if it was running smoothly without its president, and then noticed a pickup truck being unloaded in front of the former bakery. He watched for a minute or two and then crossed the street and entered the building. He found Jilly supervising the unloading.

"All that stuff goes upstairs," she said to the crew as she turned toward Jed.

"Hi Sheriff. Curiosity got you?"

"You might say that, Jilly. Where did Cassie get herself off to? She told me she'd be gone a few days. We're used to that around here, but apparently she didn't let anyone know where she was going. That Carol Morgan has been bugging me for news. Heck of a time to be leaving town, if you ask me."

"I know when she's coming home. She flies into Dulles early Saturday afternoon. She's coming straight home, so she should be here by evening."

"What are you doing to this place? I've been so busy trying to keep a couple of cantankerous prisoners from killing each other that I haven't had time to stop by."

"The brothers are at each other's throats, I take it. I know Cassie told you that she is thinking of making a career change. I'm just getting this old place ready." Jilly turned away from the sheriff for a moment to redirect a man struggling under the weight of a filing cabinet.

When she turned back, he said, "Based on all the activity around here, I'd say she's made up her mind. Incidentally, Shirley got a call from her Aunt Grace over at the Captain's Quarters bed-and-breakfast. Some fella from Washington called and rented all her rooms for the weekend. That got anything to do with Cassie?"

"Sorry, I'm not sure what's going on. Cassie did ask me to keep my calendar clear for Sunday and Monday. That's all I know right now because Cassie is out of contact."

"I'd better move along. With lawyers coming and going and reporters hounding me, it's hard to get a minute of thinking time."

Just then they heard a crash coming from upstairs. A voice yelled from the top of the steps that nothing broke.

"I'd better get back to work, too," Jilly said. One of these days, things will settle down, and I hope we can all return to our boring old lives without too much damage done."

"I'll second that," Jed said as he opened the front door to leave.

CHAPTER 60

On the last full day, Cassie checked her schedule. With one exception, it was the same as every other day. The last entry invited the occupants of the Pinnacle to dinner in the great room at six o'clock. Curiosity nagged at her all day as to who the other guest might be.

She returned all books gleaned from the shelves in the great room library, with one exception. She took it with her when the chimes signaled her rotation to the sanctum. Morning sun enveloped the glass-walled room, showcasing the mountain's splendor. A lone golden eagle circled, surveying his territory.

Cassie settled into the deep chair and opened a small book. *A Letter to America* was written by David Boren, president of the University of Oklahoma, a former senator and governor of his state. As she read, she became tearful. She stopped reading now and then to observe the eagle and ponder the majesty of her surroundings while she digested Boren's wisdom. Many are trying to warn this country of overwhelming dangers, Cassie thought. When will we listen? When will we act? Is it really possible for a few people to make a difference?

When she returned to her room, she added Boren's book to a list of books she planned to purchase even though she had just read most of them. In late afternoon, Cassie showered and then selected her navy blue slacks and pale blue turtle-necked sweater to wear in the evening. She emptied the closet and packed her bag, leaving just enough room for last-minute items. After touching up her hair, Cassie stood by her door waiting. At precisely six o'clock, the desk clock chimed. She opened the door and entered the great room.

Michael Stone stood by the fireplace. Kelly fussed over last-minute details at the library table, which had been pulled away from the back of one of the couches. With its drop sides extended, the table easily accommodated eight. Tonight it was set for four. Seconds after she entered the room, another door opened. A tall, heavy-set, broad-shouldered man entered. He had dark black hair with contrasting white sideburns. Cassie recognized him immediately.

"I believe both of you have met Kelly," Michael said.

Kelly smiled and nodded as he continued fussing around the table.

"Senator Young, I'd like you to meet Cassie Danforth."

The senator stepped forward, offering his hand to Cassie. "You look familiar," he said as he shook her hand.

"I don't think we've formally met, Senator. I sometimes cover the Capitol news conferences for NBC, and I had a Saturday morning show until recently."

"Yes, that's where I've seen you, on television. Well, I would never have guessed that I would meet you here."

"Nor I you, Senator." In fact, Cassie was amazed. Senator Scott Young was a powerful leader of the minority party.

"In the future, the two of you will be meeting a number of people whose identities may surprise," Michael said.

Kelly poured wine as each of them found a place to sit around the fireplace. Kelly sat as well.

"I'm a bit puzzled," Senator Young said. "I had heard rumors of a third-party movement, and after some investigation, I contacted Jordan Mitchell. During our many talks, I understood that most of the Pinnacle guests were to be power politicians. I fit that category. However, we politicians are leery of the press. I am a little befuddled as to why Miss Danforth is here. Am I being too presumptuous if I inquire?" asked Senator Young.

"Not at all," said Michael. "All those who join our movement toward a third party must be aware of all its facets. You, Senator, are among the most powerful of our recruits. Some of our younger recruits will be joining us on the ground floor, so to speak. Cassie will begin her political career on the state level. I'm sure she is just as surprised to learn that some very powerful leaders will be among us, since you have not announced your transition to a new party as yet."

Senator Young quickly turned to Cassie. "That's not for publication."

"No problem from me," Cassie said. "Although I would have loved to break that news, I'm leaving the journalistic field. I've been struggling with the decision to make this transition for some time. Now that I've had a week here to study and digest the works of so many wise men and women, I'm beginning to feel it is my duty. I've gotten past the feeling that I've been manipulated."

Kelly responded, "It is never easy to be a part of a pivotal era. You were wise to allow your thoughts to work their way through the dilemmas of your decision."

Michael spoke. "Let me officially introduce Dr. Kelly Lu, distinguished philosophy professor from Boston University and my esteemed colleague. He is here on retreat while writing. In exchange for his accommodations, he agreed to lend a hand. Our facility manager does not arrive for two more weeks. Kelly too is involved in our quest for a more workable government in Washington."

"This facility is so well organized, there is really little to do," Kelly said.

"It is necessary to be frugal with staff in order to maintain privacy. A well-known Denver chef prepares the meals, which are quick-frozen. The meals along with a cleaning crew are flown in on Saturday afternoon during transition periods. We opened to start preparing for our season two weeks ago. Winters tend be harsh. Spring arrives late," Michael explained. "Senator Young is here for the two weeks required for our most powerful leaders."

"Yes, and although I am ashamed to admit it, I have achieved top rank in Power Mania 101. I recently got my comeuppance at a small conference center in Virginia Beach where I attended a meeting organized by small-business leaders from several states. This hotel's only wireless hookup is in their bar area. I was at the bar with my laptop, catching up on my e-mail and at the same time talking with a colleague via cell phone. I took umbrage over some issue that was not going my way and began pacing and yelling into my phone, oblivious of my surroundings. During my tirade, I felt a tap on my shoulder. A petite white-haired lady asked me to lower my voice, as she and her friends were not able to enjoy their luncheon."

After a pause, Senator Young went on with his story. "My immediate response was to ask, 'Madam, do you know who I am?'"

"And to that statement, she replied, 'I know, sir, that at this moment, you are a pompous ass.'"

"With that, she turned and walked away. Her luncheon companions applauded."

Cassie was not sure how to react to Senator Young's story. Picturing the scene in her mind, she stifled an urge to laugh.

"It was an epiphany moment for me. I realized in that instant that my propensity to overpower was a mechanism to get my own way or my party's way regardless of the consequences to my country. I have fallen into the abyss of self-importance over common sense. However, I do feel I have much to offer in experience if I can conquer my thirst for power. I can no longer serve under the restrictions required by party loyalty. I'm offering that experience to this third-party movement with a pledge to put my country first, my ego dead last. My sojourn here and my sessions with both Kelly and Michael have encouraged me."

The four were quiet for a few moments.

Kelly rose. "Pardon me while I see to our dinner."

"Please, let me help. I've become fairly accomplished at the microwave and loading trays," Cassie said.

Dinner was lovely. The poached salmon was tastefully flavored, the asparagus tender yet crisp, the baked potato fully cooked. Conversation centered on their personal histories. Cassie helped clear. She and Kelly returned to the great room with coffee and cheesecake. The small group moved to the fireside once more.

Senator Young continued the conversation. "Much as I dislike admitting it, there are a number of well-known columnists pointing to the crisis situation in the United States. Most of them are correct in their analysis. I know that well, and so do my colleagues. We have been willing to sacrifice our political ethics for political power for too long. Our two parties are broken. Perhaps they can be mended, perhaps not. At any rate, a third party will shake the chambers, so to speak, if it's not single-issue based."

"I understand that the core members of the new party are about a hundred strong. Do those few members really have a chance to influence our politics? That thought has concerned me," Cassie said.

"Allow me," Kelly said. "Perhaps you have heard of the Italian lawyer, Gaetano Mosca. He served Italy in the political field during a good deal of his life, as well as in academia. He died in 1941. He was quite famous for his many writings of political theory. While many thought his theories elitist, he did write, 'A hundred men acting uniformly in concert, with a common understanding, will triumph over a thousand men who are not in accord and can be dealt with one by one.' I do not think we should be skeptical of our small number. History reminds us that small groups do rise to great power."

Michael added, "As you know, Cassie, each initial participant will bankroll his or her own campaign. However, we are enthusiastic in our expectation that thousands will be sending their contributions when the mission becomes clear."

"My own personal wealth is a result of fortuitous investments," said Senator Young. "I'm not filthy rich, but I have more than I need to live a comfortable life. I am willing to dedicate the bulk of it to my country. I have come to feel that I owe the American people a debt that I must pay before I retire."

The four sat quietly for a few moments, content to digest their conversation by firelight.

Cassie rose first. "Gentlemen, this has been a very enlightening evening, but dawn arrives on schedule, and with it Senator Young and I depart." As if on cue, the chimes denoted the late hour. "I trust our paths will cross again."

The three men rose and wished Cassie a good night.

"Yes, we will surely meet again, and soon," Michael said as they parted.

CHAPTER 61

Cassie's cell phone rang as she made her way to the baggage area at Dulles Airport.

"Any chance of hitching a ride to Clayton Landing?" Cooper asked.

Cassie recognized his voice immediately. "Where are you?"

"I'm standing at the bottom of the escalator in baggage. I'm the tall one with reddish hair and a big grin on his face."

"You're also incorrigible. I see you now."

She'd barely reached the bottom escalator step when Cooper pulled her aside. He swept her into his arms.

"Can you tell I've missed you?"

Although she was delighted, Cassie's face must have registered her surprise at his exuberance.

"Maybe it was the whole week of not being able to contact you. Maybe I missed your sassiness. Maybe I just need a ride to Clayton Landing," he said, grinning.

"And you couldn't rent a car, I suppose. You pay for half the gas, and you have a deal. I assumed you would be running around Connecticut this weekend shaking hands. Anyway, why are you going to Clayton Landing?" Cassie asked.

"Jordan doesn't usually do any campaign site inspections, especially for state office campaigns. However, he wanted to meet with Linwood and me this weekend if possible. Jordan's wife, Linda, learned that Clayton Landing was an option for Jordan's meeting and insisted on coming along. She had read about your town and all the bed-and-breakfasts in one of her magazines. I guess she clinched the deal."

The baggage bell sounded. Cooper retrieved her luggage, and they made their way to her car.

During the nearly five hour drive to Clayton Landing, they talked about Cassie's impressions of the Pinnacle and some of her studies. Cooper mentioned being worried about Madalaine's health. He also told Cassie that he would be meeting with Martin Lansfield during his brief stay.

"Martin says he has some kind of proposition for me to think about," Cooper said.

~ ~ ~

They decided to stop by the former bakery that was to be Cassie's campaign headquarters before she dropped Cooper off at the Captain's Quarters bed-and-breakfast. Cassie called Jilly during their drive and gave her their approximate arrival time. She parked a block away. As they got out of the car, they spied balloons tied to a container of pansies sitting in front of the former bakery door.

Cassie opened the door to a chorus of voices cheering her name along with drumbeats on pots and pans. Jilly, Peggy, Pearl, Johna, and Mary Sue were so excited they could hardly contain themselves.

"We can't wait to show you around!" Jilly declared after greeting Cooper.

Cassie looked around the front room. "This is unbelievable, Jilly! How did you manage all this in just a week? It's not like any campaign headquarters I've ever seen."

"Believe me, I had lots of help. I called in favors and offered favors. I'm slated to give a beer party for John's friends, for one thing. Anyway, except for a few minor items, it's all done. Most of the folks in town have decided that I'm opening an antique store."

"Do I recognize that antique chest and that lamp?"

"Sure. You told me I could raid your attic. Pearl and I did just that. The chest's drawers will give us more storage space for pamphlets. Besides, this room should reflect the town's unique hold on the past."

"I made the window valances," Peggy chimed in.

"And we helped scrub the bathrooms," Johna and Mary Sue said simultaneously.

"And, as you might guess, I cleaned up the kitchen," Pearl added.

Led by the five ladies, Cooper and Cassie toured the building. While the front room downstairs reflected Clayton Landing standards, upstairs proved to be a model for efficiency.

"Can I steal you away from Cassie, Jilly?" Cooper asked. "My headquarters looks like a shambles compared to this. Phones are elbow lengths apart on tables, supplies stacked in corners. This is terrific!"

"Is Jordan planning to hold the meeting here?" asked Cassie.

"I'm not sure what the plans are, but I will find out shortly and let you know. The back room upstairs will be a perfect place—plenty of table space."

"Just let him know it's available. Shall I run you over to Captain's Quarters?"

"Point me in the right direction and I'll walk. It can't be more than a few blocks, can it?"

"By the time we go back to my car to get your bag, you'll be almost there," Cassie answered.

"Good, I need to stretch my legs a bit anyway."

"Will I see you tonight?" Cassie asked.

"How about I come over after dinner? I promised Martin I would have dinner with him tonight," Cooper replied.

"I'll save you a piece of pecan pie, Cooper," Pearl said.

CHAPTER 62

True to her word, Pearl placed two pieces of pecan pie on the kitchen table before she retired to her room to watch television. It was after nine when Cooper knocked on the back veranda door.

Cassie poured fresh coffee from a carafe and served the pecan pie. She asked, "How did your dinner with Doc Lansfield go? What was on his mind that was so important?'

"He had a proposition that sounded feasible for his dilemma about what to do with Wahala Hall. He has been rewriting his will, and I have let him know that I don't wish to be remembered. I wouldn't feel comfortable taking over Wahala or any of his assets at this stage in my life. He does intend leaving Mavis a generous annuity, certainly not title to Wahala. He is meeting with us tomorrow, as his proposition will have to be presented to Jordan."

"Now you really have me curious."

Cassie put their dishes in the dishwasher and suggested that they adjourn to the front veranda.

Except for the chirping of tree frogs, the evening was quiet. They sat together in the swing.

Both were content to enjoy the peaceful evening until Cooper finally spoke. "Cassie, you must be aware that I am growing very fond of you."

"I'd guessed as much. I don't suppose you are aware that I haven't been resisting a whole lot."

"I'm much too old for you, Cassie, by at least fifteen years I'd say. That bothers me. Because of the age difference, I've been hesitant."

"I like the way you operate, Cooper Canaday. You don't find many real gentlemen these days who know how to treat a lady. I don't care for the trend of hopping in bed on the first date. I like mature. Growing up here in Clayton Landing, I've been around mature people most of my life. I haven't been comfortable with the bar-hopping, all-about-me dating environment in Washington. Besides, you have a killer grin."

"Are you saying I stand a chance despite the age thing?"

"You must not pay attention to anything but politics. Don't you know older men and younger women have been a trend for years and years? Around here we relate to the seventeen hundreds like it was yesterday. Back then men sought out younger women. Heck, Dolley Madison was seventeen years younger than President James Madison, and that worked out pretty good, I'd say. And if you want a more up-to-date example, what about Michael Douglas and Catherine Zeta-Jones for heavens sake."

Cooper laughed. "Now that's one of the things that attracted me to you. There's an answer for every argument."

He put his arm around her and pulled her over. "It won't be easy. If we are to be major players in a new political party, it will mean a lot of separation time."

"If I get elected, there's plenty of free time in the state legislature. Polls say there's not much doubt you'll be elected, even running as an independent. I plan to catch up with you in a few years, and then we can operate as one of those Washington power couples."

"There you go, rationalizing everything."

"Well, if that's settled, would you mind sealing this conversation with a real kiss? I've been patient long enough, Mr. Canaday."

Cooper obliged.

CHAPTER 63

"We have to show our hospitality," Pearl said as she insisted that she serve dinner for Cassie's friends after their meeting at Cassie's headquarters on Sunday. "It will be like old times when your father entertained his out-of-town visitors."

"It can never be the same, Pearl. Dad was a master of conversation, particularly if it turned political. I do miss him so. But you're right. I need to carry on. It's clear to me now that he would have wanted me to."

The group gathered at one o'clock in the afternoon: Jordan Mitchell, Linwood, Cooper, Jilly, and two men that Cassie had not met.

Jordan introduced the two men. "I'd like you all to meet Jim Stephens and Travis Matthews. Both of these gentlemen are professional campaign managers here to give you advice, Cassie. Travis has worked in North Carolina before and will be assigned here to get the campaign on its feet."

Cassie introduced Jilly and thanked all for helping to start her campaign. Jilly proudly showed the group around the refurbished headquarters. The tour ended in the upstairs work room, as Jilly called it. They settled in for serious discussion.

Jordan reviewed the purpose of the campaign. "The stabilization of our country is vital. Our debt is heretofore inconceivable. Our former president led us into grave danger in Asia. The 2008 election did not change the situation. It is our goal to have some of our principals elected as independents in 2010 and have our party firmly in place by 2012 so that we can make a dent in politics as usual. Meantime, we have been seeking solutions through our affiliates and forming a platform. Our immediate goal is to place as many as possible in various political positions around the country to give validity to our efforts. As you know, a few outstanding candidates have already been elected as independents. Also by 2012, we have high expectations that many in congress will walk away from their parties and join our efforts."

Linwood spoke. "Those of us who have been analyzing the political situation for years fear for our country. Politics has become a duel among the powerful, many of whom are owned by corporations. Obstinate, unyielding personalities equate to stalemate while the country flounders. There are solutions, and those solutions will take courage to offer. It will take the courage and commitment of the American people to carry them out. If we are to save this country, sacrifice will be necessary. We are talking about relatively short-term sacrifice for the future of our children, and that's a point we must emphasize."

Jordan nodded. "Well said, Linwood."

"It's still a little difficult for me to grasp how my seeking a state office will move the effort forward," Cassie said.

"Cassie, no one expects you to stay at the state level for very long, but ground-floor experience is invaluable," Cooper said.

Jordan nodded toward Jim and Travis. "Shall we begin our strategy plan?"

The two men explained the campaign plan, which included securing voter registration lists, enlisting volunteers to man phone banks and to knock on doors, organizing sponsor receptions, and encouraging supply donations. None of this was new to Jilly, who had worked as a volunteer in several campaigns, or to Cassie, who had covered many campaigns as a reporter.

Jilly spoke up. "I think you have to know your district when you're running for office. One thing folks around here do not like is receiving call after call from the same candidate. I really believe we should also try some new approaches to this campaign. Also, Cassie's personality does not lend itself to smearing another person. I strongly suggest that her own individuality has made her a natural leader, and that is what she can and should project."

Linwood laughed. "Gentlemen, you have just gotten a lecture from our county dynamo, who, small as she is, can twist a grown man's arm with abandon and make him like it."

Jordan turned to Travis. "I guess your stay here will be short-lived. It looks like the lady has her own set of plans for Cassie."

Travis replied, "I'm sure that we'll work well together—perhaps I will learn a thing or two myself. As Jilly says, every district has its quirks, and that's why we do need knowledgeable local people." He reached across the table and shook Jilly's hand. "I think we will make a good partnership, Jilly."

It was after five in the afternoon when the group finished talking.

"Cassie has allowed me to invite Dr. Martin Lansfield to dinner tonight. He has a proposition to present to Jordan," said Cooper.

"Shall we adjourn?" said Cassie. "My home is within walking distance of your bed-and-breakfast. Jilly has drawn up directions for you. I'll expect you at six-thirty. Of course your wife Linda is included in the invitation, Jordan."

As Jilly handed out the directions, she said, "I have plans for the evening, so I won't be joining you for dinner. I'll see all of you tomorrow morning and we'll get to work."

CHAPTER 64

Pearl set the table in the dining room with the delicate china, ornate silverware, and crystal goblets that Cassie had inherited from her mother, Elizabeth. Just before the guests arrived, she stood back and admired the results.

"It's beautiful," Cassie said as she entered the room. "You've outdone yourself."

"You are looking beautiful yourself. It's good to see this old house come alive again."

"Yes, you're right. Life doesn't stand still. Somehow I think Dad will be with us tonight. I feel his presence. I think he would be very proud of my decision to enter the political field," Cassie said.

After she'd been introduced to all the guests, Linda Mitchell proved to be the catalyst for starting the evening off graciously. Over cocktails, she admired Cassie's home and told of her explorations around town. "The antebellum houses are magnificent—so much history. If only houses could talk."

Martin Lansfield laughed, "There are some folks around here that are sure glad houses can't talk."

Pearl announced that dinner was ready, and Jordan raised an eyebrow when he saw Cooper take the seat at the head of the table, seemingly very much at home there. It had not occurred to him that there was more than a professional association between Cassie and Cooper.

Pearl glowed in the praise for her dinner as she served coffee, tea, and dessert.

The group adjourned to the front veranda to enjoy the evening.

Jim and Travis told stories about their many adventures with political candidates, some resulting in a good deal of laughter. Some of their stories came across as warnings about live microphones and slips of the tongue.

After their discourse, Cooper explained his relationship to Martin, the owner of historic Wahala Hall and the founder of the county hospital.

"Martin has an announcement that he would like to make," Cooper added as he closed his introduction.

Martin cleared his throat and explained. "Cooper has told me about the retreat called the Pinnacle and the need in the future for additional retreats. After talking it over with him, I want to offer a good portion of Wahala Hall land for such a retreat as well as a generous endowment toward construction. The wooded area overlooks the Pasqua River and lends itself to serenity. Further, I intend to will Wahala Hall to Cooper so that it remains in the Lansfield family as it has for generations. Cooper will accept the inheritance only if it too can be used in his lifetime as part of the retreat, perhaps for the resident director. It is my hope that you will accept my offer, Mr. Mitchell."

"You've taken me by surprise, Dr. Lansfield. That is a magnanimous offer, to say the least. Details will have to be worked out, but I see no reason not to accept your offer. Your generosity will surely help to ensure the new party's success."

"What a pleasant and invigorating evening," Linda Mitchell said. "I'm sorry to see it come to an end, but it's time to return to the Captain's Quarters."

Cooper lingered as Cassie's guests departed.

They strolled by the waterfront, hand-in-hand, savoring the evening.

"It's unbelievable that so much has happened in so little time," Cassie said. "It's almost as if I was given a big shove and propelled along a detour that turned out to be the right direction. I'm becoming quite excited to be a part of a great experiment."

"I believe that it's more than an experiment. I have faith that it will be. The people of the United States are resilient, our history shows that. I also believe that for every ranting, tax-evading citizen or tax-evading corporation, there are ten ready to sacrifice if they find a trustworthy pathway. Trust in our government, our way of life, has to be restored."

"I get chills listening to you. Or maybe I just get chills being near you."

"It's not chills I get being near you, Cassie," Cooper said as he took her in his arms.

CHAPTER 65

Cooper had his arm around Cassie as they stood silently at the Sheraton Hotel window that overlooked the nation's capital. Visible to their left, they glimpsed graves at the National Cemetery. Spread out before them was the Pentagon and a panorama of memorials, the Washington Monument, and the Capitol—the heart of the people's city.

"It's been quite a ride, Congresswoman Danforth," Cooper said.

Cassie leaned her head on her husband's shoulder. "Yes it has, Senator Canaday. We've come a long way, and there's still a long way to go."

When in Washington, they shared their new home close by in Virginia Highlands, just over Arlington Ridge Road. They arrived early for the conference of core members of the Pinnacle Seven group, numbering more than a hundred strong.

Cassie had quickly won the hearts of her district and worked hard to bring about sensible changes. When Congressman Robert Friedman died suddenly of a heart attack, Jilly insisted that she run for his seat. Cooper and Jordan Mitchell agreed. By this time Jilly's ideas on running a modern campaign were bearing fruit, and Cassie was very popular. On the night of her victory, Cooper had proposed.

~ ~ ~

Clayton Landing gloried in Cassie's wedding to Cooper. The town was at its loveliest in spring. The new town council authorized hanging baskets flowing with pansies and petunias on every lamppost. The Garden Club busied all their volunteers with fresh plantings in all the public areas and around the city dock. On schedule, the daffodils bloomed in every yard.

By the wedding date, Clayton Landing was ready to greet its distinguished guests and the national attention that this event would bring.

Madalaine tried her best not to let her fame overshadow Cassie. She stayed out of sight at Cassie's home, getting acquainted with Pearl and loving every minute of being pampered. Pearl, as a show of admiration for Madalaine, decided to share her recipe for Sunday Go-to-Meeting Coconut Cake.

As the congregation and guests arrived, the church bells pealed. The overflow waited outside for the wedding party.

Looking exceptionally handsome in his tuxedo, Cooper stood at the altar awaiting his bride. Standing beside him were Linwood Johnson and Dr. Martin Lansfield.

Madalaine held herself majestically as her escort led her to the front right pew. She smiled at her son and then caught Martin's eye and nodded as if to say, "All's well."

As her escort led Pearl down the aisle to the left front pew, she clutched a handkerchief in her left hand, ready for tears.

Mille, Selma, and Miss Maime sat just behind Pearl.

Johna and Mary Sue entered as the processional began, strewing rose petals in the aisle before they took their seats beside Pearl. Dressed alike in pale aquamarine gowns, Jilly and Peggy, as maid and matron of honor, preceded the bride to the altar. Peggy gloried in her loss of weight for the occasion.

All eyes were on Cassie as she entered on the arm of Jed Ryan. Her eyes were on Cooper as she slowly walked down the aisle. Yellow roses, closely matching her hair, cascaded from her bouquet down the front of her simple white wedding dress.

When Reverend Michaels asked, "Who gives this woman in marriage?" Jed answered, "As her godfather and in the name of her revered father, Clifford Danforth, I do."

There was not a dry eye in the church as the ceremony proceeded.

CHAPTER 66

Cassie and Cooper turned from the hotel window and began to mingle as participants arrived. There were congressmen, former congressmen, and senators who would be announcing their affiliation with the new party and their candidacy under its banner. They warmly greeted their friend and neighbor, Congressman Jake Miller. Governor Linwood Johnson joined them just as Cassie recognized two former governors from Florida and California. Cassie was surprised to see two of her former news anchor colleagues, Judy Woodmore and Alexis Thompson, who had recently won elections to their state legislatures.

Senator Young made his way to greet Cassie.

"A good deal has happened since we met at the Pinnacle in Colorado, Cassie. I managed to get reelected as an independent, and you have been on the fast track to Congress."

"Yes sir, it's been quite a ride."

"You and Cooper have taken Washington by storm. The *Washington Post* frequently refers to you two as the new power couple."

Cassie laughed. "I'm not sure that's an honor. We're here to do our job with only our country's welfare in mind."

Michael Stone entered the room and looked around. As he shook hands and greeted old friends, he slowly moved in the direction of Cassie, Cooper, and Senator Young.

"We meet again. I've been busy working with Martin Lansfield and architects on the plans for our retreat on the Wahala Hall property. We're just getting underway. Our numbers are growing, as we can see," Michael said as he gestured toward the crowd.

Just then, Jordan Mitchell stepped to the podium and invited everyone to be seated at the tables where lunch would later be served.

After everyone took their places, Jordan stood looking around the room for several seconds before he spoke.

"Michael Stone has reminded many of you that Aristotle said, 'the man or group of men noble enough to govern solely for the best interest of the people at large is rare and hardly to be found.' There were such men among our forefathers. They were men of vision willing to sacrifice their lives and their wealth to establish this great nation. There are such men and women in this room today."

Jordan paused and again surveyed the room.

"I stand here humbled by this assemblage of men and women who have pledged personal wealth and grueling personal schedules in order to bring an end to government gridlock that is undermining the very fabric of our republic. The original Pinnacle Seven has grown to over one hundred unique individuals who have been elected to significant political offices as independents. We anticipate rapid growth as we announce our affiliation as a new party.

"Our citizens recognize that we are in economic peril. Osama bin Laden is credited with saying that he could bring this country down without so much as firing a weapon. As far back as Aristotle, there have been warnings against government foreign indebtedness. The question arises: Is our economic plight due to manipulation, or is it due to ineptness on the part of our leaders? In effect, this country is in an economic war."

Jordan paused to take a sip of water.

"Having been elected as independents, members of this audience have already contributed to significant changes.

"Many are unaware that in 1843 Congress set up a special account to accept gifts from people wishing to express their patriotism. I credit Senator Young with succeeding in the passage of a bill that creates a Treasury lockbox on that account and directs those gifts to be used solely for our country's debt reduction. The law is emphatic; the funds may not be used for any other purpose."

The audience applauded as Jordan gestured toward Senator Young indicating that the Senator should stand and be recognized.

Jordan continued, "Many thought that bill laughable, but in a little over two years, the debt has been reduced by billions. Many donations to the debt have been small checks from every corner of the country. There have been some very large corporate donations as well. Voluntarily, not in the form of taxes, our citizens are meeting the challenge to save our nation and the future of our children. This is only the beginning of new ideas, new strategies.

"Many in Congress over the years have felt that government expansion equates to their own extended power. We are hiring many of the baby boomer federal employees as they retire. They are a gold mine of information that will lead us toward discovering government duplications, thus guiding us to reductions. They have knowledge of contracting abuses.

"We will encourage industry to return to this country. A capitalist democracy runs our engine, but when greed is the order of the day, then regulation is invited. Corporations, credit card companies, and banks that continue to refuse to monitor themselves—leading to the economic ruin of too many of our citizens—will find themselves scrutinized as never before.

"Unhampered by lobbyists, we will move forward unencumbered by favoritism that often dispels common sense.

"We recognize that a strong middle class is vital to our well-being as a nation.

"Education is the backbone of any country. Thomas Jefferson expounded on this subject. The young people that we have trained at the Americas World Academy are ready to go to work. We are seeking new methodologies of educating a generation who are teething on electronics and who will lead the world in furthering the technology explosion. We may have to text-message them, but we will find a way."

Jordan paused as his audience responded with laughter.

"We are gathered here today to officially announce a national third party. Each of you in this room will be running in the 2012 elections under that banner. We expect a skyrocketing growth in our numbers for future elections. Rumors are flying that independents are ready to form a third party. We are here today to confirm those rumors.

"We are not about any single issue. We are about government of the people and by the people, unimpeded by the thirst for personal power. All of you are ready for the challenge.

"The original Pinnacle Seven found themselves on a quest. Their thirst for knowledge, their search for the tools, and their love for this country has led us to this room today.

"We ask our young men and women to volunteer for wars fought on foreign soils to protect our democracy. We ask that they risk their lives.

Many have returned to us in caskets, others, maimed for life. We in this room are merely risking our wealth."

Jordan paused once more, slowly looking around the room. He took a deep breath as he continued.

"It is not our intention to buy our country. It is our intention to return our great country to its people. Ladies and gentlemen, we must—we will lead the world to a new tomorrow. Our forefathers set about to build a nation dedicated to freedom and equality for its people. They gave us the foundation on which to build.

It is in their honor that I welcome you to the *Founders Party* of the United States of America."

———————— ✦ ————————

LaVergne, TN USA
11 October 2010
200379LV00001B/116/P